MW01171353

All The Violent Ways

Ways

The Realm of Nume

All The Violent Ways

Ways

The Realm of Nume

Emma Lynn Ellis

Copyright © Emma Lynn Ellis 2024

TikTok: @ellisitstories

Instagram: @ellisitstories

All rights reserved.

No portion of this book may be reproduced in any form without written permission from the author or publisher except as permitted by U.S. copyright law.

This book is a work of fiction. Names, characters, places, and incidents are solely the work of the author's imagination. Any resemblance to actual events, locations, or persons living or deceased are purely coincidental.

Cover Art by Katie Youngblood

TikTok: @katiespoodsandspores

Cover Design by Jasmine Bender

Email: jasminebendergraphicdesign@gmail.com

Print ISBN-13: 979-8-9889673-3-0

Digital ISBN-13: 979-8-9889673-2-3

Youngblood Publishing LLC

youngbloodpublishingllc@gmail.com

youngbloodpublishing.com

If you've ever found yourself waiting on a man to save the day
and thought, "How hard can it be? Boys do it."
This is for you.

Prologue

The King had gone mad.

He had always expected it would come to this. The man always did have a darker side to him. There were glimpses of that delirium, even in childhood, and it had started with the birds. Oh, those poor birds…

That was nothing compared to the madman he was facing now. It was as if everyone else within the Kingdom was blind to it, though. Was he the only one to see the soon-to-be King for who he truly was? Or were they all just overlooking his terrors, too focused on his pretty face? His pretty words?

He did have a way with words, that man. Words that were weighted with something… more, it seemed.

He would stop him. He had to. He may be the only one who could. *He* knew him best, after all. Knew his weaknesses better than anyone could ever dream to. Understood the best way to end a King. He had done it before.

Weaving through the crowd with ease, he paid no mind to the patrons surrounding him. Bodies leapt back as he passed, parting in his wake. No one had ever wanted to be near to him. No one had ever wanted him close enough to touch them, so he moved through them with ease—a stone within a steady current. They were terrified of him, these people.

1

He enjoyed it.

He pulled deeply from the goblet he held in his hand, letting the notes of that sweet liquid spark across his taste buds. He downed the remnants in another swallow, abandoning the goblet along with his reluctance and unease. His fingers flexed, adjusting to their newfound emptiness. Warmth settled in his stomach—a gift from that amber liquid—settling his nerves. He kept up an air of indifference as he meandered through the crowd. The smiles came with ease—directed at the lovely ladies in attendance, though he didn't linger too long on any of their faces.

He only had eyes for one.

Upon the dais, the officiant droned on and on in a language no one understood. The ancient words were merely ceremonial, the ones that anointed new monarchs within the South. And there—atop a cushioned pedestal just beside the man nearly singing those ancient words—sat the sparkling crowns of his realm.

Movement in his periphery caught his attention. He slid his gaze in that direction, subtly assessing the small fluctuation within the darkness. A shadow skittered past, delicately weaving through the tangle of bodies in the throne room.

Hello, friend.

The shadow swirled ahead of him, as if leading the way. It urged him to follow, speaking in a language only he could understand. With every step, his confidence surged, signaling that he was indeed doing the right thing. Yes, he was sure of it now.

Closer and closer, he made his way to the dais. Closer to the man standing atop it and the one behind him holding court with that wicked grin. The shadow swept between the almost King's feet, unnoticed by him or the patrons in attendance tonight. Unnoticed by all except one other.

He could do it.

He would do it.

For her.

Chapter 1

*T*he *Southern Prince is an idiot*, Syrenn thought to herself as she descended the spiraling tower stairs. The summer's day was bright and warm—the air swirled through one of the many open windows that speckled the stone walls of the castle. Early morning sun glittered gracefully against the calm waves of the sea far below the castle walls where the ships at the docks bobbed up and down with the light current.

Well, Syrenn supposed he would be the Southern King soon enough, considering the untimely passing of his father just last month. That had been quite a peculiar ordeal. Syrenn still couldn't understand it all, everything having happened so quickly. Not a lot made sense about it, either.

A ship had been discovered in the waters not far to the north of the Kingdom—abandoned. It was one of the Southern trading ships, sent on a journey to the Northern Kingdom of Kahnan. The ship that was found on its return voyage looked as if it had been attacked by pirates, Syrenn had been told. She thought that seemed strange since the contents of the ship had remained untouched. If it were pirates, surely they would have stripped the thing bare.

The Southern King saw to it that the ship was still unloaded, regardless of what had taken place. The King had quite a lucrative trade agreement with the Northern Kingdom. They sent a lovely array of crops and gems in exchange for the South's rare spices.

He seemed almost unfazed by the lack of crew aboard the ship. All he cared for was his goods, not his people. The contents were inspected, and everything was in order, including a new delicacy that had been promised by the Northern King. It was said to have been a charmed tea that brought the drinker immensely good luck.

That's what did him in, in the end. The King insisted on trying out that tea and wouldn't allow anyone to inspect it for poison before he drank his fill.

It turned out to be poisoned, obviously, causing him to go mad almost immediately. He went rabid, as if his mind had shriveled up inside his head, and he no longer held any of his own thoughts. He was no longer human, but more of a mindless husk.

Or so Syrenn had been told.

It was a horrid day all throughout the castle. The West Wing was locked from the outside, barring the girls from exiting. The King had to be put down. His eldest son was the one to do it, unsurprisingly. All the horrible deeds were thrust onto the King's eldest son, as had been the tradition for centuries. Most of these Southern traditions didn't make sense to Syrenn.

This was the way of things ever since the horrible rule of the First King of the South. The First King had been an eldest son as well. He and his brother had created this Kingdom—on the edges of the land of Nume—from nothing. He, being the eldest, took on the role of leader, while his younger brother watched from the sidelines. However, that elder son was a wicked thing who used his power to take what he wanted from whomever he wanted—who tortured and killed for sport.

Or so the fairytales say. The younger brother, having no choice, usurped the crown and banished the elder brother from the Southern Kingdom and this land altogether. And so it had been ever since. The King's crown would go to his second born son, for fear of history repeating itself.

Syrenn thought it was quite queer, indeed, when she had heard about the history of this Kingdom, and the ordeal with the most recent King. She was rather sad, too. The captain of that particular trading ship had been a particularly handsome man whom she often found herself admiring from afar.

His eyes had matched the sea.

Syrenn had spent many an evening wishing she had jumped aboard that ship with the handsome captain. Most likely, she would have died with the rest of them, but at least she would no longer be caged in this castle. She hated the Southern Kingdom. She hated that her parents had sent her here. She hated their reasoning even more.

"A fine match indeed," her mother had said when she read the summons. Syrenn could have died from shock when she learned of the arrangement. Her parents had petitioned the Southern King to allow her to join in as a contender for the Prince's hand in marriage. It was maddening. She hadn't asked for it, yet as soon as they received the final word, her parents packed her belongings and placed her on a ship heading east.

She was one of six girls expected to parade around, attend dinners and balls, and entertain the Prince. After learning more about them all, he was to select the one he admired most. That poor girl would become his wife, and eventually his Queen.

Syrenn had no desire to be queen. Her parents knew this, but they sent her anyway. She thought they just wanted to be rid of her. Life would be easier without her there. They could hardly enjoy themselves with their daughter of six and twenty trailing after them everywhere they went.

They were ashamed of her, really. To have a daughter reach that age, without any man showing an interest in her hand? She was a pariah amongst her peers. She was a stain upon her parents' good name. It wasn't as if Syrenn was unsightly. On the contrary, she was quite beautiful. Her hair was a unique, bright white that flowed to her waist. Her eyes were dark, muddy puddles surrounded with long, thick lashes. Sharp cheekbones cut across her face in an intimidating manner, and those striking features were something that had been talked about amongst her male peers for years.

She had purposely sabotaged every match her parents tried to make for her, though. She kept trying to sabotage this one as well, but for some reason, the Prince had yet to send her home. It made her wonder if her parents hadn't written anything extra in that petition...

Syrenn was content to never marry. After much begging, her parents finally agreed to grant her one condition before going to the Southern Kingdom. If the Prince chose another girl, Syrenn would be allowed to come home and live out her days as she wished. There would be no more harping from her parents about the matter. She would be free.

She had been in the Southern Kingdom for just over a year now. How she had made it this long without strangling Prince Gideon, she didn't know. He was quite handsome, that was true. But she could not get over his arrogance. She tried her hardest to quell her annoyance as she reached the final step of the tower, emerging into the main castle.

The West Wing was home to the six girls competing for the Prince's hand. The royals, as well as the parents of the girls, didn't want to risk anyone being able to wander into one of the girl's quarters in secret. So, because of this, the wing was sealed off from anyone except for staff. Since each girl was supposed to still be a maiden, they thought it best to keep everyone locked together in a single wing, as well as heavily guarded.

Supposed to be, Syrenn chuckled to herself. She didn't believe a single one of the girls—herself included—still carried their maidenhood with them. None of them voiced this aloud, of course, for fear of bringing shame upon their family names.

Syrenn's shoes clicked against the marble floor as she made her way down the corridor. When all the girls had arrived, somehow on the same exact day, there had been a debate on who would get which room. If they were to be locked in a cage, they might as well each have a room they could bear for the foreseeable future. There were fights amongst the girls on who would be staying in the largest room, closest to the stairs that led away from the wing. Syrenn's guess was that they had developed plans of sneaking out. Or on someone sneaking in. *Good for them*, she thought, though she did not share in this desire.

Oddly enough, no one wanted the tower room. Syrenn was thankful for this, because she didn't feel like arguing with anyone about why she should have the tower all to herself. She did not plan on having any visitors to her room and would rather keep to herself completely if she could. It also had the best view of the sea and of the ships that frequented the Kingdom. Though it was the farthest from escape, she realized, as she headed straight for Daphne's room.

Daphne was the youngest daughter of the King's most trusted advisor. She was also the only girl in the vicinity that Syrenn could tolerate. She had beautiful hickory-colored curls and the prettiest sage eyes. Her face was slightly rounded, with cheeks that were plastered with freckles. Not only was she beautiful, but she was the sweetest girl Syrenn had ever met. She treated everyone with utter kindness and love, no matter how they treated her in return.

She was most definitely going to be the Prince's wife.

Syrenn just wished the Prince would realize it and let the rest of them go home. Instead, he seemed to be enjoying the attentions of the girls a bit too much. She wondered if that was why they were all still there, a wife unchosen even after a year. His undeniable need to be desired outweighed any wishes he had of marriage. He had five girls flocking after him. What more could the man's pride want?

Syrenn rolled her eyes at the thought as she pushed Daphne's door open without knocking. She never knocked, and neither did Daph when she came bursting into the tower. Their friendship was very open in that way—close. Neither had anything to hide from the other. They chose each other as allies amongst the rivalry of the West Wing.

"Did you hear?" Daphne exclaimed as Syrenn pushed her way further into the room. Daphne leapt from her place on the window seat. She lurched for Syrenn, grabbing at her arms.

"Yes, we're all supposed to attend breakfast with the Prince." Syrenn said, failing to hide the annoyance in her tone.

"No. Not that. About Scarlett." It was at that moment that Syrenn finally took in Daphne's features. The girl's sage eyes were rimmed in red. She was in a panic—as if she had been crying for some time.

"What about Scarlett? Did she finally let Aster have it after last week's dinner incident?" Syrenn would be happy to hear of anyone other than herself finally standing up to the wretched girl. Aster had been under the impression since the moment they arrived that she would be queen. She was not nice towards the other girls about it either and often played nasty tricks on them, all in an effort to make them look like fools in front of the Prince. Just last week she had swapped Scarlett's stew out with one containing mushrooms. Poor Scarlett was unwise of this, and being allergic to mushrooms… Well, she was unable to finish dinner with the Prince that evening.

Luckily, her allergy wasn't life-threatening, or else Aster could have killed her.

"No, Syrenn." Daph looked as if she would be sick. Her eyes welled up once more as she said, "They found her this morning. She's dead."

Chapter 2

Dead. Scarlett was dead.

She wasn't just dead, but she had been murdered. In the early hours of dawn, she was found in her room by her handmaid who had gone to wake her. The handmaid had woken the entire wing with her wails. Syrenn hadn't heard the screams, apparently. Fortunately, the guards rushed to her aid in time to keep the rest of the girls from the gruesome scene.

Syrenn couldn't process the nightmare. Scarlett had her faults, mostly she was just annoying, but she was a sweet girl. She was innocent.

The information flowed from Daphne like the rushing waters of a broken dam. Syrenn's head throbbed as she tried to sort through it all. Daphne's words surged from her mouth as fast as her thoughts from her mind, and it was hard for Syrenn to take in both at the same time. Daphne was normally good about containing her thoughts around Syrenn, since she was... *sensitive* to them. With the uptick in emotion, however, she was unable to hold them back.

Daphne had apologized profusely over it. She was still apologizing as Syrenn massaged the skin between her eyes, willing the dull pain there to subside. The two girls had descended the stairs to the main floor of the castle hand in hand and were now making their way to the dining hall.

The echo of their shoes on the hard floors synched up with that pounding in Syrenn's head.

Of course, Prince Gideon would still want to have breakfast, even after such a tragedy. Syrenn was sure the man didn't actually have feelings—or a heart—but he put on a good show. He pretended to be kind and caring, all while toying with these poor girls. He led them on, holding their hearts in his palm. It was only a matter of time before he crushed all but one.

Three, she supposed. Syrenn wouldn't be crushed in the slightest. She would be ecstatic to be let free of this arrangement and finally go home. And poor Scarlett was now unfeeling of such trivial things.

Daphne's hand was gripping Syrenn's, tears falling down her lovely cheeks. She gave it a firm squeeze in response. Their grips were unyielding, fingers laced, as they walked through the archway leading into the dining hall.

Prince Gideon was already seated at the table, holding court. The sunlight flowing through the windows reflected off his short, sandy brown hair. The light pierced his blue eyes, the affect sending out something ethereal indeed. His face was not unkind to the eyes, though Syrenn couldn't look past the harrowing thoughts that flowed from behind.

There was no denying that the Prince was beautiful, however.

The formal dining table had long been replaced with that of a circular one, so that the Prince could better attend to all his admirers. Aster sat to his right—a heap grin plastered to her plain face. Her dark hair fell just below her chin and her eyes were a pale green that pierced daggers into anyone brave enough to look within them. The two were murmuring quietly to one another.

Iris, a curly blond-haired girl with soft blue eyes, and Vera, a redhead with almond shaped eyes, sat stoically on either side of the pair. Their hard masks showed no sadness towards the tragedy of the morning.

Each of their heads slowly turned towards the doorway as Syrenn and Daphne entered.

"Ah! There are our final two beauties. Please. Sit with us and dine. The meal is quite divine this morning." Prince Gideon bellowed from the far end of the hall. He half stood, gesturing wildly towards two empty chairs across from him. Daphne stifled the blanch threatening to overtake her, though Syrenn felt her stiffen.

Syrenn wasn't so controlled.

"Do you really think, Your Highness, that we should be carrying on without regard for Scarlett? Shouldn't we have at least taken the morning to mourn her?" Syrenn's voice came out bewildered and unkind. She knew the Prince had his own priorities, but this was just downright appalling.

"Well, if the two of you had arrived on time, you could have joined us in prayer over her soul." Gideon's feigned sadness fell on deaf ears. *Ungrateful wretch.*

The thought hit Syrenn just as all the others had. She didn't roll her eyes, as she wished she could. Instead, she said with more control than she felt, "My apologies, Prince. We were overtaken with sorrow. It took us a few extra minutes to collect ourselves."

"Oh, of course. No worries. Please, take your seats and we'll try to move on from this horrible, horrible occasion." His smug grin crawled back into place. Syrenn just dipped her chin slightly and directed Daphne to the left of the Prince. She placed Daphne in the chair beside Iris, then sat on her other side. An empty remained seat between Vera and Syrenn, forever unclaimed by Scarlett.

One less witch in my way. Aster had always been the worst at keeping her thoughts to herself. Syrenn clenched her hand at the dismissiveness within Aster. She silently wished for her power to settle back down within her, to not go searching the thoughts of the people around her. But it had always done what it wanted, simply using her as a sort of conduit.

She eyed the food before them. Everything was still steaming, due to the magic of the kitchen staff, keeping it indefinitely warm for His Highness. Many of the people in the land of Nume held varying levels of magic. If that magic was useful to the crown, the King—or Prince, rather—would employ them within the castle.

It was rare for people of other lands to hold any powers, or so Syrenn had been told by those who lived in the South. None of the girls before her now had even a flicker of magic within them. This was something that did not please the Prince. He had been hoping for a bride with power, something that would bemuse or benefit him.

It was for this reason that Syrenn kept her ability from everyone within the castle, except for Daphne. It was something she never even told her own parents about—for an entirely different reason, though. But she trusted the doe-eyed girl. She didn't trust her parents or the power-hungry inhabitants of this foreign castle.

She especially didn't trust the Southern Prince.

Syrenn's head still pulsed with pain. It was more bearable than before, but the small headache was an agitation that made it hard for her to hold her tongue. She sighed, delicately slicing a piece of quiche onto Daphne's plate and then her own.

At least pretend to eat, she sent the words over to Daphne. She saw the girl go still for a fraction of a moment as she absorbed Syrenn's silent message. Then, she picked up her fork and began to cut off pieces, pushing them around on her plate. This act would please the Prince, who seemed so unfazed by the sudden murder of one of his contenders. It would also keep Daphne focused on something mundane.

Syrenn's stomach grumbled, so she did not have to pretend to eat. Yes, she was upset over Scarlett's passing, but it was easier for her to compartmentalize that sorrow. She had not been as close to her as Daphne had. Daphne had some varying degree of closeness with each of the other girls, unlike Syrenn who kept a step away.

"Is it true?" Iris's voice rang out from the clatter of metal on porcelain. "That she was murdered?" *I wonder if she had some secret lover. Maybe they felt wronged by her relationship with the Prince.*

"I heard they found her prostrate on the bed. When the maid turned her over, she had been cut open and her heart was missing. It must have been a bloody mess," Aster said, without the slightest hint of sadness. She speared a piece of fruit onto her fork. *Now if only something would happen to the rest of them.*

"Now, ladies. I don't want you to be feeding into these rumors. It is true that the circumstances surrounding Miss Scarlett's death are suspicious, but there is no cause for alarm for any of you." Gideon's eyes had turned dark as he spoke the words. "I don't think I want to hear any of you talking of it again. It's done and over. It's time we move past it." *The last thing we need is for the hysteria to spread any further.*

Syrenn thought it was strange how dismissive he was about the death. Although, it wasn't completely out of character for the Prince. He showed hardly a speck of sorrow when it came to his own father's tragic passing. Scarlett no longer benefited him in any way. Why would he waste another breath or thought on her?

"My apologies, Prince Gideon. You're right. Let's not speak of her again." Aster seemed too eager to forget her fallen comrade. She batted her eyelashes playfully at the Prince, curling her mouth into a sultry grin for his benefit.

Syrenn wished it had been Aster instead of Scarlett. She hated herself a little for the thought, but she wasn't sorry for it. If any one of the girls deserved to be murdered, it was Aster.

The hairs on the back of her neck lifted as a feeling of dread washed over her. Her arms pebbled with bumps as her stomach dropped low. She stilled, focusing on the feeling of being watched. She glanced sidelong, noting the attendees focused on each other or their respective plates. She had heard no one enter the room, and the staff graciously averted their eyes to somewhere on the floor until summoned, as they always did.

Abruptly, a shadow invaded the doorway to the dining hall. A tall, slender form emerged from the corridor on silent feet. Everyone at the table paused their eating and conversing to stare at the intruder. He was dressed from head to toe in deep purples and blacks, the colors slimming his figure even further than it already was. The clothes complemented his features well, though. His skin was pale, but it was contrasted with dark unruly waves atop his head. If his irises had been any darker, they would have been near indistinguishable against his pupils.

Ender, the Prince's older brother, glided elegantly into the room. He held an air about him that caused most people to quake with dread. The girls in attendance held their breaths as he crept deeper into the dining hall, no one daring to look away. His face was devoid of any expression as his long fingers gripped the back of Scarlett's chair. The sound of wood scraping against marble was deafening in the silence that now enveloped the room. Ender, unbothered by the screeching, gracefully folded himself into the seat without a word.

"Dear brother, have you decided to join us for breakfast?" Gideon's voice held an edge to it. *What is he doing here?* the Prince mused within himself.

"I became aware this morning that there would be an empty seat. Why let it go to waste?" Ender purred while pouring liquid into his goblet from a hidden flask within his jacket. Something told Syrenn that it wasn't tea. She watched as Ender proceeded to plate some berries and quiche, unfazed by the now open-mouthed stares of the girls sitting around him— the girls who had been warned immensely about keeping their distance from the elder brother.

"Right. Well, it will be lovely to have your company." Gideon sounded anything but happy about having his brother join their table. The girls looked towards Gideon with utter disgust on their faces. Syrenn couldn't blame them. They had all been explicitly and extensively warned by the Southern Kingdom's council about making no contact with the elder Prince upon their arrival. A warning that had only piqued Syrenn's interest on the mysterious man, if she were being honest with herself.

Chatter picked back up, albeit mostly nervous in manner. Everyone seemed on edge with Ender now seated amongst them. He was the prime suspect in regard to Scarlett's murder. Syrenn weighed her thoughts further. If the fairytales and the warnings of this kingdom were true, he was the most likely culprit. The first-born son was always evil, they said. She wouldn't put it past the man either. He looked like evil incarnate.

Syrenn wondered if Gideon would punish Ender for the murder when it came down to it. It would be hard filling that role as King, having to enact judgement on your elder brother. She hoped he would, though. Poor Scarlett...

"Why don't we play a game, dear brother?" Ender's voice caused Vera to visibly jump. The unease amongst the girls was unsettling, though it seemed that Ender was feeding off it with the way he was smirking.

"What is it you have in mind?" Gideon asked, looking bemused.

"Well, you are taking some time to decide which of these poor girls you wish to marry. Why not get to know them on a deeper level, to assist in your decision." Syrenn's body stiffened at what Ender was suggesting. The other girls looked nervous as well.

"Oh, what a fun little experiment. What do you say girls? Will you let me ask you each one question?" Gideon's eyes had become full of excitement now. Bile roiled in Syrenn's gut.

"Well, of course my Prince. Ask us anything." Aster was too eager to be put under the Prince's power. Prince Gideon had the ability to draw truth from anyone, at any time. If he chose. That influence was something Syrenn hoped to never be on the receiving end of. When his father had been alive only a month ago, the King had forbidden Gideon from using his powers on the girls. He thought it best that the Prince get to know his admirers the old-fashioned way.

Given Syrenn's own ability, she thought herself lucky to remain far away from the Prince's command. It looked as if her luck finally had run out. She only prayed he did not know to ask the right questions of her.

The other girls nodded their agreement, no one voicing their true opinions. Syrenn heard their silent disapproval all the same. Gideon was nearly bursting from his seat at this point. Syrenn shot a hateful glance towards Ender, but his face was plastered in sheer amusement at his brother's antics and he did not notice the daggers she was glaring at him.

"Aster, I'll start with you. What is your deepest desire?" he purred to her. Gideon waited with bated breath and steepled fingers for Aster's answer.

"For you to crawl into my bed with me." Aster's voice came out in a sultry purr of her own, her eyes glossed over in desire. She blinked after the words rolled from her tongue, letting out an embarrassed chuckle. Syrenn watched as heat rose to her cheeks as Ender let out a bellow of a laugh.

"Fascinating. Iris? You're next. What is your deepest desire?" Syrenn sent up a silent prayer in thanks for it seemed Gideon was asking them each the same question. His unoriginality may be his best quality, she thought as she ruminated on her own answer. She wasn't sure what it would be and the thought sent her stomach plummeting even further.

"To be your Queen." Iris didn't blush when she spoke her truth. It was obvious what she would say. No doubt Scarlett's answer would have been nearly the same. Vera responded in much of the same manner as well when it was her turn. Ender wasn't as amused with their confessions.

"Daph. What is your deepest desire?" Gideon held a sparkle in his eyes as he looked upon the pretty girl. They had grown up together and shared many intimate moments in their past. They knew each other the best out of everyone in this room, and it showed in the smallest ways.

"To be loved and cherished, as my father loves my mother." Syrenn's heart fluttered at the innocent answer from the girl. Her hand found Daphne's beneath the table and held it. The two shared a caring glance. Syrenn hoped her friend found just that.

Gideon only smirked and chuckled softly. Ender's eyes darkened.

It was in that moment that Syrenn became keenly aware of how close she was to Ender. Having taken Scarlett's chair, she could almost feel the heat radiating from his body. It was as if that heat was something physical brushing against the skin of her legs beneath the table. The feeling caused her skin to crawl as she felt his gaze land on her.

It was her turn.

"Syrenn? What is your deepest desire?" The words pierced into Syrenn's mind like an arrow finding prey. She tried to fight them, force them out, but it was no use. She could feel them sinking in deep, pulling that bit of truth from a place she hadn't known existed.

"To go far, far from here and never return." The words dropped from her tongue. She wished she could bite it to keep them inside. She knew she shouldn't have said it, but she couldn't stop them. She was supposed to be happy about courting the Prince. She was supposed to be joyful

about even being considered as a contender. She had played the part well during her entire stay thus far.

Her façade was ripped away in only a moment.

Gideon's face darkened as he furrowed his brow. His smile dropped from his face the moment the words registered. He sat back in his chair and tossed a leg over his other knee.

"Well, then. I didn't realize my company was that atrocious to you," he bit the words out and the room fell silent. No one dared say a word or look in Syrenn's direction. Her cheeks began to sting with shame and embarrassment.

"Peculiar." The word cut through the thick silence, causing Syrenn's head to whip toward Ender. His teeth were gleaming in the sunlight, his smile a sneer across his face as he repeated, "Peculiar indeed."

"Yes, brother. It is. Apparently, father should have selected a more willing participant from Farehail than Miss Syrenn here." Gideon said bitterly. Syrenn's cheeks heated further.

"I'm sorry, Your Highness—"

"No, don't give me false apologies. That's how you feel." Gideon became dismissive. "Perhaps I can try to change that. Until then, you have *my* apologies." *She really is an ungrateful wretch.*

Syrenn felt as if she had anything but. She turned her face back to her plate, now no longer interested in her favorite dish. Her stomach turned and she felt Daphne's hand grip hers from where they were still connected under the table, pulsing it twice.

Syrenn took the cue and willed her mind open to receive Daphne's thoughts.

It's okay, Syrenn. He won't hold it against you.

Syrenn glanced subtly toward Daphne, hoping she was right. She returned her grip, the only response she could allow herself. Daphne did know him the best, so perhaps she was correct in her assumption.

Perhaps this moment wouldn't be remembered by him. Though, she wouldn't soon forget the embarrassment.

Breakfast continued without another incident, but Syrenn was overjoyed when it finally ended. The girls were dismissed, all expected to attend daily classes. There were classes on dancing, ensuring the girls learned the steps contained in the traditional Nume dances. They had classes in the arts, where they had their choice of needlepoint, painting, or knitting. There was an instrumental class, where each girl was expected to master piano, the Prince's favorite. Along with each of these, the girls were expected to know the histories of the Kingdom, as well as how they were expected to act if they were to become queen.

Syrenn's favorite class was instruments. She had always loved the piano. She had already been adept at it and was eager to learn new songs from the Southern Kingdom. This was not the class they had today, however. They were heading straight for the ballroom.

Dancing. Syrenn cringed. She was a decent dancer, but the traditional dances they had to learn were cumbersome and left her sore for days. Aster was known to try and trip the girls during instruction as well.

Syrenn fumed at the thought as they left the dining hall. The girls filed out one by one, the two Princes following closely behind. Syrenn hadn't yet recovered from the intrusion Gideon's magic had caused in her mind. It felt as if his power had left a small tear in her well-crafted defenses.

It was quite startling indeed when a foreign memory that was not her own floated through that very crack and into her mind—a flurry of images accompanied by a sense of overwhelming delight. The power within her consumed the arrant thought greedily. Her steps faltered, and she had to feign a trip as everyone's attention turned on her. A guardsman's shot an arm out, grabbing her quickly and briefly to right her posture once more.

Who had that memory come from? Her eyes subtly darted over the four other girls, as well as the two Princes. None of their features gave away whose memory it had been, whose mind it had floated from. Her heart rate accelerated, sending her blood rushing. She felt a cold sweat start to bloom over the expanse of her body. The horrible images were now forever stamped into her mind. She tried unsuccessfully to shake them free.

Scarlett's smiling face as she welcomed someone into her room.

Scarlett's look of surprise and confusion as a dagger pierced her chest.

The feeling of sticky blood coating the fingers wrapped tightly around the dagger's hilt.

The feeling of pure ecstasy tied with Scarlett's unseeing eyes.

Chapter 3

Syrenn was about to be sick. Her stomach lurched, and she tasted bile in the back of her throat before she swallowed it back down. Daphne saw the change in her demeaner almost instantly and sent a worried glance her way, making to step in her direction. Syrenn shook her off before she could make it into something. *I'll tell you later.*

The girl resolved to wait and turned her attention back towards the group and intended path. No one had noticed their quick exchange, too enraptured with the Prince. It seemed Gideon would be escorting the girls to class today. His elder brother showed no desire to part from the group either. Syrenn mused idly about Ender's intentions of stalking the girls to their destination. Maybe he was feeding off the sorrow and emptiness the girls now held within them. Maybe he was deciding on who to target next.

Syrenn stole a glance at him as they continued down the corridor.

He was watching her.

Their eyes met, and Ender's held a look of puzzlement, as if he were trying to figure something out. She held his stare, pouring every bit of loathing she held in her body into him. She wanted him to understand that she was well aware of what exactly he had done.

He blinked, then a cruel smile began to slowly stretch across his lips. Syrenn's focus moved to them, unable to keep from noting how smooth they looked. His teeth flashed just behind the grin, snapping Syrenn from the thought before it could go any further.

She wondered if that smile was what persuaded Scarlett into letting him enter her room. He was alluring, and Syrenn knew from her personal experiences that his darkness only intrigued a person more. She knew this was the very reason they had been warned to keep their distance upon arrival. The council must have been more aware of his true nature than they let on. Perhaps the fairytales of the land were rooted in truth after all, and he had shown them, at some point, just how truthful they were.

The echoes of footfalls reverberated against the ceiling, bouncing around the stone surrounding them and slowly fading. It was at that moment that Syrenn realized she had stopped walking. She and Ender had paused in the middle of the hallway while the rest of the party had continued towards the ballroom. They were standing mere feet from each other, simply staring.

Gawking, a bystander might say.

Syrenn's skin crawled as she heard Gideon call from down the corridor, "Is everything okay?"

She opened her mouth to call back, turning to rejoin the group. Ender's hand on her wrist had her halting once more, the words catching in her throat. She cast him a withering look. Why did he think he could touch her so freely?

"I think Miss Syrenn here is feeling under the weather. I should escort her back to her chambers to rest. Today's events must not be sitting well with her." Ender's clear voice was a command, not a suggestion.

"Right, then. Thank you, brother. Syrenn, I hope you're feeling well enough by dinner tonight. My mother is to join us this evening." Gideon said dismissing her into Ender's care.

His mother? That meant...

"It seems my brother has finally made his decision." Ender smirked at Gideon's fading figure, then turned his black eyes back onto her. "Shall we, Miss *Syrenn*?"

A shiver ran down her spine at the venom in his voice. Her heartbeat picked up as he looped her arm in his and turned them around. He half dragged her down the corridor, away from the retreating party. She turned her head over her shoulder and caught sight of Daphne's horror-stricken expression as she was carted away.

Away from any hope of help.

She clamped her mouth shut to keep from screaming. She didn't want Ender to find out she had accidentally seen his memory of Scarlett. He was unaware of her power, and she would like to keep it that way. She focused on slowing her hammering heart and evening her breathing.

So much for Gideon upholding the council's warning. He had sent Syrenn straight into the mouth of the awaiting viper.

"I assure you, Prince Ender, I am quite well. There is no need for you to escort me anywhere." Her voice betrayed her unease. She tried in vain to keep her hand from trembling within his arm.

"Do I unnerve you?" His grin turned arrogant, and his words held an underlying amusement.

"Not in the slightest. I really should practice my dancing with the rest of them. If there is to be a wedding soon, I should make sure that I'm well-rehearsed," she said with ease.

"I'm sure you know the dances well enough. And here I thought you were nervous about being alone with me." He tilted his head towards her.

His eyelids fluttered half-closed with the words, insinuating something would occur between the two of them.

"Why would I be nervous to be alone with you, Prince?" She kept her voice light. Innocent.

Ender stopped their trek, forcing her to look at him. "Well, I wouldn't want you to get the wrong idea..." He lowered his head with condescension. He was so close that she could feel the heat of his breath brush across her cheek. She shuddered.

"I'm here for Prince Gideon. I won't be swayed by any other man, no matter how handsome or persuasive he may be." She recited the words just as she was instructed to do during her initiation into the maddening game. The words hit her own ears and made her cringe. She thought none of those things about Prince Ender. His looks intrigued her, yes, but they also terrified her. His features were all dark, and sharp. They reminded her of the dagger he carried at his side.

"You think I'm handsome? Syrenn! If Gideon were to hear about this..." He tsked. Syrenn rolled her eyes at the delight that was utterly apparent on his face.

"As if what I said at breakfast hasn't damned me already," she huffed.

"Oh, I think you have much bigger things to worry about than that." Ender began walking once more, steering her towards the stairs leading to the West Wing.

"What are you implying?" She couldn't keep the question contained. Was he really going to be this obvious?

Ender remained quiet as they ascended the steps. He kept half a step ahead of Syrenn, nearly dragging her up with him—his focus solely on the sentinels perched before the guarded door of the West Wing. Syrenn noted that the guards locked their eyes on Ender with distaste, overlooking her altogether. This was how most of the staff within the castle looked at him. It was what they all thought of him too. She had no shortage of annoyed, snarky, or even terrified thoughts that she had come across throughout her year here—all directled at or around the Prince now with her.

She took the momentary lack of attention to quickly swipe the blade from Ender's side. As she began to unsheathe it fully, she stumbled forward, bumping into Ender with a bit too much force. But the blade glided out smoothly. The jostling of their bodies ensured he wouldn't feel or notice her move the blade into one of the wide pockets of her skirt—a skill she had picked up from many of her childhood friends.

"Careful now, I don't know if Gideon would appreciate one of his ladies falling for his wicked older brother." Ender nearly purred as he helped her steady her feet again. He wound his arm through hers as he sent a devious look down at her. He said it as if it were a joke, him being wicked. As if what everyone thought of him wasn't actually the truth. As if he thought it was amusing, to be seen that way by everyone around him.

Syrenn plastered on an embarrassed expression and took the next step above Ender, tugging at their interlocked arms. When they reached the top of the stairs, Ender nodded to each sentinel before unwinding Syrenn's arm from his. His grip remained firm around her palm and he pulled her in close.

"What I was implying, Syrenn," Ender said, continuing the conversation, "Is that there's someone murdering pretty girls." His voice was soft as that cruel smile appeared once more. Syrenn was unable to tear her eyes from his face—his lush lips, those deep dark eyes. Those sharp cheekbones and that dark smattering of hair…

The way Ender murmured the words had her breath faltering. She felt her eyes widen as Ender let out a small chuckle. Her blood roared in her ears, and she willed her senses into him. She wasn't met with thoughts, but rather an overwhelming feeling of pity.

This man pitied her. Was it because he intended on making her his next victim? Or for her participation in this marital game?

Syrenn closed her mind off quickly, hiding the confusion that feeling sent through her.

Ender squinted down at her with a questioning look. He moved his free hand up to her face and brushed his index finger along her forehead. She didn't dare move as he gave it a light tap before cocking his head to one side.

"Peculiar, indeed." The words were so quiet, Syrenn thought she'd imagined them. "Do be sure to lock that tower door of yours." He dropped his hands and turned back to the stairs. As his foot connected with the first step, he said over his shoulder, "Oh, and Syrenn? Don't let anyone into your room. No matter how handsome and persuasive they may be."

With that, he disappeared. Syrenn stared after him. She heard the groan of metal as the guards unlocked and opened the door to the West Wing. Syrenn made no move toward it until one of the guards cleared their throat, catching her attention. Reluctantly, she pulled herself from the top of the stairs and entered the prison that was the West Wing. She was thankful that she had had the good sense to swipe the blade from Ender. It would be a useful tool if he did indeed decide to target her next.

"He really said that?" Daphne was perched at the end of Syrenn's bed. Syrenn sat atop the large alcove before the windowsill overlooking the boating docks, watching as ships were unloaded. Her eyes ran over the waves as they subtly crashed against the wood of the bows. She rubbed two fingers against her brow, swearing she could still feel Ender's touch there, as if it were now branded upon her skin.

"He really said that," she confirmed, turning to look at Daphne. Her eyes were wild from everything Syrenn has just told her. Syrenn even relayed the memories that she had seen of Scarlett's murder. She had left out the part about Ender touching her—caressing her—and about stealing the dagger, though she didn't know why. Daphne's eyes sparkled with something akin to a mixture of fear and intrigue.

"Do you think it was a threat?" Daphne asked.

"That's how I took it. I just hope Gideon realizes who Scarlett's murderer is and takes care of him. It's obvious to everyone else, but I could see him being blind to the true nature of his brother. Surely the council is aware and has their suspicions." Daphne nodded her agreement. Syrenn changed the subject. "Are you nervous for tonight?"

"Not exactly. We don't really have any control over who he chooses, do we? Why stress about something we can't control. Whatever will be, will be." Syrenn heard the words, but she also detected the hint of despair in Daphne's voice. She was careful to block out any thoughts that threatened to crawl from Daphne's mind. She wanted to allow her friend privacy over something as delicate as this.

"He'd be a fool not to choose you. Everyone knows that as well. That's why Aster is so bitter and conniving." Syrenn said, attempting to put the girl's mind at ease.

"I'm afraid that growing up together hurts my chance. He finds me boring. He already knows everything there is to know about me. I'm not intriguing anymore." Daphne's self-pity was so unlike her normal manner.

"Whatever will be, will be." Syrenn echoed the words back to her and sent an encouraging smile to her friend. Daphne returned the grin and rose from her place on the bed. She pecked Syrenn softly on the side of the mouth—eliciting a blush from her before heading for the door.

Daphne left then, heading down to her own room to prepare for the evening. The girls were expected to be dressed in their very best attire. Being unable to leave the castle to visit the many shops in the city, they had to make do with what they brought with them. They had been in the castle so long that they had worn the dresses numerous times already.

Unless their parents were able to send them new gowns, they had to settle for something the Prince had already seen them in. Syrenn had a deep blue ballgown selected—one of her favorites—and she didn't mind the comfort of the familiar fabric wrapped around her body.

She peeled herself from the windowsill and the setting sun. As if summoned by the sound of her feet hitting the floor, her door abruptly opened to reveal her handmaid. Maren knocked her hip into the wood, swinging the door open wider. Her blond hair swished behind her like a wild mane. Her hands were weighed down by a giant package.

"I'm here to ready you for dinner, Miss Syrenn. I was given this with the orders that you wear it tonight." Maren placed the box atop Syrenn's bed and began untying the rope that held it closed.

"Did my mother send it?" She asked. Her mother must have taken pity on her and sent something from home. What a perfect day for it to have arrived.

"It was the Prince, actually. One of his maids gave me the instructions and the dress." She opened the box and Syrenn walked to the bed for a better look. "Oh, Miss. This is beautiful."

The gown inside the box was nothing like what Syrenn would have selected for herself. It was made of deep gray silk and gossamer. The straps were nothing but thin strands, the neck plunging into a deep vee. The waist was fitted, or so it looked from where it lay inside the box, neatly folded. The skirts billowed beneath the bodice giving the impression of rolling thunderclouds in the night sky.

"Oh my." Syrenn gasped a bit nervously. "I'm not sure I can wear this." Her fingers trembled slightly as she slipped them along the fabric.

"If it's the Prince's request, you must wear it. It would be disrespectful not to." Syrenn knew Maren was right. And after the truth he had forced from her mind that day, the last thing she wanted was to cause more hard feelings. She didn't like the Prince, but he had been kind enough to take her in and appease her parents. If she were sent home early, the bargain with her parents would be broken as well. The least she could do was appease him in this way.

"Thank you, Maren. I think I best be getting ready, then." Maren gave a cheerful nod and pulled the dress from the box. The maid held the gown up, admiring it for a moment before hanging it from the wardrobe door.

"We'll start with your hair." Maren said before getting to work. Syrenn sat before her vanity and allowed Maren to brush through her tangles. The soft strokes of the brush softened Syrenn's unease slightly. When Maren finished, she began delicately twisting strands into braids. She pinned the braids into place, leaving masses of hair hanging loose.

"This is different," Syrenn commented.

"I was given thorough instructions on how you were to be presented this evening." The maid smiled at Syrenn through the mirror, a knowing gleam in her eye. Syrenn's stomach began twisting nervously. The extra fussing and instruction over her attire was completely out of character for the Prince. He normally allowed the girls to wear things of their choosing. For him to have selected her dress, he had to have something special in mind for the evening. Syrenn silently prayed that she was not the only girl who received this particular luxury. If she had been singled out for the night, that could only mean...

"Well, that's a bit excessive, don't you think?"

"I only follow the orders I'm given, Miss." Maren set about painting Syrenn's face. Syrenn tried to keep her expression from turning sour with her swirling thoughts. She chose to stay away from the maid's thoughts, as well. She couldn't stomach what she might find within them. When Maren finally finished after some time, she helped Syrenn into the new dress. The maid made quick work of the back of the dress, securely fastening each button into place. "Lovely. Just, lovely." She mused.

Syrenn agreed reluctantly. The dress had been beautiful in the box. It was downright gorgeous wrapped around her curves. Her loose white hair flowed elegantly down her back, the braids sweeping most of it from her face. The new hairstyle left her clavicle and sternum completely exposed.

"Are you sure it isn't a bit... much?" she asked Maren.

"No, Miss. It's beautiful on you. The Prince will adore it." That was the last thing Syrenn cared about. It was more of a reason for Syrenn to take the dress off altogether. She held the sentiment within herself, though, and pushed down her power that hungrily dove towards Maren's thoughts. "It's time to head out now." Maren gently herded Syrenn towards the door. "The other girls will be waiting."

With a final glance in the mirror, Syrenn couldn't help but think she was heading to her funeral.

Chapter 4

The girls filed into the dining hall one by one—sheep funneled into the slaughterhouse. Syrenn was the last to enter, her steps weighed down with the unknown. She was surprised to see that the room had been transformed since breakfast. The round table had been replaced with a long, narrow one. The table looked original to the room, the one used before the contenders arrived in the Southern Kingdom.

Each of the girls was guided to their seat. The place at the head of the long table remained empty for the Prince, as well as the seats on either side of him. Syrenn was guided to one of the many seats to the left, only one down from where the Prince was expected to sit. She watched as Aster sat directly in front of her, also next to an empty seat. Iris was placed in the chair beside Syrenn. Daphne ended up on Aster's other side, and Vera sat next to her.

The hosts had yet to arrive. Syrenn noted the gowns of each girl in attendance in more detail. She had seen every one of their dresses at some point or another during her long stay in the Southern Kingdom. Syrenn's stomach dropped. Only she had received a special dress for the evening.

Each girl looked stunning, regardless, though. They had, in fact, picked their finest gowns, some going so far as to add new embellishments in the form of beading and embroidery. The handmaids had also done exquisite work on the canvases they were given. If tonight was the end of their yearlong contention, they wanted to end it in beauty.

Syrenn could feel the tension in the room. The girls were on edge, bouncing in their seats and tapping their toes as they all waited for the Prince to arrive. She strained to keep her power inside and her mind closed off from the others. Try as she might, small snippets still broke through her ironclad barrier.

Where did she get that dress? Syrenn recognized the envy in Aster's thoughts. She focused her sight on the empty table before her, trying not to blush from embarrassment at being scrutinized. So, her new look was that noticeable, was it?

Anyone but Aster. Syrenn suspected the thought came from Vera. She wholeheartedly agreed with her on the sentiment. Any of the girls would make a better queen than Aster. She enjoyed toying with those weaker than her a bit too much to make a fair ruler. The title would go straight to her head.

The echoing of footsteps on stone had all the girls snapping to attention. She saw them straighten their spines and assume open expressions. No one looked too invested in what the evening would bring. Syrenn turned toward the archway of the dining room, holding her breath just as she knew the other girls were doing. For very different reason, though. The Prince finally graced the dining hall with a flourish, his mother dangling from his arm.

The Queen Regent was beautiful. Her hair, as dark as her first son's, was speckled with beautiful shocks of white. Her eyes were the deep blue from which Gideon's had come. A practiced smile split her face, causing Syrenn to blink. The woman was the embodiment of perfection. No wonder her sons were so handsome.

Son, Syrenn corrected herself.

As if summoned by her thought, Ender appeared on his brother's heels seemingly out of thin air. He shadowed the two as they made their way deeper into the hall. Gideon flashed each girl a smug smile, and

Ender stepped out before his brother, sliding back the chair on Gideon's right. He gestured for his mother to sit. She folded herself gracefully into the chair and sent her eldest son a sweet, appreciative smile. Every eye in the room watched the exchange.

Gideon moved just to her side, paying no mind to the woman, more interested in the chair at the head of the table. He paused behind his seat, waiting for his brother to move to his own. Ender glided around with an apologetic nod, aiming for the only remaining place.

Syrenn's blood thundered in her ears as the elder Prince scraped back the empty chair next to her. She held her eyes forward as she felt his presence settle deeper into the seat. Gideon cleared his throat, drawing everyone's attention back toward the head of the table.

"Thank you all for joining us this evening. I would like to take a moment to introduce you to my mother, Queen Estia." Gideon waved a hand towards his mother, who looked fondly up at her youngest son.

"Thank you, my dear." Her alluring voice rang from her. "It's lovely to finally put faces to names after all this time. And my, they are quite beautiful faces." She smiled at each girl then. Murmurs of thanks sounded simultaneously. "I did find it quite unfair that the late King enacted that silly rule. I finally convinced Gideon here to break it for me." She sent her son a dazzling grin.

"Indeed. My mother made a great case. How could I choose a bride without having you all meet my mother first? I wouldn't want to choose someone she despised." That was... honorable of him, Syrenn thought. Syrenn's hope spiked. He hadn't chosen yet. But that didn't explain the reason for him sending her this lavish dress.

He can't be serious? Like we care about meeting the old hag. The thought was startling to Syrenn. It hadn't been Aster, but Iris whom her power consumed it from. The year of waiting must finally be taking its toll on everyone, it seemed. Their hope of it being over diminished, and anger took root in its place.

"So, mother. What are your initial thoughts?" Ender's voice grated against Syrenn's ears. She shook off the chill it brought to her. "Does anyone stick out to you?"

"Now, Ender. Do be patient. I haven't had the chance to talk with any of them, save for Daphne." She scolded. Syrenn smiled to herself. She looked at Daphne then, taking note of her scarlet cheeks, brightening by the second.

"Perhaps I should have dined alone, then, since you already know me so well." Daphne's soft voice shook as she said the words.

"Nonsense, sweet child. I enjoy looking upon your beauty. Eat with us and take comfort in knowing you won't be on the other end of my interrogation." The Queen smiled sweetly to her. Daphne nodded her head, her blush deepening.

The servants arrived, bearing trays of food. They placed them in the center of the table and began plating the delicacies. Syrenn thanked the man spooning her greens onto her plate. As she did, she caught a flash of Ender's heavy eyes on her. She quickly averted hers towards her plate, but taking note of his amused expression.

"Aster, why don't you tell me a bit about yourself?" The Queen asked, idly pushing the food around her plate. Syrenn's power reached outwardly, curious of the Queen's intention. She noted the Queen's mind was well guarded. So guarded, in fact, that she didn't receive so much as a stray thought from her. Normally, she would be thankful for this, but she had to admit she was quite curious about the woman. She had heard tales of her from the servants throughout her stay. The Queen was said to be pleasant, but powerful.

Where Gideon could draw out the truth in someone, his mother could detect any lie. No matter how small. Together they made a fantastic duo.

Syrenn could only imagine what their powers could do on any unknowing victim.

Perhaps they could use their joint ability to force Ender to admit to his crimes.

The thought of him had Syrenn subtly glancing to her right. Ender sat stoically next to her, eating his food in the elegant way only a trained prince could do. She scooped a bite into her own mouth, the movements not as practiced as the Prince's.

When she noticed his clothes, she almost choked on her bite of food. She coughed softly, trying to clear her throat, the debris now ash on her tongue. She reached for her goblet, but a long-fingered hand was already grasping it and bringing it to her lips. The tendons beneath the smooth, pale skin rippled as his grasp adjusted. She tried not to acknowledge how pleasing the sight was.

She ripped the glass from Ender's hand, careful not to brush his fingers with her own. He chuckled at her aggression. She tipped the goblet, letting the liquid trickle down her throat.

"Are you alright, my dear?" the Queen trilled.

"Apologies." Syrenn rasped the response.

"Why, you two match!" The Queen exclaimed, noticing her and Ender's attire for the first time. Her features twisted in delight as she realized the same thing that caused Syrenn to choke. Ender was wearing pants and a jacket in the same stormy gray as her. The silver strands and buttons decorating his jacket twinkled like stars in the night sky in the same way her gossamer shimmered in the dim lighting.

"What a happy accident," Ender purred next to her. *Now, Now, Syrenn. That scowl you're wearing is quite unbecoming.*

Syrenn blinked back her surprise as Ender's voice was pushed into her—her power lurking just below the surface, ready to consume. Unable to quell the shaking of her hand, she placed her goblet back onto the table before she sloshed its contents all over its surface. Her hands found their way beneath the table and into her lap. The biting pain of her nails digging into her skin brought her back to attention.

Aster continued her ramblings to the Queen. Syrenn could feel Daphne's eyes on her, so she shook her head back and forth. *I'll explain later. I'm not sure what's happening, but I'm alright.* She pushed the thought to Daphne, hoping there was enough sincerity in it to reassure her friend.

Syr-enn. Her name was drawn out and melodic—taunting. She squeezed her hands tighter into fists and tried to reign in her power to block Ender from her mind. *I know you can hear me, Syrenn.*

He didn't. There was no way he could know that. She hadn't told a soul besides Daphne about her ability, and Daph would never betray her trust in that way. She pulled her hands back onto the table to continue eating. She would prove to him that he was mistaken about her. The only way she could do that was to ignore him completely.

Oh, come now, Syrenn. Play with me.

Syrenn didn't taste the food she shoveled into her mouth. She simply scooped morsels onto her fork, then deposited them onto her tongue, blocking out the conversations around her, along with the one being forced inside of her mind. Distantly, she wondered if perhaps Ender had been watching her all this time, the way she had always tried not to watch him. Perhaps he, too, had been eager to learn if a power lurked beneath her surface.

She's trying to talk to you. Are you just going to ignore her like you're ignoring me? How do you think Prince Gideon will feel about you being rude to our dear mother?

Syrenn started, blinking back into focus.

"I am so sorry, Queen Estia. What is it you were saying to me?" Syrenn said in an even voice.

"Don't worry, my girl. I was just wondering what it is you like to do in your leisure time?" The Queen held Syrenn's stare, and it dawned on her that the queen was checking for lies in each of them. She wondered if this was another way for Gideon to learn more about the girl he planned to marry. Undoubtedly, he and his mother would convene after dinner to discuss what she had learned.

"I enjoy watching the ships at the dock." Syrenn replied. "I only see them from my tower window, since we aren't allowed out of the castle, except for the courtyard gardens. I do find them fascinating, regardless."

"You come from the Islands, is that correct? Are there many ships that visit there as well?" The Queen tried to keep the judgement from her voice. Syrenn noticed it anyway. The Islands were small—quaint, rather. Not many people visited, and there wasn't much trade.

"No, there isn't. Maybe that's why I find them so fascinating." Syrenn mused.

The little Island heathen. Aster's thought wasn't anything she hadn't voiced directly before. Syrenn learned to shrug it off long ago.

"Do you like it in the Southern Kingdom?" The Queen asked. Syrenn chewed over her response for a moment. She didn't want to lie to the Queen. She didn't want to tell her the truth, either.

"I haven't seen anything like it before. But, after being here so long, I am starting to become homesick."

"That's to be expected, dear. Maybe once my son here finally makes his decision, you can go home for a visit." Her warm voice was motherly as she said the words. Syrenn smiled genuinely in response.

Ah. So, you're aware of my mother's abilities. Ender's voice pierced into her mind more forcefully this time, as if he were shouting at her. He'd grown tired of being ignored it seemed. *Did anyone enlighten you on mine?* There was a dark humor to his words.

Intrigue sparked in Syrenn, and she dampened it down as fast as she could. No one in the castle knew Ender's power. At least, no one she had talked to or overheard knew what they were. She had tried for nearly her entire stay to uncover them but had failed miserably. Why it mattered to her, she chose not to think about, but it was a task that kept her mind busy during the daunting days caged inside.

Before Syrenn knew it, the servants were clearing away the now empty plates. Gideon rose from the head of the table, beckoning for everyone to do the same. Where had the time gone? She hadn't even noticed Queen Estia talking with any of the other girls.

"Thank you, ladies, for humoring me this evening. I do apologize if anyone got the wrong idea about tonight. I assure you, though, I will have my decision soon." His smile plagued the room once more before he departed from the table. There was not a bit of regret in his tone. Lacing his mother's arm in his own, the two floated from the room.

Syrenn stole a final glance towards Ender. She expected to see his smug expression, or at least have another thought thrown towards her. Instead, his eyes were focused down the table. Syrenn turned, following his gaze.

Daphne stood before her seat; hands clasped behind her back. She watched as the Prince disappeared around the corner and out of sight. Syrenn looked back towards Ender, confused. Their eyes met this time. Syrenn found herself lost in their darkness for a moment. He was staring at her with such focus, she felt herself swirling into his irises.

He broke their connection first, moving his eyes lower along her body. She felt their heat land on the exposed skin of her chest. Her pulse quickened as the sting of blush crept across her clavicle and up her neck, nearly reaching her cheeks.

The corner of his mouth quirked up.

"Have a lovely night, ladies." Ender said, the sound just as hypnotic as his mother's voice. He moved around his chair and departed from the room in long strides, not sparing another word to the group.

Sleep tight, Syrenn.

Chapter 5

Sleep tight. Sleep *tight,* Syrenn fumed. She wanted to pierce Ender in the neck with his own blade. How could he be so condescending and so unfazed by his own actions? Did the dead girl's life mean nothing to him? He had to be toying with Syrenn. Perhaps something like this had been done to poor Scarlett before he murdered her.

Syrenn pondered Ender's strange behavior on her way back to her room. She bid Daph goodnight and ascended the stairs of the tower, too mad to linger with her friend for long like she normally would have. She made sure to double check her lock as she closed the door behind her— just in case. She couldn't wait to be out of the godforsaken gown Ender had sent her.

It truly *was* the Prince's wish that she wear the damn thing. Maren had just forgotten to ask *which* Prince had sent it. She ripped at the front of the gown causing the back buttons to tear free. They skittered to the floor, falling like pebbles onto stone. Rolling along the floor, they were swallowed up by the darkness. Silk and gossamer slipped from her body like water as she crumpled it up and tossed it into a corner. She didn't even want to look at the thing.

She dressed for bed quickly but paced her room for hours before finally calming her whirling mind. Her bare feet padded against the floor, grazing over the rough fibers of the many rugs scattered about. They did little to block out the chill emanating from the stone.

Starlight glimmered through the open window, a chilly breeze blowing in the salty scent of the sea. The glittering light reminded her once more of the dress and Ender. She inhaled the briny smell of the sea, allowing it to cleanse her mind and wash Ender from her thoughts. She wouldn't get worked up, wouldn't allow Ender to frighten her in this way. If he chose to come for her next, she would be waiting—ready.

She crossed to the bed, lifting the pillow to uncover the blade she had hidden beneath. It was made of steel etched with a watery pattern; the hilt wrapped in a dark leather. It glinted in the moonlight, the gleam almost searing her eyes in the near darkness of the room.

She grasped the hilt, bringing the dagger closer to her face for inspection. The weight was heavy, almost too heavy for a dagger. The blade itself was longer than any dagger she'd handled herself, though it was still too short to be considered any sort of sword. It was rather remarkable. Though, she wondered why Ender carried it like a badge of honor.

Syrenn abruptly dropped the dagger back onto the bed. Had he used this on Scarlett? Was she now looking at the very blade that pierced the girl's heart? She shuddered and stepped back, dropping the pillow back over the blade. She needed to push the thought from her mind. This weapon, even if it was the murder weapon, was better than being defenseless if Ender came searching for her next.

She fell to the bed, ready to try and succumb to sleep, leaning back on the pillow now covering the dagger. The feeling of the hard metal digging into the back of her head was surprisingly comforting. She rolled to her slide, sliding her hand beneath the pillow, and grazed her fingers along the hilt, savoring the rough feel of the leather.

The salty breeze whipped lightly around the room. Even though it was still the height of summer, the air contained a slight chill brought in by the expansive sea. Syrenn pulled her thick blankets over her body, settling further into her bed. She closed her mind off from the day. It had been a long one, and the memories left a bad taste in her mouth.

She recited her favorite story from childhood within her mind. It had always brought her comfort, had always settled her when she was uneasy. It was her oldest trick for falling asleep, even on nights when sleep seemed so out of reach.

Once there was a queen who was fair and true. She loved her people, and they loved her…

The chill in the room deepened, brought in by a ghastly bit of wind. Syrenn shivered, closing her eyes tighter and nestling into the blankets.

The queen fell in love with a woman just as fair. Or so she seemed. Unwise of her true allegiances, the queen invited her into her home. The woman sought to overthrow the queen and take her kingdom for her own. And she did.

Syrenn thought she heard a noise then. Her eyes sprang open, and she sat up, alertly scanning the room. It must have been the wind rustling her things about. There was nothing there. She let her head drop back against the pillow.

The queen was cast out, but she did not give up hope. She rallied her people, storming the castle in the dead of night.

Syrenn could feel her mind drifting off. Her body had become so heavy, relaxing further into the thick blankets. She pulled in a long, smooth breath.

The queen pulled her lover from her bed, ready to pierce a blade into her heart. But she could not. Her hand froze, inches from the woman's flesh. The two stared into each other's eyes for so long, they turned to stone…

Syrenn's eyes flicked open for an instant before sleep fully claimed her. She didn't have time to panic over what she saw. What she thought she saw. Perhaps it was a dream.

Shadows couldn't move on their own.

Syrenn woke with a start, the morning sun blaring through her single window and lighting her entire room. She shot to her feet, darting around the room, checking every corner. Perhaps she had been dreaming. Yes, surely, she had been asleep already. There hadn't been anything in her room.

Syrenn checked the lock on her door. It was secure, and she let out a breath. There was no way anyone could have entered unless it was Maren. She was the only person with a key, other than herself. Checking the top of her dresser, she found her key was sitting exactly where she had left it.

Yet, Syrenn still held tension all throughout her body. She couldn't let go of the feeling of being watched. But that couldn't be possible. She was just paranoid from Scarlett's murder. She was safe in her tower. It was too cumbersome for Ender to climb the stairs while remaining out of sight. He would likely kill her somewhere else.

Syrenn dressed for the day and descended the stairs, pushing her lingering fears from her mind. She wound round and round, collecting herself with each swirl of the passageway. By the time she reached the end, she felt saner than she had in her room.

That shadow had definitely been a piece of her dream creeping out.

Daphne was outside her door, waiting for Syrenn as she did most mornings. The two walked arm in arm to breakfast together daily, the rest of the girls leaving much earlier to await the Prince. Syrenn had no such compunctions, and Daphne had spent plenty of her life wooing the Prince. If he didn't love her by now, he never would.

The girls emerged into the dining hall. The narrow table from the previous night still remained. This put a sour taste in Syrenn's mouth. She bit back the acid creeping up her throat and took in the people already sitting.

The queen was amongst them, as was Ender. Gideon sat at the head, flocked by Aster and Vera. They giggled superficially at whatever Gideon was saying. Syrenn rolled her eyes at how fake it sounded even to her own ears. Yet the Prince was eating it all up. The flash of Ender's eyes on hers sent a jolt through her.

Its pathetic, really. The way they simper.

Syrenn tried to claw her powers back inside to no avail. She saw a smile crawl onto Ender's face, much to her dismay. How had he figured it out?

"Ladies! Please have a seat and join us." Gideon splayed his hands out, as if the two girls didn't already know where to sit.

"Is Iris not with you?" A hint of worry flicked across the Queen's face for a moment as she looked upon the pair.

Syrenn glanced about once more from her chair. Indeed, Iris was not amongst those in attendance. She had always been one of the first to join. She felt her face slacken, dread pouring through her veins. Her head whipped to Ender's, but he only stared at her with a curious expression. Was that concern?

"No, we assumed she had already come down." Daphne's voice clanged through Syrenn like lead. Her hand clenched in her lap.

"Someone should go search for her." Syrenn spoke with an authority she knew the Prince was not fond of. "Someone who is not sitting in this room." Gideon stared at her, as if deciding whether or not to heed her command or lash out against her.

"What a good idea, Syrenn. Elliot, good sir, will you please see what is holding up Miss Iris?" It was not Gideon who made the request of the servant, but Ender. Gideon's mouth hung open like a fish out of water. He must have realized because he proceeded to snap it shut with an audible click.

"Yes, Elliot, please go check on Miss Iris. Hurry her along." Gideon resolved. The servant looked hesitant but proceeded into action without question. No one was allowed to question the future King. The man left the room on near silent feet. "Well, there is no point in waiting. Eat." Another command, but this one Syrenn could not follow. Her stomach was twisting into knots. Her jaw was clenched so hard it ached.

The minutes ticked by slowly, the only conversation was that of Aster, Vera, and Gideon. Everyone else seemed as if they were waiting with bated breath. Until they heard the screaming.

Syrenn eyes dropped closed, the anguish searing into her like a knife. She knew those screams. She had heard screams like them before. The screams of absolute terror.

The room fell quiet as the others processed what those screams meant. But Syrenn knew already. Iris was dead. She was sure of it. She could feel it in her bones. She had suspected it from the moment she noticed the girl's absence. How the Prince didn't realize was beyond her. He had always been so blind to anything but his own priorities.

No one moved. No one dared breathe too loudly as they all sat around the table and waited. Hurried footsteps banged down the hallway. Syrenn could tell whoever they belonged to was running. Her hands trembled as the sound grew closer. Finally, Elliot's shouting burst into the dining hall.

"She's dead! Your Highness, she's been murdered, just like the other." His hand was clutching his chest, his eyes wild with fright. He lingered on each of the girls around the table, as if he expected to find them murdered as well. He waited for the Prince to respond.

"Take me to her." The words came out strained and unbelieving. The Prince looked as if he would be sick. He lifted himself from the chair and

Ender followed his lead. He reached a hand to his elder brother, grasping his upper arm, as if he were drawing strength from him. The sight made Syrenn want to laugh. Why was he not locking his brother up? Instead, he was leaning on him for comfort!

Gideon walked around the table, and no one else dared to move. Ender cocked his head, watching him leave but didn't trail after him. Syrenn thought she saw regret in the elder Prince's eyes before they found hers. She expected to hear his voice in her mind, but it remained silent. She looked to Daphne. The poor girl appeared as if she might faint, her face was so pale.

"Dears, why don't you all accompany me to the tearoom. We can pray for Iris there, together." Estia rose from her seat, putting out a hand to guide the girls forth. They rose silently and followed the Queen Regent from the room.

Syrenn paced her bedroom once more. The day had dragged by. The girls were sequestered to the tearoom and questioned by both the Queen Regent and Prince Gideon. They were questioned in private, so Syrenn wasn't privy to the other girls' responses. Not that she thought any of them were at fault. She knew the true murderer was Ender.

Why was the Prince not questioning his brother? Perhaps he was, but out of sight from prying eyes and ears. But surely with his gift, he would be able to draw the truth of the matter from him easily. Unless he hadn't been the one...

Syrenn didn't even want to waste her time considering it. It had been him.

She finally gave up her pacing. Her arches throbbed from the repetitive back and forth she had done for hours. It was well past midnight at this point. She resolved to try and get some rest, throwing herself onto the bed praying for sleep. But she knew not even her silly bedtime fairytale would soothe her today. Not after a second murder.

She closed her eyes and draped her arm over her face. She thought she could almost hear the crashing of the waves far below her window, and she imagined herself on a ship, sailing home. Sailing away from this nightmare. Sailing anywhere.

Something tickled Syrenn's arm, causing her heart to stutter. She flew upright, scanning the room.

It was empty.

She was paranoid, she thought as she shook her head. She laid back, staring up at the ceiling and steadying her breathing. Her chest rose and fell with the crashing of waves within her mind. That eased the tension that had been steadily growing.

Syrenn. The singsong voice had her eyes snapping open. It took only a moment for her periphery to register something to her right. Her body chilled and her muscles constricted. Her head dropped to the side, unveiling what—*who*—was now in her room.

Ender.

He stood next to her bed, leering down upon her body. He was studying her—though his face remained impassive. She bolted upright, snatching the knife from beneath her pillow in a swift movement. On her knees, she thrust the blade into his abdomen without a second thought. Her hand shook with the effort, but she felt the tip pierce his flesh. She heard him grunt deeply as she thrust it in further.

"Play nice, Syrenn," he whispered. Her name sounded like sin on his tongue, but she ignored it. Their eyes met, and he held a wicked look.

Her teeth chattered with fear. Gripping the blade harder, she dragged it upwards, slicing Ender in half. She didn't stop pulling the blade higher until it reverberated off his sternum, never taking her eyes off his. She finally ripped the blade free. She looked toward her hands, at the dagger grasped between them.

It was clean.

There wasn't a speck of blood on it.

She looked to the wound that should have been marring Ender's skin beneath his shirt. The wound wasn't weeping blood, as a wound that size should be.

No. That wasn't blood pouring from his flesh. That was smoke.

Not smoke.

Shadow.

The dagger clattered to the floor and Syrenn scrambled backwards, nearly falling onto the bed beneath her. She watched as Ender melted into nothing but blackness, disintegrating into the darkness and dispersing. She began to hyperventilate. She couldn't breathe as she frantically searched for where the shadows had hidden.

She scrambled about on her bed, turning in all directions. The shadows were gone. Or were they everywhere? She couldn't tell, not when everything was cast in darkness.

"Don't tease me like this, Syrenn." The purr sounded from behind her, and she felt his breath graze her ear. She whirled around, but nothing was there. "You are so enticingly *violent.*" The notes brushed along the skin of her exposed back. She swung her arm behind her, but it met with nothing.

She could feel the thunderous pounding of her heart. She was in a panic. He could be anywhere, everywhere, watching her and she would never know. His presence was evident in the room. The air was ignited with his essence, but where?

A soft whisper of shadow flicked along her jaw; the feeling liken to a finger. She shuddered.

Chapter 6

Syrenn didn't sleep that night.

She started at every shadow she saw flickering in her room. She wasn't sure if they were normal shadows, or if they were pieces of Ender skittering along her walls. The thought made her shudder. Was she no longer safe in her own tower?

With two of the girls now dead, the entire castle was shrouded in an air of unease. Scarlett hadn't been an isolated incident, as the Prince had insinuated. Someone was targeting the girls. Ender was targeting the girls. Was he jealous of his brother? Was history to repeat itself, in that the elder son would go mad with power?

It was still quite early in the morning, but she was wary of being left alone in her room. It was no longer her haven. Syrenn bounced ideas around as she paced the corridors of the castle. She had no destination in mind but soon found herself in the courtyard. The early morning light was soft, casting shadows along the many pillars that surrounded the enclosed space.

Warm air brushed against her skin, though she still felt a chill when she looked towards those shadows. The scent of the flowers in the garden sweetened the air. She wasn't fond of the smell, much preferring that of the ocean. But alas, she could not get close enough to the ocean to touch it. These flowers were the only bit of nature she was allowed. Oh, how she missed her home...

"You know, if anyone else would have stabbed me like that, they wouldn't have awakened this morning." The voice had Syrenn's hand freezing midair, mere inches from the flower she was about to pluck. "You're making me soft, Syrenn." The notes tickled her ear, sending a chill down her spine.

"What do you want from me? Or am I to be your next victim?" She whirled around to face him. He was leaning casually against one of the stone columns surrounding the courtyard garden, arms folded over his chest, nearly invisible within the darkness there. Syrenn watched as he pushed off from the stone, beginning a slow, predatory stalk closer to her. He stopped just before her, close enough that she could smell him. He smelled like pine, and it made Syrenn suddenly homesick.

Ender brought his face to hers, their lips nearly brushing as he said, "There are so many more enjoyable things I could do to you than kill you." It was a whisper—his exhale pressed against her lips as she drew in sharp breaths, the scent of him driving deeper into her mind. Her lids lowered involuntarily as her heart pounded in her chest. When she opened her eyes no more than a moment later, Ender was gone.

Footsteps echoed as someone else approached the garden, so Syrenn turned her attention back to the flowers, swallowing down her terror. She plucked a rose from the bush harshly, the thorns sinking deep into her skin. She paid no mind to the pain, or the blood that flowed from the wounds. Bringing the flower to her nose, she inhaled deeply, trying to erase the lingering smell of Ender from her nose.

"Syrenn, I hoped to find you here. Will you walk with me?" Gideon's voice reverberated against the walls around them, eliciting a cringe from Syrenn. He had come searching for her. To know she was here and not still in her tower, he had to have gone to the West Wing first. If she were truly outside, she could run. But she thought that was the idea on keeping the girls locked inside. They were contained. They were isolated.

They were his.

"Of course, my prince." Her voice sounded hollow, a bit shaky, but she knew Gideon wouldn't notice. He never noticed how uncomfortable he made her. He never noticed how his presence rubbed her in such a rough way. He only saw what he wanted to see when he looked at Syrenn.

Her beauty. And someone willingly flocking after him, just like every girl did.

She squeezed the rose tighter between her fingers, the pain searing into her and making her focus on the present. Gideon had his arm outstretched, waiting for her. She closed the distance and gracefully looped her arm within his. He gave her an arrogant smile and led them from the garden. Syrenn threw the flowers one last longing look before falling into step with him.

"You look lovely today, Miss Syrenn. And you looked lovelier yet the other night. That dress was a sight, though I do prefer you in red." Of course, he did. It was his favorite color, and the girls had been taking to wearing the many different shades. Syrenn preferred blue.

"Thank you, Your Highness," she said softly. From the corner of her eye, she swore she saw a shadow skittering across the floor. She whipped her head to it, but nothing was there.

"Syrenn? What is it?" Gideon came to a stop, searching the hallway beside them.

"Nothing. I thought I saw a mouse, but I must have been mistaken."

"You must be on edge after Iris. Such a tragedy, but I do promise nothing will happen to you. I have brought more guards into the West Wing. You are safe." His fingers brushed down her arm, causing her hair to stand on end. She shoved down the cringe threatening to overtake her body. The touch was… claiming.

"Have you caught the culprit?" She made the question as innocent as possible.

"Not yet, but I have faith that we will. I think it was an intruder in the castle. There is no other explanation."

"What about Prince Ender? Could it have been him?" Syrenn braced herself for the backlash she knew was about to come.

"I have had my suspicions, but I questioned him myself." *Will she shut up about it already?* Gideon had continued walking, half dragging her along with him.

"I'm sorry for throwing the accusation, Your Highness, we have just always been warned to be aware of him. And now with the girls being murdered—"

"I said it wasn't him. We are done with this conversation." The words felt like a slap with how much venom was in them. *As if he would hurt a fly, the dim wretch.*

"My apologies. I was out of line." Syrenn lowered her eyes and hung her head in a show of mock shame. She wanted to press him, but it was as if some force was urging her to remain silent.

"Don't worry your pretty little head about it. I know the histories and traditions of this land can cause people to feel a certain way. But I don't think I've ever known my brother to hurt a hair on anyone's head. Without cause." The Prince's mood had changed back to cheerful so abruptly, it gave Syrenn whiplash. "I asked you on this walk because I wanted to know what you thought of my mother? She was quite taken with you."

Syrenn paused. She had barely spoken to the queen. They had exchanged more words during the murder interrogation than at dinner. "She seems lovely, my prince."

"She thought the same of you. She says you are by far the most beautiful of my contenders, but she also thinks you are the most intelligent. She saw a sort of look in your eye, and she has always been able to notice these sorts of things."

"Your mother is too kind. I will have to thank her the next time I see her." Syrenn felt an uneasiness crawl up her spine.

"I do have to agree with her. There is definitely something different about you than all the rest. *What is it?*"

The command knocked into Syrenn before she knew what was happening. Her heart raced as she felt the words being pulled to the surface. She knew her face was horror stricken by the delighted look that now rested on the Prince's face. She bit down on her tongue as hard as she could, trying as she might to keep the truth inside herself.

But it was no use. She felt her jaw loosen, her tongue relax as the words tumbled from her mouth. "It must be my powers."

She could be sick. Her stomach lurched as she saw the words click into place behind the Prince's eyes.

Powers. The wretch has powers *and has been hiding them from me.* His lip curled into a sneer as he said, "Why haven't you told me of these *powers?*" Another command, and Syrenn didn't fight it this time. It was too late for her, and she knew it.

"I wanted to go home, and I knew you wouldn't let me if you found out the truth." She felt tears slip down her cheeks. The Prince smiled deeper when he noticed them. He reached a hand up and dragged a finger under her eye.

"Don't cry, my dear. Why would you think I wouldn't let you return home? What kind of monster would that make me?" He said this with a façade of offense, but it wasn't a command this time. Syrenn answered truthfully regardless.

"I know you value power."

Smart girl. "You're correct, I do value power. But I'm not heartless. I would never keep someone from their family." Syrenn tried to let the words calm her, but she had such an unsettled feeling within her. She had guarded this from the Prince for an entire year, and just like that, everything was ruined. She was so close to leaving this place. She was so close to returning home and to her freedom. Now, something told her that she never would.

"Thank you, Prince." It sounded false, but she knew that he wasn't expecting her gratitude.

"Of course. I appreciate your honesty. And thank you for the lovely walk, Miss Syrenn. Do enjoy the rest of your day." The Prince bowed his head slightly toward her before turning on his heel and retreating down the hall.

Syrenn stood in the center of the corridor, completely defeated. She didn't feel the sting of the thorns digging into her palm. They would be imbedded into her skin from how tightly her fist was gripping the stem. She didn't feel the blood trickling down her fist or hear it plinking onto the floor beside her.

But she did feel a ghostlike touch brush the curve of her neck and swirl around her ear.

She leaned into it.

The Prince would take his father's place as King once he selected a wife. That had been one of the terms when the idea was enacted, when the King was living and ready to give up his reign to his son. Now, the Southern Kingdom of Nume had been without a ruler for months, due to the tragedy of his early death.

The council made all decisions, heavily swayed by the Prince, since he was the eventual ruler anyway. The Queen Regent sat on the council as well, as did the elder Prince. It was they who would make the final approval over the Prince's selected wife. If they decided the woman he chose was not fit to be Queen, they would choose another for him.

Syrenn knew the Prince would take the information of her powers directly to the council. She knew this would not be in her personal favor.

She stood upon her windowsill, the open ocean crashing far beneath the tower. She debated jumping. If she ended her life now, she would not be subjected to Gideon's marriage. She would be free. Not to go home, but to move on.

Her toes inched forward, grazing the ledge and open air just beyond. The crashing of the waves was faint from this high up, but she could still hear their song. She closed her eyes and let the warm air melt into the skin along her cheeks. She smiled and moved ever so slightly further into the open window. Her hand dropped from its place on the trim...

"If you don't step down from there, I will pull you back myself."

Syrenn stumbled back, nearly falling to the floor as she whipped toward her room. Ender stood in its center. "How did you get in here?" Her voice was hysterical.

"Hop down from there and I'll tell you all of my secrets, Syrenn," he purred. His hands were tucked into his jacket pockets, but his body was not at ease like he tried to portray.

"Maybe I'll just fall backwards, rather than let you end me yourself." Syrenn took half a step back to the open windowsill. Ender was suddenly there, his face inches from her. The shock had her foot slipping, unable to catch herself by the stone frame. Her body swayed abruptly away from him, back toward the open air. She had the sickening feeling of falling.

Everything around her swirled with blackness. She kept falling, backwards. She shut her eyes tightly, ready for the impact of the cold water on her skin. Would she die instantly? Would she drown slowly? She did not care.

Her back smacked onto something hard, pushing the air from her lungs. Her eyes burst open. The ceiling to her bedroom loomed above her, as did Ender's body.

She looked around, noting she was still in her bedroom. Ender's hand was cradling her head, protecting it from smashing onto the floor. He was pressed firmly to her front, caging her between him and the stone.

"How—"

"Were you really about to kill yourself, Syrenn? What a waste that would have been." He stroked his fingers through her hair as a smile curled his lips. She shoved at him harshly. He laughed, then fell to the side. Leaning back onto his elbows, he surveyed her as she got to her feet and brushed out the wrinkles from her dress.

"How did you do that?" She spit the question down at him.

"Oh, Syrenn, don't pretend with me." His body swirled into shadow before her eyes, then reformed atop the bed. He patted the place next to him. She didn't budge. He sighed but relented. "The darkness consumes me, pulling me into its depths. It allows me to move within it, to become one with it." He didn't pull his eyes from hers.

"Why is it some big secret?"

"Why is your power?" He quirked an eyebrow at her. She blushed, but her face remained neutral—waiting. He sighed. "Cranky today, are we? My ability can be advantageous to our kingdom. The less people who know, the better."

"Why are you showing me, then?" Syrenn crossed her arms and furrowed her brow.

"I like that you know all my naughty little secrets. And it was only fair," *since I know yours.* Ender gently pushed the words to her.

"It was you."

"Mmm... I don't know what you're referring to, Syrenn, but it can be me if you want it." He laid onto his side at the end of the bed, balancing his head on his hand and kicking his feet up. He fluttered his eyelashes at her.

"You told Gideon about my powers. Because of you, I'll be stuck here forever." Her voice broke, and she clamped her jaw shut on the feeling of hopelessness curling around her throat.

Ender blanched. He dropped his feet to the ground and cleared the distance between them in an instant. "He knows?" The alarm in his voice threw Syrenn off balance.

"Yes. Because you told him." The words were unstable as she began to doubt his part in it.

"No, Syrenn." His voice was low—calming. He placed his hand along the outside of Syrenn's crossed arms. "I would never betray your trust."

"I don't trust you." Syrenn wrenched her arms free from his grasp.

"You should. I think I'm the only person within these castle walls who doesn't intend you harm." Ender let his hand fall back into his pockets.

"But you killed Scarlett and Iris." Syrenn's conviction was beginning to waver. Ender let out a bellow of a laugh.

"You think *I* killed them? Really?" He was still laughing, one hand still in his pocket while the other fisted and came up to his face. He bit his knuckles trying to stifle the snickers. Peeking at her under his hooded lashes he said, "You are quite a treat."

"Then who did it, Ender? If not the dark, broody, *elder Prince?*" Syrenn had become irate.

"I don't know, *Syrenn*, that's what I'm trying to figure out." He dropped his fist and prowled closer once more. "That's why I'm here. I need your help."

Syrenn let out a laugh this time. "What can I do?" she asked, bewildered.

"You can use that pretty little head of yours and pry into some minds for me." His finger tapped against her forehead, as if reiterating what he just said.

Syrenn blinked back at him. "You want to use me, then?"

"Yes. You can use me in return if you like. Think of it as a mutual user, use-e relationship."

"What could I possibly want from you?" Syrenn felt her face contort in disgust.

"Oh, I could think of a few things." He was suddenly behind her, crooning the words into her ears. "But it's whatever your heart desires. Use my body..." He wisped into nothing, reforming on her other side, "Use my powers..." again, he disappeared, reappearing with his body pressed solidly into her front. His hand held her by the neck, tilting her head up to meet his stare. "Use my position. I will do as you wish. Just help me. Please."

"Why are these deaths so important to you? Why do they matter? It doesn't concern you if you aren't the one murdering them." Syrenn didn't step back but held her ground.

"I have more of a stake in this than you realize. I have my reasons." He didn't say more, instead peering down into her face with a guarded expression. "So, will you help me? Or do you still plan on killing me, and yourself?"

"If I help you find the culprit, will you get me out of here?"

"Of course. Shall we seal our bargain with a kiss?" His eyes sparkled. Syrenn shoved him back. He stumbled, grabbing at his chest in mock hurt. Laughing, he said, "You could have just declined, Syrenn. But I appreciate your knack for violence." He winked at her.

"Come into my room uninvited again, you shall see the extent of my violence," Syrenn spit out.

"Don't entice me like that. I quite like the way you stab me." The words were rough, coming from deep in his throat. He burst into shadows, then vanished entirely. Syrenn could feel the absence of him almost instantly. She was alone once more.

Chapter 7

Daphne's silken sheets brushed softly against Syrenn's skin as the two girls stared at the ceiling. They hadn't spoken in the last few hours, simply taking comfort in the communal silence.

Daphne had fallen asleep at some point while Syrenn was reading one of the many books she had snagged from the library. When Syrenn finally gave up on the story and tossed the tome on the side table, Daphne awoke.

"Will it ever end?" Daphne nearly whispered the words, but they startled Syrenn regardless.

"What?"

"The waiting? I'm so tired of waiting on him to decide. It's agony." Syrenn could hear true heartache in her voice.

"It's all a game to him," Syrenn said, thinking on Gideon unkindly. "I know how you feel about him, but he's a bit of an ass."

"Yes, he can be." Daphne sounded defeated.

"Daphne?" Syrenn's heart started pounding in her chest. She was terrified to ask the question, though she knew it was necessary after her run in with Gideon yesterday.

"Yes?" Daphne waited patiently for Syrenn to continue. She laced her fingers with Syrenn's, idly stroking the back of her hand with her thumb.

"Would you still be my friend if he chose me and not you?"

Daphne's fingers stilled, and Syrenn felt her hand become rigid. Her palm started to sweat as she waited for Daphne to answer. After an excruciatingly long pause, Daphne said, "I'll love you no matter what. But why do you ask? I would say you're the last person on his list of potential brides." She laughed as she said this, though Syrenn could tell it wasn't wholehearted.

"I just don't want to lose you." Syrenn could feel tears stinging her eyes. She knew she should tell Daphne the truth. She knew she should voice her fear, and what happened yesterday morning.

Gideon had discovered her powers, and he would not let them get away.

Syrenn knew why she was being summoned into the throne room.

She tried not to think about it as she forced herself forward. It felt as if she were moving through stone. Her feet were weighed down with each step, her heart thundering uncontrollably in her chest.

Daphne, Aster, and Vera trailed behind her. If they thought it strange that Syrenn led the group today, they didn't let on. Syrenn always took up the end; she never cared for their assemblies with the Prince.

If Daphne was beginning to put Syrenn's question from yesterday and the sudden summoning together, she did not show it.

She felt as if she were walking to her death. Her mouth was dry, her tongue sticking to its roof as if it were glued there. She couldn't scream even if she wanted to. If she stopped, if she tried to turn back, she knew one of the many guards along the walls were under strict orders to drag her back kicking and screaming.

The doors to the throne room were pulled open as the girls neared. Syrenn didn't let her steps falter. She would not be afraid. She *could not* be afraid.

The Prince sat upon his father's throne, his mother at a smaller seat just to his left. His elder brother stood off to the side, flanking him. Many of the councilmen flanked them on the sides as well, smirks upon their faces while they watched the approaching girls.

Ender's look could only be described as murderous.

Syrenn swallowed any fear she was holding onto. She cleared her mind of the dread, opening it to the thoughts surrounding her.

It's time, fucking finally. Aster seemed more annoyed than anything. She was positive the Prince was about to name her queen. As if spreading her legs entitled her to anything in the Prince's eyes.

Oh dear. He isn't, is he? Daphne's thoughts trembled. Syrenn glanced back at her and saw the tremors vibrating through her hands. She shoved away the guilt clawing at her throat. She should have confided in Daphne about the Prince discovering her powers the other day. Should have prepared her. Regret twisted around her heart at the thought of Daphne's reaction to what was about to happen.

What the Prince was about to do.

Vera only stared blankly before them, eyeing the Prince. She was still in shock after losing Iris. They had been inseparable. As close as Syrenn was with Daphne. Syrenn couldn't imagine losing Daphne—the thought terrified her. And for that reason alone, she would work with Ender. She would find who was murdering the girls. She would suffer what was about to happen in order to gain better access to the people of the castle.

She had decided.

"I'll save you all an introduction. You know why you've been summoned. I have chosen which of you shall be my wife." Gideon rose from his father's throne with an arrogance only he could manage. Gliding down the steps of the dais, he came to a stop before the gathered girls. Aster took a step forward, and if Syrenn didn't already feel like she was about to dissolve into a puddle of dread, she would have laughed at the audacity of the girl.

Gideon reached out, grasping Syrenn's hand within his. "Syrenn, it will be my honor to have you as my wife. To have you bear my heirs. You shall reign at my side from now until your dying day. Our wedding will take place at the end of the month! We've already sent word to your parents. They will be on the next ship from Farehail."

Syrenn couldn't stop her hand from shaking. She didn't grip him back, only let it lay limply within his. She stared past his head, unseeing, feeling the sting of tears prick her eyes. Syrenn heard someone gasp behind her as they realized what Gideon was doing.

The room was silent. No one said or thought a word. Syrenn felt as if she were spinning. Blinking the tears from her lashes, she tried to focus. She tried to bring herself back into her body. She blinked rapidly, her eyes landing on Ender.

He was studying her, that look of rage still etched into his features. He shot a look of warning at her, pushing her back into the task at hand. *Speak.*

Survive the night.

The smile on her face was anything but genuine as she looked at Gideon. He was leering down at her, waiting for her response—her acceptance of his proposal, if it could even be called that.

"It's an honor, my prince." Her voice was a whisper. She couldn't refuse him, per one of the statutes of consenting to the competition. She had never expected to be chosen and hadn't thought anything about signing her name upon the contract. "I will not disappoint you."

That absolute bitch! That liar! She pretended she didn't want this, but apparently, she's been plotting behind our backs! I hope she gets murdered next. Aster was seething, though she still had a false smile plastered on her face.

Syrenn felt total despair leaking from Daphne. She was trying so hard to contain it, but the heartbreak within her was evident. She could feel Daphne trying to put up walls, to block Syrenn's power from reaching to her, from knowing how she felt. *I'm so sorry,* Syrenn gently floated the words to Daphne before she blocked her out completely.

Vera was still numb.

"Now, the rest of you! You shall stay with us until after the wedding. Afterwards, you are welcome to head home. I appreciate each and every one of you. It has been a delight getting to know you all." Gideon said the words halfheartedly, almost as an afterthought.

Gideon gripped Syrenn's hand, pulling her along as he introduced her to the many councilmen—the men that basically just signed her death certificate. For she would die being caged in this castle for the rest of her days. She floated through the evening as if in a dream. Or a nightmare. She was barely coherent enough to acknowledge their names. She had seen some of their faces before, though some were still new to her.

After their initial rounds, she found Queen Estia before her.

"Congratulations, my darling. The two of you will make a fine match. With those powers of yours, your children will surely be gifted." She smiled sweetly at Syrenn. She tried to return the sentiment. The Queen squeezed her hands and patted her son on the back before sauntering off to talk with someone.

Gideon finally left her alone. She tried to hide herself from everyone. Her back pressed to the stone wall, the chill of it biting into her skin. She closed her eyes and drew in a breath.

I tried to stop it. The words swirled around her mind causing her power to greedily reach for them. Her body deflated further.

A lot of good that did. Syrenn pushed the words back towards Ender.

I am so sorry. I will still uphold my end of our bargain. I will get you out.

Syrenn snorted. *I will not hold onto that hope.*

You need to trust me, Syrenn.

"Did you know?"

Syrenn's eyes bolted open. Daphne stood before her; arms crossed over her chest. She looked on the verge of tears.

"No. I would have never guessed he would pick me."

"What changed? I thought he hated you. We all did." Daphne's words were cruel.

"He found out about my powers, Daph. I don't know how. He pulled the truth from me two days ago." Syrenn's voice sounded dead. She was numb.

"So, he chose you because of your powers?" Her brows knit together in confusion.

"Does that surprise you? He's always valued power. That's why I didn't want anyone to know. But now it seems everyone knows." Her voice trailed off.

"I just can't believe it. I thought it would be me. Even after everything, it was supposed to be me." Daphne said the words more to herself than Syrenn. She shook her head, as if she could will this night into a dream and walked off with wide eyes. "It was supposed to be me."

The night passed so slowly. Syrenn collapsed into her bed and sobbed when it was finally over. Her face pressed into her pillow, and she gripped the dagger beneath. She cried for the two dead girls. She cried for the hurt in Daphne's eyes over not being chosen. She cried for her lost freedom.

When she couldn't cry anymore, she closed her eyes and tried to fall asleep. She didn't bother changing. Her body ached, and she was too exhausted to remove herself from the bed. Her head began to throb from all the crying.

She drifted in and out of consciousness, slowly becoming aware of a light pressure on her back. That pressure turned into a rubbing sensation in the area between her shoulder blades. It was delicate, yet firm, and she was already growing accustomed to the feel of it.

"Did he say how he found out?"

"No." Ender's voice sounded from across the room. She pushed her head off the pillow, spying him sitting at her vanity. The brushing along the skin of her back continued.

"I assume the approval was unanimous."

"Everyone agreed except for me."

"Why didn't you? Like my comfort really matters." Her voice was hollow as she spit the words at him.

"You despise him. You shouldn't be tethered to someone you loathe for your entire life." Syrenn heard as he got to his feet. She felt as his body lowered onto the bed beside her. "He isn't fond of you either. You shouldn't be in a loveless marriage just because he wants your power bred into his line." Ender sounded resentful, almost disgusted as he spoke.

Well, here we are. She projected the thought into him. He chuckled in response.

Shall we leave, then? The thought was bemused.

"Did you forget? I'm not allowed to leave. Especially not now." Syrenn huffed and rolled onto her side so that she was facing Ender.

"What they don't know, won't hurt them." He flashed her a wicked grin before snatching her hand. Before she could protest, the heat of his skin seeped into her, and they were gone.

Blackness whipped around them. When it cleared, Syrenn became suddenly aware of a rocking sensation beneath her. Startled, she looked about.

They were on a boat, still tethered to an abandoned dock. Ender was already unfastening the rope holding them to the post. He grabbed each of the oars and began rowing with ease as Syrenn's face tilted to the sky.

The stars glittered endlessly above them; their beauty had the breath catching in her lungs.

"Ender. How?" Words were escaping her.

"I can take you anywhere. It's such a beautiful night, I thought we shouldn't let it go to waste." Syrenn didn't look at him as he spoke. She couldn't tear her gaze from the night sky. There were clouds, deep and dark, almost the color of the dress Ender had sent her.

"Thank you," she whispered to him.

"Do you finally believe that I don't intend to kill you?" She could hear the humor in his words, and she looked at him. His eyes glittered beneath the stars, his shadows swarming around him as if he couldn't contain the pieces within himself. Blushing, she nodded. She had to trust him. She had no other choice. He was her only hope at getting far, far away from the Southern Kingdom.

"Couldn't you just take me away now? Hide me, so that I wouldn't have to marry him?" she asked, so full of hope.

"I can't stop the murders without you here." There was defeat in his words. "You are our best chance at ending this."

"You think there will be more, then?" She shuddered to think about it.

"Yes, Syrenn. I have no doubt about it."

"Who do you think it is?" It had only been Ender capable of such atrocities in Syrenn's mind. He was able to wander about unnoticed. She couldn't begin to think of who else it could be.

"I think it's the Prince." His words were barely audible. Syrenn gasped. His eyes connected with hers and held her stare, unblinking. His jaw was set, his brow hard.

"You think Gideon is killing the girls?" She couldn't believe his accusations.

"Yes. I have my reasons why I think it's him, but I'm almost certain. I just need your help in confirming it. You and that little power of yours." His voice had gone soft. "Since you're to be his wife, you should be safe to get close to him. He wouldn't dare harm his future bride with our mother and the council watching. Eventually, he'll let something slip, and you'll be there to figure it out."

"So, you're sending me into the viper's den?" Her stomach dropped. She focused on the sound of the oars cutting through the water.

"Yes. But you won't be alone." Syrenn watched as the muscles in his chest moved with each turn of the oars. "I'll always be there, with you."

"Creeping in the shadows?"

He smirked at her, and that was all the confirmation she needed. She mulled over her task, staying quiet for so long. Ender let her think as he rowed her along the coast. She could barely make out the silhouettes of the mountains that surrounded Nume. She saw them on her journey in from Farehail and had wanted nothing more than to get close to them, to walk beneath them—between them.

"How far can your power reach?" Ender finally broke the silence as Syrenn was dipping her fingers into the chilly depths below.

She contemplated the question for a moment. "I'm not sure." She skewed her mouth to the side, thinking. "Normally I try to keep it inside and block people out. I don't like invading their privacy like that. So, I've never tried to listen to people intentionally. Usually, their thoughts just... invade me."

Ender smirked. "Well, we should test it out. I want you to be able to hear me from far away. I want to be able to hear you from far away." The words held an undertone of something Syrenn couldn't place.

"I guess you can just try shouting at me within your mind all day. You have nothing better to do with your time, do you?" Syrenn chuckled to herself.

"I live to annoy you, Syrenn." He flashed a smile her way. Her heart fluttered at his beauty. She tried to ignore the reaction he drew from her. But in the starlight alone, on the sea, she couldn't help but feel genuinely at ease with Prince Ender. The easiness beginning to settle between them was so calming and unexpected that it scared Syrenn.

"You really never tested out your power before?" Ender asked.

"No. My parents don't even know about it. No one except an old friend back home and Daphne."

"Daphne knows?" Ender's eyebrow quirked up.

"Is that a problem?" Syrenn felt herself becoming defensive, just like any other time Daphne was involved.

"Well, don't you think that's your answer on who told Gideon? They've been inseparable since they were children. She's always followed him around like a lost puppy." Ender seemed perturbed about his brother's relationship with Daphne.

"She wouldn't do that to me." Syrenn's vehemence had Ender reassessing her.

"I hope you're right, Syrenn." His face was stone as he continued rowing them to nowhere.

Silence fell between them again, neither one feeling a need to fill it. They each gazed at the night sky and breathed in the salty sea air. There was a chill blowing off the water that had Syrenn shuddering slightly.

Letting the oars rest, Ender gracefully removed his jacket and handed it to Syrenn. She was thankful it was dark, or else Ender would have seen the red stains that appeared across her cheeks. Slipping the prewarmed fabric up her arms, Syrenn inhaled the earthy scent that clung to it. It was intoxicating, the fresh pine smell of him.

"Thank you."

"You already said that."

"I know. But I want to make sure you know I mean it. No one has ever done anything this nice for me. Especially not a dark, broody prince."

"I told you. I'll give you anything you want."

Chapter 8

Screams pierced the air, causing Syrenn to leap from her bed.

The light filtering through her open window was dull, the sun barely creeping over the horizon, causing a pink glow to emanate through the room. The shadows were still so dark, and she tried not to think of Ender lurking in their depths.

She threw open her door and flew down the stairs. The screams were continuous, their cadence haunting. They echoed through her spiraling stairwell and bounced off the stone walls as her bare feet pounded down the steps as fast as she could will them.

Those were Daphne's screams.

Everything around Syrenn turned dark for a second, then she was suddenly bursting through the bottom of the stairwell. She didn't pause to catch her breath or even try to make out the mayhem around her, she only surged toward the screaming.

The West Wing was in chaos.

Servants and guards were running every which way, yelling commands. *"Get the Prince! Alert the Queen! Lock the girls in their rooms! Another murder, there's been another murder."*

Syrenn couldn't differentiate between the voiced words and the thoughts. "Daphne!" she screamed, the sound so guttural it burned her throat on the way up. A guard noticed her frantically searching amongst the chaos. He grabbed her, hoisting her over his shoulder and began running with her. "Daphne!" she screamed again, pounding her hands into his back with bruising force. He did not loosen his grip even a fraction.

"You can't be out here, Miss. You're too vital." The guard ran from the West Wing, but not quickly enough. As they passed by Vera's room, Syrenn saw what caused such chaos to ensue.

What was once Vera now lay limply across the bed. Her eyes were unseeing, shock and terror forever twisting her features. She was so pale, a stark contrast to the deep red that had since stopped flowing from the wounds marring her and was now pooling within the sheets beneath her.

There was so much blood.

A puddle surrounded her on the floor around her bed. Right where Daphne now sat, crumpled on the floor. Screaming. She was staring into her hands, her trembling body covered in blood. Fear so stark hollowed out her eyes.

Guards swarmed and blocked the view from Syrenn, but she couldn't blink back the images. This murder was so like that of Scarlett's. Those foreign memories still stuck in her mind, joined by these new gruesome ones. Syrenn could see the similarities clearly enough.

Her body bounced against the guard as he ran down the stairs that connected the West Wing to the remainder of the castle. She had stopped striking the guard who carried her. His grip was too secure, no amount of thumping would get him to drop her so that she could go to Daphne. But Daphne was alive, and that's all that mattered to Syrenn.

Daphne was alive. Daphne…

"Take her to my private chambers. Guard the door. No one is to enter but me." Gideon flew past Syrenn, and she felt the chest beneath her rumble in response.

Syrenn's eyesight began to grow black. She couldn't seem to pull enough air into her lungs as she fought against the darkness closing around her.

When she opened her eyes again, she was being sat delicately upon a settee in a lavishly decorated bedroom.

There was so much red. All Syrenn could see was blood coating the walls, the bed, the couch she was sitting on. It dripped and oozed from every surface.

"I think I'm going to be sick," she whimpered. The guard quickly conjured a vase from somewhere, just as Syrenn's stomach lurched uncontrollably. She heard different sets of feet rushing her way. She watched with bleary eyes as guard after guard filed down the hall to stand outside the door.

The man holding the vase offered her a handkerchief, which she took without thanks, too morose to speak. She felt a pressure begin to rub along her back, stroking gentle circles against the cloth of her nightgown. She glanced quickly at the guard, taken aback by his forwardness, but his hands were still wrapped around the vase before her, ready to shove it at her if she needed it.

Syrenn leaned into the ghostly feeling creeping along her spine. The touch was as comforting as she could expect after what she had just seen. Her body was trembling. She wasn't sure if it was from witnessing Vera's murder scene, or from the fact that she was now alone in Prince Gideon's room.

Though, she supposed she wasn't as alone as she appeared. The steady presence of Ender still gently tickled along her shoulders, trying as he might to calm her wrecked nerves.

The guard left once Syrenn assured him she wasn't going to vomit again. She heard as he locked the door behind him, caging Syrenn within the four bleeding walls.

Something brushed the hair from her face, and Syrenn leaned into the touch without thinking. *You can come out now.*

Ender draped a blanket around her shoulders before settling himself beside her.

"Vera." Syrenn choked out. Her throat was raw. Had she been screaming?

"I saw." Ender's voice was a hushed whisper. "Did you catch anything from anyone as you were brought here?"

"I was a little preoccupied." Syrenn tried to sound annoyed, but the words came out flat. "I thought someone was attacking Daphne. I didn't think, I just ran. I didn't think about searching anyone's minds."

"I know. I shouldn't have asked." Ender curved his arm around Syrenn and pulled her into him. "Take comfort in knowing that if the murderer is indeed my brother as I suspect, he won't harm Daphne. He loves the girl too much."

"Then why didn't he choose her?"

"She doesn't have the power you do. The council was adamant he choose you once they learned the truth. But there is no doubt in my mind that he intends to string her along on the side, even after the two of you wed." The comment turned Syrenn's stomach. Gideon was terrible.

"Why would he be killing us? I don't understand."

"There has always been something... different about Gideon. He has always had..." Ender stopped speaking for a moment. She looked at him, and he seemed far away. The pull of her inner power stretched toward him. *No,* she told it.

"He's always had sadistic tendencies. He hid it from mother and father, but he couldn't hide it from me. When we were younger, I think he believed a little too much in our histories. He thought I was like him. He thought I liked..."

"He thought you liked hurting people," Syrenn guessed. Ender nodded, looking away. "Are you all sure he isn't the elder brother?"

"We're sure." Ender found no humor in Syrenn's attempt to ease his tension. "It scared me, to see what he would do. To see what was left of the creatures he collected. I reasoned with myself, though. They were only creatures. Birds, woodland critters... never people. He never hurt people." His pain-filled eyes flicked to hers. She fell into their darkness, the pain, his sorrow for his younger brother. Her power won. She now felt his agony as if it were her own. Her power swirled within him while he stared at her, unwise of the invasion.

"You didn't stop him?" She tried to keep the accusations at bay. She felt his internal flinch as her words stung.

"I tried. I tried keeping animals from him. I tried explaining to him the fear and pain he was causing them, moments before he snapped their necks. He pretended to understand, but I think it only intrigued him further. After that, he kept it from me as well. But I've always been cautious with him. I knew it would resurface at some point." Ender dropped his face into his hands. "I never thought it would be people. I never thought he would do this."

Footsteps echoed behind the closed door, and Ender disintegrated where he sat in the blink of an eye. She pulled the blanket tighter around herself, the absence of Ender's warmth startling. She shivered and clenched her jaw to keep it from rattling. Perhaps she was going into shock, she thought.

The door burst open, and Gideon entered with a flourish. He steered directly for Syrenn, kneeling just before her, collecting both her hands in his own.

"My dear Syrenn, are you alright? I'm so sorry you had to see that." Gideon seemed genuinely concerned for her. His eyes held unease, which was so out of character for him.

"I think... I think I need to lie down." Syrenn's voice shook. Her entire body was wracked with tremors she was unable to stop. Gideon stuffed a pillow behind her back as he lowered her down into the settee. He rushed to his bed and quickly gathered his duvet. The weight was so comforting atop Syrenn as he tucked each side beneath her. Taking a seat on the floor, he rested a heavy arm across her body. His fingers dragged down the skin of her cheek.

"You poor girl. I'm so sorry." He whispered the words as he stroked her cheek. *She's petrified. I should get a healer.* "I'm going to call for a healer. Your color is draining." He summoned a guard from the open doorway and had them go to fetch the castle healer. Syrenn's teeth chattered audibly, but she was unable to clench her jaw tight enough to stop them.

"Sweet girl, we will get you something for your nerves. The healer is coming." *Hurry, hurry, hurry...* He repeated the mantra over and over in his head. Syrenn saw as his eyes grew more terrified with each passing moment her trembling didn't subside.

Someone entered the room, and relief washed over Gideon. The fear dancing in the edges of his eyes didn't diminish fully, though. The woman swept in, robes billowing out behind her. Her dark hair was braided in a crown around her head. Syrenn noted her copper, uptilted eyes and broad mouth. Her power stretched towards the beautiful woman. Syrenn had to use all of her strength to pull it back.

"She's in shock," the healer said in way of greeting.

"Fix her," the Prince commanded. Pleaded, actually. He stood and began to pace the floor. The healer took Gideon's place next to Syrenn and gripped her by the back of the head, hoisting her up. She was much stronger than she appeared, to Syrenn's surprise.

Syrenn's muscles spasmed. More pillows were placed behind her to wedge her into a sitting position. The healer pulled the blanket from her and Syrenn began shaking more from the chill in the room.

"I think it best we light a fire. Her skin is cold and clammy, and it will help comfort her after I do my healing." Gideon only nodded and went to converse with one of the guards still standing in the hall. Syrenn could only watch, taking in the workings of both the healer and the guard—the one who had ran with her, bringing her here. The guard stormed into the room and stood before the hearth. Syrenn blinked, then noticed a fire crackling within. Gideon patted the guard on the back then dismissed him back to his post.

The heat of the fire was almost immediate. The healer grasped Syrenn's hand within her own, ignoring the guard and Gideon altogether as she worked. Her eyes closed and Syrenn watched her face contort with concentration. A tingling sensation began to creep into her finger, slowly making its way up her arm. Syrenn's heart fluttered frantically as the woman's healing powers danced with Syrenn's own force, then enveloped the entirety of her body.

The sensation was warm and prickling, like drinking cinnamon tea. The trembling in her extremities subsided as the healer's powers spread throughout. Syrenn's body ached, and she couldn't stifle her groan, feeling so unbearably tired and heavy.

There you are. "Your body will be sore for a while. You'll need to rest. A warm bath with soothing salts may do you a load of good as well." She rubbed her fingers along the back of Syrenn's hand. "Don't hesitate to call for me again for anything, Miss."

The healer left with a bow to the Prince before Syrenn could even ask her name.

"How are you feeling?" Gideon was now perched on the edge of the settee, cradling Syrenn's hands in his own.

"Sore, but better." She tried to sit further up but winced with the effort. "You had me worried."

"What about Daphne? Is she alright?" Syrenn began to panic once more. The Prince rubbed the length of her arm, trying to sooth her.

"She's being cared for by another healer. She'll be okay. It will take time, but she'll be alright." *The poor girl.* Syrenn didn't know if Gideon was referring to her or to Daphne.

"I thought you said no one could get into the West Wing? You said you added more guards."

"The guards are there, but apparently it wasn't enough. I'm beginning to think you were right, Syrenn." The Prince shook his head before meeting her eyes. "The only person who could get in there unnoticed is Ender."

"What do you mean? You said you questioned him." Syrenn's gut twisted.

"I did. But it seems he's found a way to trick me. You know, his powers are quite extraordinary. He can melt into shadow and move about unnoticed. We don't tell people about it. The council says it could be useful, and to keep it secret. But I wonder if that doesn't just enable him," he contemplated. *He has been known to take advantage of his ability to lurk about undetected…*

Syrenn filed away the Prince's stray thought. Perhaps Ender was, in fact, tricking her to keep her off his trail. She hoped she was wrong.

"I don't feel safe, my prince."

"Maybe we should move you from the wing…"

"No!" Syrenn shouted the refusal before she could even think. She loved her room; she didn't want to give it up. "I mean, surely no one will be able to climb all those stairs unnoticed. And wouldn't anywhere else be even *less* guarded still?"

Gideon sighed. "I just don't know how to keep you safe." *If anything happens to her...* "I'll put your own personal guards outside of the tower. Maybe we can get you a chime, something you can ring for help if something happens." *Surely Ender wouldn't be daft enough to go after my betrothed.* She noted how concerned Gideon seemed about her. It was so out of character from the Prince she had been forced to court this past year.

"I'll feel much safer." Syrenn placed her hand atop the Prince's. "You're doing everything you can. Don't blame yourself." Syrenn wasn't sure if Gideon was being honest or trying to trick her. Regardless, she needed to get closer and gain his trust to find out.

She could play that part, for now.

Chapter 9

A silhouette flitted through the halls, unseen by those around it. Even in the daylight, the space it assumed turned into a void; the eyes of those near simply skimming over it without even registering its existence.

That had always been one of its best qualities—going unnoticed in the masses of people. Unnoticed even when it was the lone entity within a space. Able to sneak about and act without consequence.

There was a murderer within this castle, and it had to prove who was killing these girls.

It was easy for that silhouette to fall back into its old routines. Though they had remained unused, unpolished for so long, it felt like slipping back into an old skin. Oh, how that silhouette wished to be home. To be back in those trees, that forest. Being caged here was a prison unlike any other. Bound by something it could not control. Something it could not deceive.

Though it had tried. Numerous times.

Not only was it bound into staying, but it was also bound into silence. Bound by the thing the silhouette knew was murdering those girls. But that silence made it unable to tell. That binding made it unable to lift a finger against the menace. It needed to find a way to stop the murdering—though it couldn't be by its own hands. It needed to find a way around that binding in order to do what it craved most.

Enact justice for those who could no longer defend themselves.

From down the corridor, the silhouette spied the guard with fire in his veins. The silhouette knew that fire so well. That knew *it* so well. That fire enraged the silhouette every time it glimpsed it.

He wasn't supposed to be here.

He was never supposed to be here. But now, that fire was bound to this Southern Kingdom just as the silhouette was. And there was nothing either of them could do about it. That fire was another reason it needed to rid itself of the binding. The silhouette always had a knack for saving those around it.

Though the silhouette was invisible to everyone within these walls, that fire saw the silhouette. He always saw it.

The silhouette scurried into an empty room. It waited, leaning casually against one of the stone walls.

One. Two. Three.

The door opened. Three heartbeats was all it took for that fire to find it. As it knew he would.

"What are you doing?" that guard asked it.

"I am doing what I can, since no one else seems to be lifting a finger to stop this madness." And it was madness, the silhouette thought to itself. How nobody could tell what was going on, that these murders we're coming from one person and one person alone. How everyone was so blind to that person made no sense to the silhouette.

"You are endangering yourself; you are disposable." He knew what the silhouette was talking about, without a word having been specified. That connection between them ran deep.

Fire gleamed behind his eyes. Usually well-guarded, they now shone with unease and concern for the silhouette. It bit it's tongue in retort, wanting to thrust out its fist in response.

"It's in my blood, I can't just let this keep happening." How could it let the murders continue? It had been one to kill at one point so long ago. But those deaths had been justified. These murders were just for sport.

For pleasure.

"You can, and you will. You are just as bound as I. What do you plan to do? Skulk around the castle and eavesdrop?" The guard stepped closer, pinning the silhouette against the wall. It leveled a glare at him. "That's the extent of your ability currently, and you know it."

"Yes. But the girl. If I learn something, perhaps she can see it and—"

"The elder prince has already asked for her assistance."

The silhouette blinked back it's surprise. The girl, she was already trying to get to the bottom of this. It never would have pegged the quiet, sad girl as the vigilante type. She was from Farehail, though. Perhaps the way of the island was bred into her in some way.

"I hope he offers his protection. This is a dangerous game that he's roped her into."

"Of course. Prince Ender wouldn't risk an innocent life like that." The guard's body tightened with defensiveness.

"I don't trust anyone here. I'm not as willing as you seem to be."

"I'm not willing, I'm making the best of a shitty situation." The guard stepped back, allowing the silhouette to put space between their bodies.

The silhouette said nothing more; it simply floated from the room on its catlike feet. Back down the hall.

It wouldn't listen to the guard. It was intent on its path. It would be the eyes in the darkness, even with its hands tied. Unable to do what it did best.

Unable to eliminate.

Chapter 10

Syrenn spent the entire day sleeping on Gideon's settee.

She was almost afraid she wouldn't wake up. But at the same time, she felt safe within his walls. His room was the most secure place within the castle besides the West Wing. And, if he were the true killer, then her death would be the last. He was the only one permitted to enter his room while she was resting there, so the question of who killed her would be of no issue.

Syrenn was now being escorted back to her own room by two guards. They flanked her as they walked through the dark, quiet castle. It was late, but the Prince felt it was best if she didn't spend the night alone within his room. Since she was still supposed to have her maidenhood, it would be unbecoming for her to stay overnight with him, no matter the extenuating circumstances.

The guards at her back were silent as they walked into the West Wing. Syrenn paused when she passed by Vera's room. It was now closed off, with more guards stationed before the door barring anyone from entering. Syrenn swallowed back her sorrow.

She noticed then that each of the girls had guards stoically standing before their doors. This calmed Syrenn, albeit slightly. It would take some plotting to get beyond the doors and murder the remaining girls.

Or someone like Ender.

The guards before the stairwell parted for her as she came to the tower entrance. She nodded her thanks to each of them as she began to ascend the stairs. The two following remained at the base of the stairs, leaving her to climb the way to her room alone. Her bare feet made no sound on the stone steps as she spiraled higher and higher. Suddenly, the hairs on the back of her neck raised as the feeling of being followed resonated with her. She stopped and turned abruptly, stifling a gasp before it escaped her parted lips.

No one was there. She turned back towards her room, shaking her head in annoyance.

Ender leaned against the stone wall; his arms crossed over his chest. A smirk cut across his lips.

"How can you be smiling after another girl was murdered?" Syrenn demanded.

"Because that girl wasn't you. And you're gaining his trust, Syrenn. That's a step in the right direction." Ender took two steps down, coming to stand just above her. "If you keep this up, we'll have what we need in no time. He'll slip up if he thinks you're falling for him." He was staring down at her. The step between them only added to the way he towered over her. Syrenn was not short by any means, but Ender dwarfed her immensely.

"Gideon made a good case, though. The only person capable of getting into these rooms and committing these crimes unnoticed is *you*. How do I know this isn't just some trick? Perhaps you *do* plan to kill me next." Syrenn whispered the last words and instantly regretted them. She knew it wasn't true. It was as if some force were pushing her and Ender together, urging her to trust him.

Stone pressed into Syrenn's back as Ender materialized before her in the blink of an eye. He didn't touch her, only loomed down above her, seething. Syrenn watched as shadows slithered around her waist, then continued upwards, finally gliding between her breasts. She shuddered and sucked in an audible breath, her body melting at the lightness of the shadow's touch.

Ender brought his face to hers, their lips nearly brushing as he said, "I told you already, Syrenn. There are so many more enjoyable things I could do to you than kill you." It was a whisper. His exhale pressed against her mouth as she drew in sharp breaths. Her lids fluttered closed involuntarily, and her chin tilted ever so slightly higher.

The pressure of the shadows intensified, and she heard herself gasp. His hands joined the shadows, the touch just as soft as they drifted along her stomach and up towards her chest. She felt his heat move closer, but she didn't dare open her eyes. Syrenn gave over to that touch; gave in to her gut when it screamed at her that none of this was Ender's doing.

His face nestled into the crook of her neck where he inhaled deeply, causing her head to fall back and rest upon the wall. A hot, wet trail was dragged up the column of her neck as he licked his way to her jaw.

"Stop," Syrenn breathed as she crushed her mouth to his. His tongue dipped between her lips and she ran her own along his and tasting him. He groaned into her mouth—her body tighten at the sound, and she deepened their kiss further. Tangling her fingers in his hair, she tugged harshly. His body slammed into hers, pressing her roughly into the wall. He gripped onto her neck, her breasts. His hands were everywhere and Syrenn only wanted more.

More.

She must have said the command into his mind because he obliged without hesitation. His hand drifted lower and began bunching up the nightgown she was still wearing from the night before. His fingers dipped beneath it and onto her exposed skin. They found their way between her legs, and she whimpered at how soft they felt against her thighs.

He brushed his fingertips along her center, feeling her arousal. She tightened in response and dug her fingers into his shoulders. He pressed his body further into her, and she felt his hardness digging into her hip. Letting go of his hair, she began clawing at his trousers. The fastenings gave way almost instantly, and Syrenn had the feeling Ender's shadows had provided their assistance.

She pulled him free, wrapping her hand around him and stroking him roughly. His hand looped around her backside and lifted her from the ground. She enveloped him between her legs and pulled him into her. She groaned as he slid deeply inside, the heat of him near scalding.

"*Syrenn*," he hissed into her mouth and into her mind. It was a plea, and she bit down on his lip in response. He moved inside her, slowly but not gently. Syrenn moaned and heard the sound echo against the walls. She bit her lip to try and quiet herself.

Footsteps began to stampede up the steps and Syrenn was abruptly dropped back to her feet. Her exposed body chilled from the emptiness. Ender was gone, leaving her hollow, but the shadows surrounding her deepened. She smoothed her dress and began to ascend the stairs once more, as if nothing had just transpired.

"Miss Syrenn, are you hurt?" The call rang loudly and Syrenn turned to see the guards a few steps below.

"I'm fine." Her voice sounded gravelly. She winced.

"We heard a noise; it sounded as if you were in pain."

"I'm still sore from this morning. I think you just heard me overexert myself," she lied easily. She felt Ender's amusement in her mind, and violently pulled her power back inside herself.

"Do you need our assistance to make it the rest of the way?" This guard took his job too seriously, Syrenn thought. *She looks flustered. I hope she doesn't pass out on us. The Prince will have our heads.*

"I'll be fine, I assure you. I just need more rest." Syrenn swallowed down her smirk. "Thank you for your concern." She nodded and turned away, dismissing the guards back to their posts.

When the guard was out of sight, Syrenn ran the remaining way to her bedroom. She could strike Ender for leaving her like that, hollow and wanting, stumbling like a fool in front of the guards. She ripped her door open, knowing he'd be there waiting.

Ender was sprawled across the bed, a taunting smile on his face.

"Miss me?" he crooned.

She slammed her door then lunged at him. She watched as his face contorted in a mix of shock and enthusiasm. She straddled him, then smacked him across the face. The sound reverberated throughout the room.

"Ow! That actually hurt." He had the audacity to feign offense as he smiled a wicked grin. "You are a violent, little thing." His teeth gleamed from the moonlight filtering in through her open window. He grabbed both her wrists, twisting his body so that she was beneath him. She thrashed halfheartedly against him.

He looked at her in awe before crushing his mouth to hers. She bit him, but that only made him hiss in pleasure. *Don't you fucking leave me like that again.* She slammed the thought into his mind, and she felt him tense for a second while he absorbed her words and their force.

He responded by dragging his shadows up her body. He broke their kiss long enough to let them tear the nightgown from her skin. She grabbed his face and brought it back to hers, pressing her mouth into him. She yanked his shirt over his head, and she felt as he slid his pants down his legs. She spread herself for him, and he nestled into her.

Hooking her legs together behind his hips, she pressed into him as he drove into her. She yelped in pleasure, and Ender's hand abruptly covered her mouth.

Groaning, he whispered in his ear, "I swear if you make them interrupt us again, this won't continue to happen." He nipped her earlobe playfully.

Liar. She said into him.

Yes, I am, he chuckled back. He quickened his pace and Syrenn whimpered in response. His body ground against her with every thrust, the heightened sensations sending her into spasms. *I crave you, Syrenn.*

She bit down on his shoulder to stifle the cries from her climax. She shuddered around him, but his movements didn't falter—only dragged out her pleasure further. She was on the edge of tears, her body convulsing beneath him before he finally fell over the edge with her.

Shuddering, he stilled above her. He held his weight on his elbows and peered at her as she breathed heavily, staring back at him.

"That wasn't your first time, was it?" His mock concern had her shoving him away. He laughed, "Aren't you supposed to be chaste?" He rolled onto his back and placed his hand onto his chest. He grinned at her.

"Would your brother have your head if it were?" Syrenn spat.

"Probably, until I told him that you initiated it." He rolled to face her. "Then he might have yours." A bit of the playfulness left his features. *Maybe we should keep it between us. I'll be pissed if you wind up murdered next.*

"How gallant of you."

"So, my body then? In exchange for your services? Or is this just a perk of the arrangement?" Syrenn shoved him again and tried to roll away. He grabbed her and dragged her into his chest. He pressed his face into her hair and inhaled deeply. *Don't worry, my violent Syrenn. I'll get you far from this mess. You have my word.*

Exhaustion swept through Syrenn, and she chose not to answer. The warmth of his body lulled her into sleep. It had been so long since she had been held like this. He remained with her for the entirety of the night, watching over her. His shadows swirled around the room, standing guard, a protection from the unknown.

Syrenn awoke naked and alone. Her body was still sore from the tremors of the day before. Her head held a low throb as well. She stretched her body across the bed, trying to loosen her muscles.

A stray shadow bounced across her exposed skin, brushing along the curve of her breast. Syrenn smiled to herself as she brushed it away. It swirled once in the air before her, then disappeared beneath her bed.

Come find me. The thought swam on the edges of her consciousness, so quiet it was as if it had to travel a long way. Her powers reached out, consuming it greedily.

Where are you?

It's not a game if I just tell you where I am, Ender teased.

Let me dress.

Now, where's the fun in that? She could feel the wanting in his words. She couldn't stop the blush from creeping up her neck and onto her cheeks as she departed the bed in search of a suitable dress. *I can still taste you, Syrenn.*

Her blush deepened and she pushed him from her mind while she slid the dress up her legs. For just a moment, the horror of recent events didn't weigh as heavily. She found herself almost floating down the spiral stairs connecting her tower to the rest of the West Wing.

When she emerged at the bottom, however, the gravity of the situation swarmed back around her. There were guards everywhere. Two stationed before each of the girls' bedroom doors. She was thankful, knowing it would take someone either ruthless or insanely cunning to get past them.

Or a Prince.

Daphne would be safe. That was all Syrenn cared about. Daphne was so pure, so kind, she did not deserve to be another forgotten victim. She didn't deserve to be tossed away by the Prince either, Syrenn thought. She would fix that part of things, she just needed to find a way, though she didn't want her friend tied to a murderer.

I'm waiting, Syrenn. The voice in her head was slightly louder now. Syrenn bit back her smirk. The somber West Wing was not the place she should be seen smiling, if only to avoid the suspicion of others. She knew that everyone was dumbfounded about who the murderer was. No one suspected the Prince like Ender apparently did. The last thing she wanted was for everyone to assume it was the Prince's betrothed. The girl who had always seemed so uninterested but was now the future queen. It did seem suspicious, looking in from the outside.

The most likely assailant was the Prince, though. This notion made sense in Syrenn's mind as well. She would not put it past the egotistical, arrogant, power-hungry man. When playing with dolls gets boring, what else is there for a man to do but break them?

Syrenn hurried down the hall and out of the West Wing. Her back prickled as she noted the guards flanking her. Would they follow her everywhere she went? How would she find Ender and keep her dealings with the dark, broody Prince secret if she was being followed and watched at all times?

She stewed internally as she descended the stairs and started for the main castle. *Dark, broody Prince,* Syrenn thought in a singsong voice, willing her power to project toward Ender. *Come out, wherever you are.* She could almost feel his chuckle inside her mind. She had never dreamed her power would be this enticing. *Give me a hint,* she pushed toward that feeling of amusement, just on her edges.

That would be cheating, and I am no cheat. We're trying to see how far away you can feel me. A shadow tickled the sensitive place behind

Syrenn's ear. Her flesh tightened into taut bumps, and she shivered. *And it seems like it's quite the distance.*

Are you staying in place, or are you moving? The sound of his voice within her ebbed in a wavelike pattern, as if he were moving between rooms of the castle as she searched.

I'm moving. So, you better be quick.

Without thinking, Syrenn burst into a run. She thought she saw a trail of shadow skirting around a corner. She leapt after it, startling the guards at her back. Their shouts of protest rang out, but she paid them no mind. She was faster, and she knew it. Even in the dress she wore. She had spent two decades running about the forests of Farehail, chasing after friends, running from her title and the expectations of her parents.

Syrenn rounded the corner, then another, taking a door just to ensure she lost them. She pressed her back into the door of the room, listening as their thundering steps faded down the hallway. Prince Gideon would have their heads for this, figuratively speaking. He wasn't one to waste good help, even if they failed to protect his future bride. She knew her place. She was a throwaway.

I give up. Syrenn shot the words to wherever Ender was hiding and waited.

"But you've already found me, Syrenn." The whisper pulled a smile from Syrenn before she could stop it. "Happy to see me?" Ender's body materialized on the couch, just before the empty hearth.

"Don't flatter yourself." The words fell flat, but Syrenn didn't care. She was annoyed with herself, but she couldn't deny the reaction the elder Prince pulled from her. She had always been... intrigued by the idea of him. She never guessed him to be so evocative though.

"Your guards will be in trouble." Ender crossed one leg over the other and lounged back into the couch.

"I don't think I need them, anyway. Surely Gideon doesn't plan on offing me until *after* he's made me bear his children." Syrenn gagged on the words.

"I won't let that happen."

"Which part?"

Ender became deathly still as he held eye contact with her. "Either. I won't let him touch you."

Syrenn couldn't stop the fluttering in her heart, and she hoped he spoke true. She also hoped it had to do with his feelings for her, and not because she was an innocent girl who shouldn't be murdered. Or be forced to marry against her will.

"What do you need me to do?" Syrenn swallowed the lump in her throat.

"Just spend time with him. Get close to him. Keep your mind open. He's bound to let something slip."

"That's it?"

"Well, if you get the opportunity, you can rifle through his thoughts. Search for something. But do be discrete. You don't want him to know you're in there. That might put a target on your back."

"I already have a target on my back." Syrenn felt a calmness as she said it, as if accepting the fate.

"I promised I would get you out. I will not break that promise, Syrenn." The words were hushed. Syrenn trusted him. Against everything she had learned while in the Southern Kingdom, against what logic said, she trusted Ender to keep his word. "Now, I'm sure Gideon is waiting for you to join him for breakfast." Ender's eyes took on a far-off look. "Yes. They're all waiting on you. Daphne looks like a wreck. You probably should calm her fears."

"Can you see through your shadows?"

"Yes. They are a part of me." Ender smiled knowingly at Syrenn.

She felt her mouth gape open. Ender laughed as she turned and angrily shoved out of the room. She slammed the door behind her. A shadow followed her down the corridor, and she shot it a dirty look.

After arriving to the dining hall, Syrenn noticed a tension to the atmosphere surrounding the room. Both Aster and Daphne wore sour expressions, while Gideon sat at the head of the table unwise to their displeasure. Syrenn tried her best to not let it bother her. She knew her friend was going to be upset and had yet to find the time to talk with her about it.

"Daphne, would you join me on a walk later today?" Syrenn asked as she took the seat Gideon now held out for her. She ignored the feeling of triumph and arrogance coming from Gideon as he admired her body. Her jaw tensed all the same though, and she silently cursed her power for latching onto Gideon.

"I am quite busy today. Since Prince Gideon has chosen *you,* my parents are rather keen on spending more time with me. Since it seems I've wasted the last year in the castle, and not with them." Her words were bitter, and Syrenn's stomach plummeted.

"Daph—"

"Now, Daphne. There's to be no hard feelings. Syrenn wasn't the one who made this decision. If you wish to be angry with someone, be angry with me." Gideon said sweetly, while fluttering his eyelashes at her. She blushed and turned away, focusing instead on the plate before her.

Syrenn remained silent. Daphne would come around, she had to believe that. She couldn't lose her only friend over something that she had no choice in. She would gladly hand Gideon over to her on a silver platter.

Although not if he truly was the murderer. Syrenn really needed to remember that part.

Daphne needs to quit her crying. As if the Prince won't still sleep with her once he marries the dumb bitch.

Syrenn tried to hide her shock as her powers latched onto Aster's thoughts. Were Daphne and Gideon sleeping together? Why hadn't she said anything, and how did Aster know?

Syrenn stewed on the information all through breakfast. She offered conversation where needed, focusing on delving into Gideon's mind. It was tough, trying to dance around the outer edges, avoiding his own power sensing her, while he talked with each of the girls in turn. Diving straight in might alert him to what she was doing.

She learned nothing. Other than the fact that Gideon was completely full of himself, which she already knew. He had no plans of being faithful to her. She heard the thoughts he had for Aster, and even Daphne. He didn't plan on letting them stay home for long. He intended to keep them on as her ladies in wait.

For better access.

Syrenn was disgusted, but not surprised by his thoughts at all. She was surprised to learn that Daphne indeed had been meeting with Gideon in secret, though. Gideon was careful not to linger too long on those memories, aware that Syrenn could hear them if she chose to. She found him thinking on her power multiple times throughout the meal. Never about how he learned of it, only that he knew of what she could do.

That was something she wanted to find out for herself during her time snooping for Ender. How had he found out about her powers? Did she slip, and he felt her power in his mind on one of the many occasions she deigned to listen in? Or had he been informed by someone?

Ender had discovered for himself almost instantly after officially meeting Syrenn. Maybe she wasn't as careful as she liked to think herself.

"Syrenn, since Daphne seems to be busy with her family this evening, I wondered if you would join me on a walk tonight in the atrium?" Gideon had sidled closer to her, nearly whispering the request into her ear. "We could star gaze together."

She looked at him sidelong. He wore a gentle smirk, almost completely devoid of his normal arrogance. He lowered his lids, looking down at her body. "Of course, my prince. It sounds like a lovely time," she whispered back to him. She offered him a small smile of her own.

Good Girl.

Enders voice in her head nearly caused her to jump, though her powers perked up at the sound. She really should shut him out.

Don't you dare.

How are you reading my thoughts now? Syrenn shot the words out into the abyss.

I'm not. You just looked annoyed when you heard me, so I just assumed what you were thinking. The smugness coating the thought had Syrenn rolling her eyes. *You are getting quite good at hearing me easily, though.*

The more we use this connection, the stronger it gets. My power gets attuned to yours, so it's easier for it to pick up on you. That's why I try not to use it. I can hear Daphne easily, too, though I keep her blocked out most of the time to respect her privacy.

It is quite interesting, how your ability works. So, the more we speak like this, the more of my naughty little secrets you'll be able to uncover? Ender was amused now.

Precisely. The stronger this bridge between us gets, the harder it is for me to block you out, or you to block me out. Unfortunately.

She felt Ender chuckle in her mind. *Do make sure you pay attention to the present, even when I'm distracting you in here. Daphne is staring at you.*

Syrenn's eyes shot to Daphne, who was indeed staring at Syrenn. She offered her a small smile, but Daphne only continued to stare. Syrenn opened her mind to Daphne, assuming she wanted to share something privately.

Are you talking to someone?

Syrenn blushed and subtly nodded her head.

Who?

I can't say.

You're keeping so many secrets, Syrenn. It wasn't a nice thought. Syrenn refrained from throwing the accusation back at her. Daphne put up her own walls, blocking out Syrenn before she could retort, anyway. Syrenn swallowed the sour taste it left in her mouth.

Chapter 11

The atrium was beautiful at night. This wasn't Syrenn's first time walking the open expanse at nighttime, but it was her first time strolling about with a partner, flanked by guards.

The room opened above them to the night sky. The warm air slowed around Syrenn's body, and she could smell the sea just outside the castle walls.

Even though they were surrounded by an ungodly amount of bodies, it was silent. The only sounds were that of their feet and their even breathing. Syrenn could hear her heart beating in her ears. She was walking next to an odious man, but it was an otherwise peaceful night.

Gideon looped his arm through hers, stopping her. "Have you ever just stopped to admire the constellations?" Syrenn tilted her chin to the sky. The vast expanse of the stars loomed above them, glittering starkly against the surrounding blackness.

"I used to often when I was a girl." She couldn't make her voice raise above a whisper; afraid she might scare them away.

"It's fascinating to think about, wouldn't you agree? How something so small can bring so much joy to people." Gideon remained staring up at the sky. "Do you think these are the same stars you saw as a girl?"

"I've always thought of the stars as being constant. Never changing. They are the same stars I have at home."

"Tell me what you're thinking."

Syrenn closed her eyes, letting the command pull her truth forth. "That even though these are the same stars, I would much rather be looking at them from my home."

"This is your home, my dear. You need to dismiss those notions from yourself." Gideon's tone wasn't harsh when he said it, though his slight annoyance was there. "I can give you so much more than you ever dreamed of in Farehail."

Syrenn chose to remain silent. Yes, he could buy her any tangible item she wished. But Syrenn was never one to want *things.*

She wanted her freedom.

And you'll have it.

The sound of Ender's voice caused her heart to skip a beat. Her power danced around the notes, pulling them deeply into her. Eventually, Ender would become undeniably aware of the reactions he caused her. The more the connection was used, the more he would be able to dig into her own mind as well.

This was one thing about her ability she did not enjoy, nor was she willing to tell him about it just yet.

You want to know my *naughty little secrets, but I can't know* yours?

Syrenn ignored him. She didn't shove him from her mind because she knew it didn't matter if she did. He was lurking somewhere in the shadows. Watching.

Always watching.

"I can make you happy, Syrenn." Syrenn flinched. She had almost forgotten she stood with Gideon, and not Ender.

Gideon's arm untangled from hers. She faced him, curious to see where his thoughts had gone while she was preoccupied with Ender. She pushed her power into him, gently.

So beautiful... Syrenn blushed. Gideon's eyes had softened, admiring her in the starlight. She saw herself from his perspective—her bright hair almost shimmered beneath the stars, her dark eyes like the abyss between the glittering starlight. She watched as her own lips parted slightly and saw the blush as it crept onto her cheeks.

She pulled from his mind, but not before she heard his intentions.

Gideon dipped his head low, closing in on her. Syrenn stared in horror as his eyes fluttered closed and he continued across that distance between them. She froze, taking a moment to accept that this was a part of getting closer to him, of gaining his trust.

She closed her own eyes as Gideon's lips met with hers. He pushed them against her, the hard lines of his lips foreign against her own. His arms draped around her; his hand gripping the back of her bicep, tugging her closer as he moved his mouth to deepen the kiss.

She reciprocated. As best she could. Her nerves were knotted into a tight ball. She didn't like this. She wanted to shove him off her but couldn't move. Nor would he take kindly to her rejection.

His tongue darted out and she gasped at the abruptness. He mistook the noise for that of enjoyment and plunged his tongue further into her, groaning into her mouth. He stroked it along her own. Syrenn could only focus on how wet it was. How stiff it felt. She wanted to gag.

She felt as if she had been stabbed in the gut, with the way she was twisted inside. Her hands trembled from where they remained on her sides. She should move them onto him, she thought. She needed him to believe she wanted this.

She pressed her hands into his chest, gently enough to seem accepting, but firm enough to make the trembling stop and to keep him slightly at bay. He pulled her even closer, roaming his own hands down the length of her back. He stopped them at a place too low to have been considered appropriate.

Syrenn waited for the kiss to finish. Her eyes opened and she stared at his closed ones. When Gideon made no inclination of stopping anytime soon, she pushed herself back into his mind to pass the time while he was otherwise preoccupied. She disconnected herself from her body, piercing her power into his mind.

Her body... Mmmm. Could I take her? Here, now? Syrenn almost choked. *That would be too forward. She isn't like Aster. She would be put off by it. And I need her.*

Syrenn dug deeper, behind his current thoughts of her body, and into his memories. She was flooded with images of Aster, naked and entangled with him in his bed. *In Aster's bed. Late at night in the garden.* Syrenn would never look at the bench by the roses the same again.

When she delved even further, she saw glimpses of Daphne. Sweet, stolen kisses. Some recent, some of them as teenagers—children.

"It's you, Daphne. It will always be you. Until my last breath. I promise." Syrenn heard the words, uttered by Gideon as a young teenager as he coaxed her into his bed. She didn't sense a lie behind them, though. Her heart ached for her friend.

"I don't want to do this charade, father." Syrenn fell into a different memory. *Gideon stood in the throne room at the bottom of the dais. The King loomed above, lounging in his throne. He sipped dismissively from his drink.*

"I don't care about your wants, boy. You will do as I say. It is tradition. If you end up still being set upon the girl, you can have her. But surely, we can find you a better match. Someone with power. Not someone as common as the Delphi girl."

Gideon scoffed. "Just because she doesn't hold an ability like us, doesn't mean she is common. An allegiance with her and her family would be very valuable—"

"Her father and I are already great allies. A marriage to his daughter is unnecessary. Now leave. The girls will arrive within the week. And you better play along." The King's command held an underlying threat.

Syrenn dug further into the memories. She was chasing a feeling of grief. *She saw Gideon, standing once again in the throne room. Only this time, his father did not sit upon the throne. The King was convulsing on the floor. His skin turned gray and shriveled before Gideon's eyes. Syrenn could feel the sting of a wound marring Gideon's abdomen. She could feel his horror as he processed how his own father had plunged a sword into his gut.*

Ender swept in on a cloud of shadows, flanked by many guards and the Queen. "Do something!" The Queen was screaming, sobbing the words. A healer rushed in, heading for Gideon. It was the same healer that had helped Syrenn just yesterday.

Syrenn didn't hear Gideon acknowledge the healer's name. "No, go to my father. Something is wrong." The healer obeyed the command, coming to a kneel before the King's body. She placed her hands on him. She turned to look at the Prince, then shook her head.

"Tell me what's wrong." It was a command, drawing the truth freely from the healer.

"Poison. It came from that retched tea. There isn't anything I can do." The healer looked on the verge of tears as she spoke.

"Ender." Gideon resolved to the only action he could take. He hated to do it. His body was riddled with absolute anguish and horror as he gave the command, "Put him down."

Syrenn leapt from the memory just as Ender drew his dagger from his side, and back into the one's surrounding Daphne. *Daphne ran through the corridors of the castle, Gideon chasing after her. They were young, Syrenn noted—during their mid teen years. Gideon finally caught up to Daphne and swung the girl into his arms. The trill of Daphne's giggle ring* through the corridor as Gideon ushered her into a room. He closed the door behind them, whisking Daphne towards the settee before the fire.

"I love you, Daphne. I can't wait to make you my wife when the time comes." Gideon murmured the words into Daphne's ears, drawing a blush from her.

"You think your father will allow it? What of the traditions?"

"I'll convince him that there is no one better for me than you." He dragged his lips along her throat, nipping the skin lightly.

"I'd do anything for you to make that happen, Gideon. Anything." Daphne grasped his face and brought it to meet hers. "I would be nothing without you. You are my everything."

Gideon's face held so much love, and Syrenn felt for the first time she shouldn't be prying. The two kissed, then began dropping to the couch, tearing at the other's clothes.

Syrenn leapt forward in time. If she were looking for something to condemn Gideon, she needed to go to a time after his father's demise. Everything was out of order and running together. Syrenn rifled through the memories that rushed passed. *More intimate moments with Daphne. Moments in the city beyond the castle walls. Moments in the forest, picnicking beneath the summer sun. Finally, the arrival of all the contenders. Gideon's annoyance at having to learn names, then his intrigue at being able to sway them into his bed. His dismissal of Daphne's feelings on the matter. He was only doing as his father wished, after all.*

Syrenn internally rolled her eyes at his logic, launching away from those feelings of entitlement. *The morning Scarlett was murdered, Gideon sat at the breakfast table with a feeling of exhaustion and unease. His hand trembled beneath the table as he talked with Aster. The girl was dead, he thought. She was really dead. He couldn't believe it, even though he—the thought was cut off as Daphne and Syrenn entered the room, fingers tightly laced together. A bolt of jealousy lanced through Gideon as he noted the girls clinging tightly to each other.*

Slipping from those memories, Syrenn's power began unlatching from Gideon's mind. She saw a quick flash of long, silky black hair against the crashing waves of the sea before falling back into herself.

She became undeniably aware of a pain in her lips so fierce as she came out from Gideon's mind. Her head was beginning to throb. As she fully settled back into her own body, she felt how strongly she was gripping the Prince's clothes.

His hand was a vice on her backside. He must have been encouraged by how forcefully Syrenn had started kissing him. She pushed him away, as gently as she could manage.

"We can't," she breathed. Her heart pounded in her chest.

"I'm sorry. I got carried away." His apology was genuine. Syrenn straightened her clothing and dragged a hand through her hair. She had lost control over her actions while her power took its fill. "Let me take you back to your room."

"Thank you." Syrenn was thankful he relinquished and didn't press her for more than she could give. He looped his arm once more in hers, and she turned her head towards the shadows. She used the back of her free hand to wipe her mouth, noting how swollen they now felt.

A shadow skirted its way around the foot of a guard and into the surrounding blackness.

Syrenn reached the top step of her tower. She pulled her key from her pocket, but the door clicked open from the inside. Letting herself in, she braced for Ender's taunts.

"Did you enjoy my brother?" The words were clipped.

Ender sat on the window seat. His hair danced in the breeze blowing through the open window. Shadows shrouded his face, so Syrenn couldn't make out the expression that sat upon it.

Syrenn glared at him. "You asked me to get close to him. So, I'm getting close to him."

"I didn't tell you to do *that*."

"What are you talking about?" Syrenn pulled her nightgown from her chest drawer. "Can I change in private, or do you plan to spy on me through your shadows?"

Ender dissipated without a word.

Syrenn turned her back to the room, knowing good and well Ender was still there, somewhere. She pulled her nightgown down over her head before letting her dress fall to the floor. When she turned back around, Ender was sitting atop her bed.

"I thought I was about to see something that would forever scar me, with how deeply you slammed your tongue down his throat." Syrenn could almost taste the bitterness thrown her way. She felt her power writhe beneath the surface in response.

"Are you *jealous?*" Syrenn accused. She was astounded by the idea, especially coming from the dark, broody Prince. One that only just deigned to get to know her, and for his own gain at that.

"No. I just don't think you need to make a fool of yourself in front of those guards. They're going to talk, you know. They'll tell everyone about how loose the Prince's betrothed is," he spat.

"So, it's only okay when I'm doing it to you, then? You had to know this would be a cost of our arrangement. And as you said, I'm his *betrothed*. No one would have batted an eye if I had stripped down right there and let him fuck me on the floor." Syrenn was nearly yelling now.

"Did you at least gain any sort of information?" Ender dismissed Syrenn's anger.

"He was not happy about keeping up with Southern tradition. He wanted to marry Daphne."

"I knew that already. Did you get anything useful?" Ender said, belittling her.

"The only other thing I saw was the King's end, and the anguish Gideon felt over it." Syrenn crossed her arms, still standing in the middle of her room.

"Useless," Ender mumbled under his breath.

"I'm sorry it isn't enough for you. Maybe when he fucks me, he'll be distracted enough so that I can dig deeper."

Ender was before her in an instant, materializing out of darkness. He slammed her against the wall, careful not to let her head hit against the stone. His hand was around her neck, squeezing tightly enough that Syrenn could feel a growing pressure in her eyes; the feeling exciting a small, dark place deep inside of her.

"Let him fuck you, and I'll slit his throat." There was such venom in his words, Syrenn was almost afraid. Almost. Behind the venom was indeed jealousy, and that caused Syrenn's heart to flutter. Her vison started to go black around the edges, but she still saw the flicker of regret as it passed over Ender's features. Then, the surrounding shadows consumed him, and she was alone.

Chapter 12

Syrenn was now free to walk about the castle as she wished. While she still had to attend some classes and was trailed by at least two different guards everywhere she went, she wasn't expected anywhere else other than meals. She relished her newfound freedom, no matter how limited that freedom actually might be.

Syrenn sat behind the grand piano, fingers dancing over the keys. The music filled the parlor, bouncing off the walls and reverberating back into her. It was an old song. Something she had learned as a young girl. The melody was soft, almost somber at times. It was a comfort piece to Syrenn. She didn't have to think much as she played—her fingers ghosted over the keys, finding their way on memory alone.

The bench creaked beside her, and she felt someone take a seat. Her fingers stumbled, causing an atrocious noise to emit from the piano and echo throughout the room.

"That was beautiful." Gideon placed a hand upon her thigh, gently gripping her flesh. "You have a talent, my dear." He leaned his face into her neck, inhaling and parting his lips into a kiss. He pressed them firmly against her, sliding closer to her upon the bench.

Her skin pimpled and she froze, allowing him to taste her as he wished. She dipped into his mind while he was distracted.

Lavender... He noted her perfume, then pulled away from her before she could dig further.

"Will you dine with me tonight? Just the two of us." It wasn't a command, neither from his ability nor his position. It was a question, one Syrenn thought she might truly have a choice in.

"Just the two of us?" she asked, considering actually denying him. She didn't want to be alone with him, not after what had transpired between them beneath the stars. With every moment they shared like that, she had no doubt word would get back to Daphne, and her only friend would start resenting her more.

"On the terrace in my wing of the castle. I'll have the kitchen make something special. We haven't celebrated yet."

"Celebrated?" Syrenn asked, confused.

"Yes. Our engagement. Shouldn't we celebrate something so joyous?" he asked, innocently. *She doesn't believe I want this.*

Syrenn flinched inwardly. Was he being truthful, or trying to manipulate her?

"Of course. Tonight. Will someone come to collect me?"

"I'll send my guard to your tower. He'll escort you directly to me." Gideon brushed his lips across hers in a back and forth motion. "Maybe we could pick up where we left off last night." The whisper caressed her lips, his breath hot and not unpleasant on her mouth.

She shivered, and Gideon smiled.

"I'll see you tonight, my bride."

Daphne sat upon the chest at the end of her bed, leaning back against the foot board. She had a book open on her lap, but she stared out her window—unseeing. Trees nearly blocked any view she had, anyway. Critters scurried about the branches, fighting over a morsel before scampering away and out of sight.

"Can we talk, Daph?" Syrenn asked.

Daphne jumped, knocking the forgotten book from her lap. It landed with a thud. "Syrenn. Why are you here?"

Syrenn closed the door behind her, ignoring the look the guards stationed beyond exchanged. As if she would hurt her dear friend.

"I want to apologize to you."

"For what?" Daphne gave her an annoyed look.

"For the Prince. I didn't want this. You know that." She projected every bit of hopefulness she had into her gaze as she closed the distance between them.

"I know, Syrenn. But I'm still allowed to be upset. It was supposed to be me..." Her voice became pained as she spoke. Syrenn stepped up to the girl, grabbing her hand and clasping it tightly in her own.

"It should be. I'm trying to find a way out. I swear it to you." She chose not to mention the allegations Ender had of his brother. She didn't need to worry the girl.

"I don't think you can, but I admire you for trying to save my feelings." Daphne slipped her hand from Syrenn's, lacing them into her lap.

"You're my only friend. I don't want to cause you pain." Daphne offered her a tight smile in response. "I do have to ask, though. The Prince only chose me because he discovered my powers. You didn't tell him about them, did you?"

Daphne remained quiet for longer than necessary. Syrenn watched as her face ran through a series of emotions. Her shock contorted into anger before she said, "Do you really think I would betray you like that?"

"I'm sorry. I just don't know how he figured it out." Syrenn moved her gaze to the floor, ashamed for even asking.

"Well, you keep checking out at dinner talking to whoever else it is that knows your secret. Maybe he's noticed, or maybe the mystery person told him." Daphne scoffed. "I can't believe you thought it was me, even for a moment."

Syrenn dropped to the chest, head in hands. "Please don't abandon me, Daphne. I don't want to be alone in this."

"Who else knows about you?" she asked, gentler this time.

"I don't think I can say just yet. Don't be angry, but I think I need to respect their privacy." The girls looked into each other's eyes, communicating with more than just their words.

"Is it a lover?"

Syrenn stiffened. Was he a lover? Or was he simply using her, just as his brother was using her in another way.

"I'm not really sure." Syrenn answered honestly.

"I don't follow. Either it is, or it isn't."

"We haven't talked about it." Syrenn saw something flicker from the corner of her eye. When she looked, there was nothing there.

"Well, if it is, just know I'm happy for you. You've been alone this entire time. No one should be alone." Syrenn didn't point out that Gideon was making sure she wouldn't be alone, even if she wanted to be.

"I'm supposed to have dinner with him tonight." She gave Daphne a pointed look. "You know I despise the man, right?"

"I'm well aware." Daphne smirked at her. "Oh, Syrenn. I was never mad at you. I'm mad at myself for allowing him to lead me on."

"You should be mad at him. He should have known better. If he didn't plan on choosing you, he should have broken it off."

"Yes. I am mad at him. But I still love him. Does that make me daft?"

"No. I understand how you feel." Syrenn ignored the shadow lurking beneath Daphne's chest of drawers.

Daphne leaned her head against Syrenn's shoulder, curling her arms around Syrenn's frame. She nuzzled her face into Syrenn's collarbone and breathed in deeply, right where Gideon had just been. Her fingers traced along the exposed skin of Syrenn's arm.

Syrenn reciprocated the embrace, her heart skipping a beat as Daphne sidled closer. The two clung to each other as tightly as they could. It had only been a couple of days, but Syrenn had grown distraught while being separated from Daphne. They had always shared this closeness, and it ached to be parted.

"Promise me we'll never fight again. My heart can't take it," Daphne's breath tickled Syrenn's neck as she spoke. She hoped the girl couldn't feel the pounding of her heart from where they were pressed so tightly together.

"I promise, Daphne."

Daphne pressed a soft, wet kiss onto the crook of Syrenn's neck, the touch so much sweeter than Gideon's. Her lips lingered a bit longer than was necessary, though their friendship had always scathed the line into something more. Syrenn's hand traced its way to Daphne's hair, clutching the curled locks between her fingers while Daphne's fingers swirled circles along Syrenn's shoulder.

"Do you hate me?" Ender asked in way of greeting as Syrenn entered her room.

"Of course, I do," Syrenn dismissed.

Ender's mouth opened and shut, like a fish trying to catch particles floating within water. "I beg your pardon. What have I done to deserve such feelings?"

"You exist."

A shadow swirled around Syrenn's hand. She batted it away, but it had already latched onto her. It circled around her wrist like a bracelet. Or a manacle.

"This is because you're mad at me, isn't it?" Ender was in front of her now, stopping her from walking further into her room.

"Yes, I am mad at you. But no, that isn't why I hate you."

"Then what is it, *Syrenn*?" The voice vibrated from deep within his chest. Her eyes fluttered up to his.

"You're angry with your brother for using us girls, then disposing of us, yet here you are doing the same."

"I'm not using you," he said indignantly.

"You aren't? Then what is happening here?" Syrenn quipped back.

"I'm paying you for your services, rather handsomely I might add. And this is mutually beneficial to us both." His fingers tilted her chin up further. He examined her face with a neutral expression.

"What payment have I received? I know when we're finished, you'll be happy to dump me off somewhere, but I haven't received anything for my services thus far, other than your disrespect after doing what you *asked* me to do." Syrenn set her jaw in defiance.

"Oh, sweet Syrenn. You've received my *services* in exchange for your services. Or was it so lacking that you've forgotten already?" His smile was wicked. "Would you like me to remind you?"

Syrenn laughed aloud. She laughed harder seeing the puzzled look that appeared on Ender's face. She pushed away from him causing him to drop her chin. "Oh. That was supposed to be payment?"

"You really are a vicious one." Ender sneered at her. Shame coated her tongue like acid. "I apologize if I left you wanting, and I apologize for how I acted last night. Now, would you prefer a different form of payment while you await your freedom?"

Before Syrenn could respond, shadows swirled around her, and she was being tugged away. The air whipping around her stole the breath from her lungs. The darkness clung to her eyes, a temporary blindfold depriving her of sight.

Sunlight burst through that darkness, equally as blinding. Syrenn felt the softness of the ground beneath her feet as her vision cleared.

Everything was green around her. She was in a forest and could hear the crashing of waves onto the shore somewhere in the distance. Ender stood behind her, so close she could feel the heat of him.

Run. She made no move. *Have a taste of freedom, Syrenn. This is what we're working towards. Run.*

Syrenn ran. Ender's shadows followed closely behind, but she managed to stay a step ahead of them. Her feet stumbled over the uneven ground. She slowed long enough to gather up the skirt to her dress, then continued forth. She careened between the trees, having no inclination of where she was going.

Only that she wanted to be far from the castle.

She flung herself into a tree and disappeared in an instant. The shadows following her faltered and scattered around its bark. They circled the tree as if searching for Syrenn on the other side and dissipated when they couldn't find her.

Syrenn emerged miles away. She kept running, heading straight for another of the large pines within the forest.

She ran directly into Ender instead.

"How the hell did you just do that?" He loomed over her from where she had fallen to the ground. His expression was guarded.

"Do what?"

"You just ran *into* a tree." His voice had risen a few octaves. "And then you came out all the way over here."

"Says the man who can turn into shadow." Syrenn pulled herself from the ground and dusted the back of her dress.

"Do you realize how far you've traveled?"

"How did you find me so quickly?"

Ender didn't respond, but instead dipped his head towards the shadow that was still daintily wrapped around her wrist. It had solidified into a dark, black band.

Syrenn was disgusted. She projected as much hate into her gaze as she could. Ender looked pleased with himself.

She shoved him, hard. He stumbled, but still smiled at her. She shoved him again, then darted past him straight into the tree.

She didn't hesitate this time, only disappeared once more into a third tree. She kept this up, no longer greeted by Ender on her appearances back into the forest.

The sky opened before her, and she ran into it. She pushed all her might into her legs, ignoring the barking of her disused muscles. Her feet pounded against the dirt. She made it to the edge of a cliff but made no effort to stop herself, instead projected herself forward with all her strength.

Falling was such a sickening feeling, Syrenn thought as her body plummeted down, down, down. She let go of all her rage, all her longing as she braced herself for the impact.

She didn't feel it.

She was consumed by darkness, and she let out a sigh. Her body floated within that void. It pressed against her skin in such a comforting way that she was confident she was dead.

What am I going to do with you, Syrenn?

Her eyes burst open a moment before her body was dropped into ice cold water. The shock caused her to suck in a breath. Water plunged into her mouth, pouring down her lungs—the salt stung her eyes. She thrashed, kicking her legs and clawing towards the surface.

Her head broke free; then her surroundings swirled into black once more.

"So, you don't actually want to die." Her body was gracelessly dumped onto the ground. Sand stuck to her wet skin and clung to her dress. Her face turned to the side, and she purged the water from her lungs. The salt stung her throat and nostrils, causing her to cough repeatedly.

Ender lounged on the beach beside her, unruffled. He looked at her expectantly. "Fuck you." Her voice croaked.

"Please do," he smirked.

She wanted to hit him, but she was too exhausted. Her head fell back into the sand. She closed her eyes and listened to the waves crashing. The sound was near deafening at this distance. She smiled to herself.

"Don't do that again, Syrenn." Ender's voice was nearly inaudible. She felt his shadows wrap around her like a blanket, holding in the warmth from the sun.

"Why?"

"Just... don't." His voice had such a finality to it, she didn't question him. She didn't tell him that it wasn't her plan to jump from the cliff. She just did, as if compelled.

"Thank you." Her voice was raspy, rubbed raw by the salt water. "For taking me out here. You don't know what it means to me."

"I see what being caged does to you. Obviously, it makes you a little bit... impulsive. And not in a good way." He laid on the sand next to her. She felt his fingers brush hers.

She pulled her hand onto her chest.

"I grew up in the forest, much to my parent's dismay." She smiled with the memory. "I always snuck out of our house. They would be so cross when I finally wandered home."

"Is that when you discovered you could travel through the trees?"

Syrenn opened her eyes to look at Ender. He was studying her face. "Everyone with powers can walk through the trees. Is that not how it is here?"

"Not that I've ever seen." His expression was serious. "It's commonplace, then?"

Syrenn only nodded.

"How?"

She propped herself up onto her elbow. "Our histories say that our powers come from the trees. Because of the connection, they allow us passage."

Ender laughed. "As if they're sentient?"

"Why couldn't they be? Aren't your shadows sentient? Don't they move by your command?" Syrenn pierced him with a stare.

"Interesting."

"This sand is drying to my skin. Will you take me back to the castle now?"

"So soon?"

"I have dinner with the Prince. I'm sure he'll expect me to look my finest. I should probably spend some time checking my crevices for sand." She got to her feet. Her dress was heavy from the water and sand still tainting it.

"As you wish." Ender didn't move, but darkness began to swim from him.

They were back in the tower in an instant. Syrenn stared at him, expectantly.

"What?"

"Do you really expect me to walk out from my tower wet and covered in sand? Take me to the baths," she demanded.

"Only if I can help," he said as he swept them away.

When they appeared in the bathroom, Syrenn swatted him away. "Come back when I'm finished. I know you're watching, but you don't need to be obvious about it." He left with a smirk.

After the tub was filled with steaming water, she undressed and climbed in. She scrubbed her skin with the soaps, but didn't plunge her head beneath the surface, still rattled by her fight for the surface in the ocean. When she was finished, she submerged her dress under the water, trying to rinse the sand from the fabrics. She wrung it out as best she could, then hung it upon the rack.

She listened as the water droplets plinked onto the floor.

She'd forgotten to bring a clean dress to put on.

Ender appeared a heartbeat later, holding a swath of fabric between his fingers while his other hand was draped dramatically over his eyes. She ripped the robe from him and wrapped it around her body. His fingers parted, and he peaked out at her.

"How are your crevices?"

Syrenn rolled her eyes. Ender took them back to her tower without another word, chuckling to himself through the darkness.

Syrenn moved straight to her vanity, and the lavender oil atop. She unstopped the bottle and let the oils drip into her palm; the pungent aroma filled the air. Replacing the bottle, she warmed the oil between her hands and began to press it into her skin.

Ender swirled before her, half shadow, and plucked the bottle up. He sniffed it, then wrinkled his nose. "Would you like my assistance?"

"You can get my back," Syrenn said, turning from him and letting the robe slip from her shoulders. She stopped it at her waist. He didn't touch her initially, so she looked over her shoulder towards where he had been.

He stared back at her in disbelief, still clutching the tiny bottle. She watched as he blinked back his surprise. Her lips curled as he approached her. His fingers brushed her still damp hair over her shoulder. She looked away from him as he began dripping the oil onto his palm.

His hands were soft when they connected with her shoulders. He rubbed his thumbs in circles, pressing deeply into her muscles. She let out a sound of contentment, unable to keep from leaning into his touch. She could feel his breath skating across her skin as he massaged over her skin.

"You won't be alone tonight," he whispered to her. "I'll be watching."

"Always watching."

His hands gripped her shoulders and twirled her around. She scrambled to cover her breasts with the robe. His lips connected with hers, devouring them. She tangled herself with him, drawing him into her, ignoring how her robe parted. Her body was flush with his, his hands snaking around her waist to hold onto her backside. He squeezed and she groaned.

He pushed into her, forcing her to relinquish step after step. Her legs made contact with her bed, and he shoved her back onto it. She pushed herself back, lifting her legs from the floor. He crawled over her, covering her body with his own, dipping low to continue their kissing. She spread her legs, allowing him to nestle closer to her. His clothes were rough against her sensitive flesh.

Her hands dragged low, fingers itching to pull the fabric from his body. She gripped his pants, but something pulled her hands away. They were tugged above her head and pressed firmly into the mattress.

Shadows.

"Now is not the time for that, Syrenn," he said into her mouth.

She made to protest, but he drank it down. His kiss deepened, and she couldn't taste him enough. Her tongue ran along his, their lips crushing harder together. Her hips thrust upwards, eager to make contact with him. He moved farther away.

He disconnected from her, leaving her panting and empty on the bed. She pulled her robe closed, glowering at Ender as he stood and admired her.

"That wasn't nice," she hissed.

His lips parted and his eyes trailed over her exposed skin. He looked... hungry. "I'm not a nice person, Syrenn. Remember that."

He was gone before she could let any other words leave her lips.

Chapter 13

As Gideon promised, a guard retrieved her when it was time for dinner. She followed as he led her through the halls and into the Prince's private wing. They bypassed his room and continued to a library.

It was enormous. Shelves towered high above Syrenn's head, and she was awed by the volume of books lining them. The guard continued to the double doors at the end of the expansive library. They opened, revealing a terrace alight with dozens of candles. Each flame flicked in tandem with the stars above.

Gideon stood before an ornately decorated table. The table itself was small, crowded with dishes and more candles. He greeted her with a pleasant smile, and her answering one was not completely false. Rounding the table to meet her, he grasped her hands in his.

"You look lovely, my dear. Please, have a seat." He pulled out one of the chairs and guided her into it. Before he sat in his own, he poured her a glass of red liquid.

Wine.

The girls weren't allowed to drink wine during the competition. It was said to make them act unbecoming, or something Syrenn couldn't remember. She'd had it a few times back home. Usually, on nights she'd snuck out with one of her friends.

Maybe there was logic to the rule after all, Syrenn thought. She hadn't acted very pious on those nights long ago.

She thanked Gideon as he took his seat before her. Servants came forth to plate their dishes. The meal smelled divine. There was smoked fish with a garnish of lemon, potatoes that had been roasted in some sort of savory sauce, and a pile of fresh greens. There was a mountain of fresh bread between them as well.

Syrenn could feel her mouth begin to water.

"It smells wonderful, doesn't it?" Gideon's teeth gleamed in the light of the candles. "Eat. You look hungry."

Syrenn nodded and began spearing her food onto her fork without a word. She made quick work of the food. Gideon offered commentary on the mix of flavors during the meal, but it was otherwise silent.

Syrenn enjoyed the silence, though. Too often, Gideon wouldn't shut up. When he was quiet, he was rather nice to be around. He smiled more when he was alone, too, she noticed.

"How is your dinner?" Gideon's voice was gentle. He looked almost amused, and that's when Syrenn noticed she had eaten at least twice what he had. She swallowed, then sipped on her wine to clear her throat.

"It's amazing. All of it. It's breathtaking up here, my prince." She dropped the piece of bread she was eating back onto her plate.

"Will you please call me Gideon already?"

"Am I allowed to?" Syrenn felt silly asking the question, but she also genuinely didn't know.

"You can if I command it." Gideon took on a devilish look. "*Call me Gideon.*"

Syrenn couldn't help the blush that crept across her cheeks at the sultry tone he commanded her in. She smiled as she let the words roll from her tongue. "Gideon," she breathed.

His smile became almost feline in response. "You have such a lovely voice, Syrenn. I could listen to you talk for hours and never grow bored."

Syrenn wiped her mouth on the napkin, then placed it over her plate. "While it is lovely out here, I wonder if you would mind me exploring your library?" She couldn't help her intrigue. Gideon could see the anticipation written throughout her body. She was nearly bouncing with excitement.

"Of course. Asher, would you please start the fires inside the library so that Miss Syrenn can see what titles I have?" The same guard as before came forth, then receded into the library. Syrenn stood and was soon joined by Gideon. They walked arm in arm into the library.

Asher stood before the hearth, going still as death for a single moment before flames burst from the logs. He moved to the hearth on the opposite wall, doing the same. The room warmed noticeably from the crackling fires.

"That is quite impressive," Syrenn said in awe.

"Isn't it? People with abilities in fire are quite rare. When we discovered Asher here, we had to hire him on. He's aptly named, as well." Gideon smirked. "I believe he comes from Farehail, too. Isn't that correct, Asher?"

The man silently nodded in response before taking up a post by the terrace doors. He was the same man who had taken her from the West Wing and into Gideon's rooms after Vera was murdered, Syrenn noticed.

"You two don't know each other?" Gideon seemed confused.

"I don't believe so." Syrenn was sure she had never seen Asher before arriving at the Southern Kingdom.

"I thought Farehail was quite small. My healer is from the island as well. And you didn't recognize her either?" Gideon raised an eyebrow.

"My parents were the hovering type. I wasn't allowed out much and barely had any access to people I wasn't related to," Syrenn lied.

"That makes sense. I've heard the island is savage as well. I could see them wanting to protect you by keeping you locked up." Gideon placed a hand on Syrenn's back, guiding her toward the towers of books. She was thankful he was so dismissive.

Syrenn crept to the towering cases of books. Running a finger across the many spines, she admired his expansive collection. He had everything from histories to fairytales it seemed. She plucked one of the many whimsical titles from the shelves, opening it to the first page.

"So, you like the fairytales?" He sent her a condescending smirk.

"Yes. That's mainly what I read back home. I like the escape from reality." She smiled to him, batting her lashes in the way she knew he liked. She had seen the other girls do it many times before, and it made him mad with lust.

He pulled the tome from her hand, flipping the pages idly. He stepped away from her before dropping the book onto a side table. "Tell me about the ones you had back home. Which was your favorite?"

Syrenn followed his lead, sitting down on the couch next to him. "Well, there was this one about our old queen. Long before the fall of Farehail."

"Ah, yes. Where she turned to stone?"

"That was always a favorite of mine."

"Why is that, Syrenn?"

Syrenn blushed before explaining, "Well, she didn't have to choose between her true love and her kingdom. It was either kill her lover or give up her kingdom. The trees turned her to stone before she had to make that choice."

"The trees?" Gideon furrowed his brow.

"Another tale in our land. The trees have power over us. It's where our power originated from." A burst of laughter exploded from Gideon. Syrenn blushed and turned away.

"I'm sorry, sweet Syrenn. I don't mean to embarrass you. I do love your simple tales."

Syrenn bit her tongue to keep from retorting. The weight from Gideon's hand plopped onto her shoulder, and it took everything in Syrenn not to cringe and brush it off. His fingers gripped into her flesh, urging her to turn toward him.

"Really, Syrenn. I'm not trying to laugh at you. I've just always found those stories amusing."

"Right. Well, as you said, they are quite silly. They just comforted me as a child."

"I can see that. Well, just know that you will never be in that position. This is all yours. I am all yours. You get both." He smiled, trying to reassure her.

Syrenn didn't want his kingdom, or him for that matter. But she gave him her best smile in return. "Thank you, Gideon. I am not worried about either." Lowering her eyelids, she peeked up through her lashes.

Gideon's smile faltered. Glancing at her mouth, he slowly dipped his head to meet her lips. Syrenn was ready this time and devoured them as soon as they connected. His body was against hers instantly. Arms tangled around her back, and she began clutching at his chest in response. Swinging her leg over his lap, she pressed her core into his hips. He sat back deeper into the couch and his hands roved over her body hungrily.

Her lips pressed so hard into his that they hurt, and he opened his mouth for her tongue. Her arms were wrapped around his head, clinging to his hair. She felt his hands trail down her back and rest onto her hips, his fingers digging into the flesh of her backside. He pressed his hands forward, and Syrenn knew what he wanted.

Her hips rolled forward; her core connected with his hardness. She was thankful for the clothes between them but smiled to herself, taking the moment of his snagged focus to dip into his mind. She rolled her hips subtly—slowly—again and again as she speared her power deeper.

She felt her body flying around in midair as he flipped her beneath him. She yelped, and her power was effectively flung from his mind from the shock. She heard the door to the terrace silently open, then close once more.

Asher, trying to give them privacy.

Syrenn's heart began to thunder, but she continued kissing the Prince. She tried pushing her power back into his mind, but then he thrust himself against her, pulling a different sort of yelp from her mouth. He groaned against her lips and thrust again. A jolt of pleasure pulsed through her where they were connected.

Gideon reached a hand between them, feeling for her over her dress. Her head dropped back into the arm of the couch when he connected with her sensitive flesh. She stifled her moan. He moved his mouth to her ear, nipping slightly at her lobe.

She didn't want to do this.

He removed his hand and continued thrusting against her, his rhythm unrelenting. She tried to push her power back into him, but it was useless. She couldn't hold onto a thought for longer than the break between each of his thrusts. The sensations were building, her mind was growing more and more numb, and she was so angry with herself.

Her body tightened, stiffening as the sensations peaked beneath him. She clamped her mouth shut to keep from crying out, and the sound she made was a strangled sob. Gideon thrust against her a few more times before shuttering with a grunt. They both let out heavy breaths, and Syrenn's gut sank with the knowledge of what she had done.

What he had pulled from her.

She pressed gently against him, trying to wriggle free from beneath his weight. "I need to go back to my rooms." Her voice was trembling, and she refused to look at him. She could feel the sting of tears threatening to overflow from her eyes.

Gideon sat up and pulled her to him. He hugged her into his chest and began petting her hair in a soothing manner. She rested her head on his shoulder and blinked back her tears.

"Let me walk you—"

"No," Syrenn cut him off harshly. "I'm sure Asher could escort me well enough."

Gideon looked into her eyes, and she noted as a flash of hurt blinked across his face. She felt bad for only a moment before she stood and crossed her arms expectantly. Gideon rose to his feet and walked to the terrace without another word. She listened as the door clicked open and the Prince's muffled words floated into the night air.

Two sets of boots sounded, closing in on her. Asher stood and avoided meeting her gaze. She brushed off the sorrowful look Gideon gave her and headed for the library doors.

Her room was empty. She hated herself for the sinking feeling it left inside her. She had expected that Ender would be waiting, just like the time before. But she was alone. She couldn't even sense any of his shadows, save for the one around her wrist.

She had stopped at the bathing room on her way up to wash the feel of Gideon from her skin. She felt wrong—used. After quickly changing, she folded herself beneath her blankets. There, she finally let the tears fall, thankful no one could see.

Her nights with Gideon were proving useless. She had found nothing—had only been taken advantage of on both occasions. She felt awful, and she attributed it to the fact that she had failed in her one job. If she failed, she wouldn't make it out of this castle alive.

She was not upset because it felt like it was a betrayal of Ender.

No. That definitely wasn't it, she thought.

Her body became heavy, her eyes so sore she couldn't keep them open. Sleep finally began to claim her, and there was not a thought in her mind. She felt a softness brush along her cheekbone but was too exhausted to flick her eyes open. Just as a deep warmth settled next to her, she drifted off into a dreamless sleep.

Her room was still dark. Her head still ached. She could tell she hadn't been asleep for long. She could smell the unmistakable pine scent of Ender. Idly, she wondered if he spent a lot of time outdoors or if he had a special soap made.

Her bed was warm, and she could feel Ender's breath against the back of her neck. It was deep and even, and Syrenn could tell that he had fallen asleep next to her. She rolled within his grasp, turning so that she faced him. Her eyes stayed closed as she nestled closer, moving her own hands so that they pressed into him.

The fabric covering his body was soft, almost silky. Her face pressed into his neck, and she inhaled more of his woody scent. She imagined large, domineering trees surrounding her. She imagined running through them and escaping far, far away from this wretched castle.

She imagined Wren, and her chest constricted.

Ender's grip tightened on her, easing that constriction within her just a bit. His fingers brushed along the skin of her back, the feeling of it so comforting. Syrenn let loose a long, shaky breath and sidled ever closer. His hand moved to the back of her head, tilting it upwards where he met her lips in a kiss. His lips pressed lightly into hers, parting ever so slightly as the kiss deepened.

He kissed her slowly—unhurried. She hooked her leg around his hip, and somehow, Ender pulled her even closer to his body. His hand rested on her thigh, his skin hot against hers. She melted into him—his kiss, tasting him. He was sweet on her tongue, and she couldn't drink enough of him in.

I'm sorry.

She wasn't sure if the thought was hers or Ender's. It didn't matter. His fingers were tangled in her hair, pulling gently, causing Syrenn's mouth to part from his and emit a small gasp. He rolled on top of her, dipping his tongue between her parted lips. Their mouths collided hungrily as Syrenn slipped her hands up Ender's shirt. She traced her fingers along his skin, feeling the ridges of muscles spanning his slim torso. She could almost feel the dips of his ribs beneath his flesh.

Her power brushed along the inside of her ribs, reaching out towards the man pressed against her. A fluttering sensation began inside her stomach, and she felt nervous with Ender for the first time. He continued to kiss her thoroughly, as if unaware of this change. But she noted how his intensity softened, as if he too could feel her power clawing at him.

Something touched her between her ribs. She didn't know how, with Ender so closely pressed to her. But then she understood.

Go, she said to that force inside her. It obeyed.

She felt that power spear towards Ender. Not towards his mind, but towards his own dark power. She felt as they intertwined, not unlike the way she was now intertwined with Ender's body. He gasped into her mouth, causing her to shudder beneath him.

That's when she finally opened her eyes. His tousled hair framed his face, and Syrenn couldn't help but comb her fingers through it. As she was admiring his long eyelashes, his eyes flickered open as well. With the minimal light from the moon filtering through her window, they looked like two endless black holes.

She wanted to lose herself in them, and never come back out for air.

He broke their kiss, but still loomed over her, trapping her to the bed. He twined his fingers into hers and pressed her hand into the bed. His face pulled back, studying her.

"I don't want you to ever feel like you have to do that again," he whispered. His eyes were full of sorrow, and Syrenn watched as his lip trembled slightly. "Don't ever do that again." It was a plea, not a demand.

Syrenn felt her heart crack, and then the tears began to flow from her eyes. He pressed his mouth back into hers, and she could still feel their power dancing together between them. She should recall it, but she couldn't. She didn't want to. She wanted to remain wrapped up in Ender wholly like this until she took her last breath.

She kissed him back harder than before, ignoring her tears as she ripped the shirt over his head. Their lips only parted long enough for the fabric to run between them, then they collided again. Syrenn locked her legs behind Enders hips and squeezed her arms around his back. The weight of him atop her made her unable to pull in enough air.

She didn't care. He was all she needed to survive.

She pulled her lips free from him before connecting them with his shoulder. They parted and she bit into his flesh. Her tongue flicked over his salty skin and her body writhed beneath him. A guttural sound rumbled in his chest as he kissed the side of her head. She sucked at the skin she had just marred, savoring the taste of it on her tongue.

His body began to tremble and Syrenn felt as he pushed her nightgown up higher. She arched her back so he could slide it further up her body. The fabric was pulled from her shoulders, and she was bare beneath him. Their skin stuck together, the heat nearly fusing them everywhere they touched. His forearm settled between her breasts as he grabbed her by the throat. His long fingers guided her head to the side so that his tongue could lick up the column of her neck.

She was gasping. *More.*

He pushed his pants down his body, losing them within the tangle of the sheets. She met him halfway, pushing her body so that she could envelop him faster. They groaned in unison with pleasure, each tensing with the sensation. His body shivered above hers, and still she could feel her power tangled with his. It felt dark, almost like the black holes within his eyes.

She stared into those eyes as he began to move inside her. Their mouths were no longer touching, though their arms were still wrapped tightly around each other as if they were afraid to let go. His hand still gripped her neck, but this hold was gentle. She gave herself over to the feeling of him moving atop her. Her eyes fluttered closed, and she gripped his wrist.

He tightened his hold around her neck in return. She pulled his hand into her throat, savoring the pressure. His pace quickened in response, causing her head to lull back against the pillows.

Do you like the feel of me inside you? His tone was deep and hypnotic. Syrenn nodded her head against his hold on her throat. She felt his tongue against her breast as he licked his way to her nipple. His mouth closed around her and sucked gently. She moaned and ground her hips against him.

She wanted him to make her come. She wanted him to wash away the memories of his brother atop her. She wanted him as the only man to know her this way, so thoroughly and deeply.

I will kill him if he touches you again. She had the feeling Ender could hear her thoughts through the connection of their power. She could feel how vehement his words were. *You are mine.*

Syrenn erupted with his words, unaware of anything else but him. But Ender did not let her fall over that edge alone. He would never allow her to be alone again.

Chapter 14

Syrenn knew she was dreaming by the vibrancy of the colors alone. Not only was she dreaming, but her power was leading her dream, it seemed. Syrenn allowed it to take her along for the ride—to show her what it wanted her to see. What it wanted her to remember.

It was quite odd, Syrenn thought, watching as a younger version of herself crept out of her parent's manor. She had done it so often, that Syrenn couldn't pinpoint which time this had been. She was young, perhaps seventeen.

Dressed in dark pants and a shirt, she almost couldn't make herself out against the blackness of the wildlife surrounding her. The trees had always been thick around the manor. They were thick everywhere in Farehail, but their branches were almost touching in places as Syrenn floated behind herself, carried forward by her powers.

She had been bold for someone so young and unskilled. Though, a girl didn't need any skills when she had the assassins looking out for her. Shuffling within the underbrush to the side had young Syrenn darting behind a tree and waiting for the intruder to unveil themselves.

Out stepped Wren, and Syrenn's heart tightened with the memory. The self within her memory leapt forward, encasing the assassin in an all-consuming embrace. Syrenn watched as Wren dragged her through a tree, her and her power following after.

They emerged miles away in one of the many outposts that surrounded the island of Farehail. The two walked hand in hand into the building, welcomed by the excited shouts of the many inhabitants. Inside, there were many candles glowing, as well as a hearth at each end of the room. The fires cracked and cast shadows upon the walls but still created a cozy effect. Even in a building full of deadly people.

How many nights had Syrenn snuck out to meet Wren, journeying miles away to whichever outpost was that night's home? She couldn't remember but was thankful for every one of them. Syrenn had met so many different people on those nights. Had encountered so many different types of powers.

None of the assassins were aware of her own power, save for Wren. She didn't dare tell them for fear they would report her, and she would then be recruited in some way or another. Syrenn knew well enough that she was not cut out for that type of lifestyle. Wren—though sent away much later than most of the others—adapted rather quickly to what was expected from the assassins.

If there was a threat to their way of life, the assassins were unleashed. If there was a threat on another continent that could potentially affect the island, they were dispatched to take care of it. Farehail kept its secrets well-guarded—no one outside of the island knew of the guild. Everyone suspected the island was still as dilapidated as it was after the fall of their small kingdom.

They couldn't have been farther from the truth.

Syrenn focused on her current dream—memory—whatever it was she was now experiencing. She was draped across Wren's lap, drinking from a goblet, and eating off the many plates covering the long wooden table. The men and women were playing some sort of drinking game.

Yes. Syrenn remembered this night perfectly now. Wren never participated in these games. As a healer, she was there to patch up the assassins when their powers—mixed with their drinking—got out of hand. Which happened.

Often.

A young man with charcoal hair was setting fire to another man's boots, the two trading blow for blow. The goal was to see who could outlast the other. After using water he manifested out of thin air to extinguish the flame, Syrenn watched as the man with charcoal hair began sputtering. Coughing repeatedly, he finally spewed the contents from his lungs. Water splashed onto the floor.

Barbaric, Syrenn felt her younger self thinking. She smiled, rememebering how much fun she was having regardless.

The two finished their spar, the winner remaining in place for the next challenger to emerge. This time, it was an even younger blonde girl. She was petite, and young Syrenn sat up within Wren's lap to get a better view. Syrenn felt the memory of panic, her past self fearful of the young, petite girl being irreversibly hurt.

Wren nudged her, smiling slightly and urging her to watch.

The champion from the first round—the man with charcoal hair— looked uneasy as the girl made the first move. His look of uneasiness washed away almost instantly, and the man stepped toward the table. Syrenn thought he was simply getting a drink before starting the duel.

That was, until he picked up one of the many blades, bringing it up to his own throat. He held it there, eyes unfocused, before sliding across the skin.

Syrenn jumped up and screamed. The knife clattered to the floor, and everyone cheered—the young girl pronounced the winner.

It took her past self a moment to calm down enough to see that the slice was superficial.

"How?" Syrenn croaked.

Wren chuckled, pulling Syrenn back atop her lap. "She can manipulate people into doing her bidding. Amazing, right? Rarer than fire, even."

Syrenn sat back down, watching as the next competition started. The petite blond opted out of another round, leaving two new abilities to go against one another. This time, a girl who could conjure wards was against someone who could float objects. The latter favored sharp and pointed objects, it seemed, as well as blunt ones.

Waiting until the ward user dropped her guard, she was the first to need treatment from Wren. She had taken a metal chalice to the head and was bleeding profusely. Wren worked quickly, sending her healing power into the girl, the wound knitting together before their eyes.

Syrenn assessed her memory, focusing on Wren. She re-memorized her face. Her mouth—her smile. Syrenn missed her so much that the memory was almost too much for her to bear.

Taking pity on her, her power pulled her from the past gently. No more dreams plagued her for the remainder of the night, but the feeling of loss still clung to Syrenn within her unconsciousness.

Chapter 15

Ender was still wrapped around Syrenn when they awoke in the morning. Neither gave any inclination of getting out of bed. Or opening their eyes.

The chill of the morning air blew through the open window, circling around their intwined bodies. Syrenn shuffled closer to Ender, leeching his warmth. He chuckled softly as he folded her into his arms and buried his face in her pale hair. His shadows swirled above them as they held each other.

The door to Syrenn's room creaked quietly, jolting both of the inhabitants into a sitting position, still naked from the night before. Syrenn grasped at the blanket, pulling it to cover her chest as the door slowly opened, unveiling Daphne. The girl paused, taking a moment to process the sight of them before her eyes widened in utter terror.

"What the hell are you *doing*?" Syrenn didn't know if Daphne was talking to her or Ender. She scurried in and slammed the door behind her. In a flash, she had a knife in her hand, aiming it at Ender. "Are you here for her next?" Her voice was hard.

When had Daphne taken to carrying a knife with her, Syrenn wondered. Probably the moment the girls had started being slaughtered.

"Daphne, it's alright. He's not here to hurt me." Syrenn sat up straighter, as if that would help relay her point.

"I'll leave you to it," Ender mumbled before disappearing into nothing more than a cloud of shadow. The shadows skittered off and out of sight. She could still feel a piece of him in the room with her, though. Along with the small piece of her power he now held within him. A fraction of his darkness brushed along the inner wall of her ribs in response.

"What the fuck, Syrenn. Are you really that dim?" Daphne was nearly yelling as Syrenn searched for her discarded nightgown. She found it amongst the tangle of sheets and stuffed herself back into it.

"Daph, it's okay." She dismounted the bed and approached the girl, motioning for her to put her knife away. Reluctantly, Daphne did as instructed.

"You realize he's probably the one who killed Scarlett? As well as Vera and Iris. You're probably next. I would bet he bedded both before offing them, with how twisted he is." Daphne's fists were clenched at her sides, her brow furrowed in anger.

"Daphne, it wasn't him."

"How can you be so sure? Did he tell you that?"

"Well, no." Syrenn felt stupid admitting it. Ender never had denied killing the girls, only ensured he wouldn't kill Syrenn and eluded that it was his brother who had done the murdering. "We have a suspect, though."

"A suspect? Are you two playing spy?" Her eyes had gone wild, her mouth gaping as if she couldn't believe what Syrenn was telling her.

"Daphne, I *can* read people's thoughts. Who better than me to get to the bottom of this?" Syrenn crossed the room to her wardrobe and pulled the doors open. A shadow weaved between the cloth inside, attaching itself to a blue knee length dress. She plucked it from where it hung and began dressing, paying no mind to Daphne watching her like she had gone mad.

"Syrenn, I don't want you to be next. Please don't trust what he says."

"Do you know something?" Syrenn turned around after she pulled the dress over her head. She stuffed her arms into the sleeves and smoothed the fabric down her body.

"You've heard what everyone says. He's evil."

"Yes, that's what the fairytales say. But are those always the truth?"

"They are here, Syrenn. Gideon always told me of his knack for violence. How he would prey on innocent animals, working his way up to servants and the like." It was Syrenn's turn to furrow her brow. Hadn't Ender said that it was Gideon who had done those things?

"I can take care of myself, Daphne. And he seems like the only person who can get me out of this betrothal to Gideon." Their eyes met and she saw sadness pass behind Daphne's. "You know I don't want to be stuck with him. If Ender can get me out, I need to try."

"Even if he kills you?"

"At least I wouldn't have to marry Gideon."

"That isn't funny, Syrenn. I'd rather you marry the man I love than find your mutilated corpse."

"With any luck, neither of those things will come to fruition." Syrenn smiled to Daphne, hoping to reassure her. "And I trust Ender. You may think I'm crazy for it, Daph, but I trust him with my life." Syrenn hoped her gut was right about the dark, broody Prince.

Daphne shook her head in defeat. "Who is your suspect?"

Syrenn faltered. "Um. I don't think I should say until we have proof. I wouldn't want to cause an uproar if it doesn't turn into anything."

Daphne looked annoyed, then left the tower without another word. Syrenn stared after her, confused. She wondered why Daphne had originally come to the tower. She'd have to hunt her down after breakfast to ask. Maybe she would be slightly less angry by then.

What if Daphne was right? Perhaps Ender was trying to pit her against Gideon, and it was truly he who was the murderer? Syrenn couldn't deny the logic. She already hated the Prince, so just the suggestion from Ender that Gideon was the murderer was enough to persuade Syrenn. And it was such an easy way to overthrow a Prince in order to steal his throne.

The images of Aster and Gideon tangled together on the bench plagued Syrenn when she steered herself toward the garden. Squeezing her eyes shut, she tried to bar the memory from her mind.

She walked along the trails, brushing the tips of her fingers along the many different flowers as she went. The perfumes mixed with the air as she inhaled deeply. An ache for her home throbbed in her chest—to be back in the woods with the many wildflower graves. She missed lying between the stems, her body completely out of sight from those who would come searching for her. She missed the feel of the magic pulsing beneath the earth, stabilizing her and awakening her own power within.

She felt a tickle along her wrist. Looking down, she smiled to herself at the shadow that still swirled there. To any onlooker, it was simply a black cord tied neatly around her skin. If they would look closer, they would see how the darkness still swirled like smoke. She brushed her fingers across it, feeling only a minute brush of dense air.

I miss you.

Syrenn heard the words more clearly than she had ever dreamed possible. *Where are you?* She asked.

In the forest. He was so far, yet sounded like he was standing right next to her. *You know, where you performed that little trick of yours?*

What are you doing there? Syrenn couldn't keep the smile from breaking through her lips. She hoped Daphne was wrong, for her heart wouldn't be able to bear Ender betraying her so completely.

Experimenting.

Alone?

With a friend.

Syrenn's gut wrenched. Was it another woman? Had he taken someone—

Don't worry, my violent girl. You are the only person I'll allow to stab me, then fuck me.

She blushed, deeply. The darkness inside of her laced itself around her power, almost like a web. She felt her heart flutter in response.

"How are you today, my bride?" The voice echoed off the pillars and Syrenn almost jumped out of her skin. She whirled, clutching her throat to stifle the scream forming there.

"Prince, I didn't hear you approach." Her voice came out breathy, and she felt a spike of anger that was not her own spear through her.

"I can see that. Apologies if I startled you." He examined her face. She could still feel the burn of her blush there. It deepened under his gaze. "Are you alright?" He took a step closer to her, and she fought her foot from inching back.

"I am. Just admiring the flowers and missing home."

"Ah. I see. But there is good news, sweet Syrenn. You parents should be arriving in a few days." He was before her now, grabbing the arm she had wrapped around her middle. "Won't that make you happy?" His voice had lowered a few octaves, and he dipped his head closer to hers. She jerked hers back out of reflex. Offended, he gave her a quizzical look.

"Yes. I do miss them very much." She tried pulling her arm back, but he tightened his hold on her.

"Syrenn, about last night..." She looked away from him, not wanting to remember what transpired. "I'm sorry if that's not what you wanted. I may have taken it too far."

She blinked back tears, cursing herself for letting him affect her this much. For letting what had happened affect her so much. As if she hadn't already been at the receiving end of a male's cruelties on more than one occasion in her short life.

"Syrenn," he whispered. He pulled her into his arms, and she held her breath as they connected. Her body ached from how rigidly she was standing. "It won't happen again. I should have showed you more respect than that."

She only nodded into his shoulder as she continued to fight against her tears. She hated herself for it, but the thought crept in anyway. Perhaps Gideon truly was innocent in these murders. Perhaps her power consumed that thought from someone else that morning.

Footsteps reverberated around them, and Gideon pulled back. He threw a look over his shoulder, annoyed at the intrusion. Dropping Syrenn from his grasp completely, he turned to face whoever it was coming toward them.

Ender wove through the bushes of flowers and into view. His face was unpleasant as it fell on his brother. "Can we have a chat, brother?" Ender asked between clenched teeth. Syrenn took the moment to push into the Prince's mind.

She gasped and stumbled back. With quick thinking, she lunged for the roses and wrapped her hand around one of the spikey stems. She didn't feel as the thorns dug into her palm.

"Syrenn! Are you alright?" Gideon was beside her in an instant, cupping his hands around hers. She didn't let go of the stem, using the pain to focus—to calm her mind and racing heart. Ender looked at her in horror, so confused by her seemingly irrational behavior.

"I'm sorry. I didn't think. It was just so pretty I wanted to pluck it." Gideon gingerly opened Syrenn's fingers, prodding at the damage. Blood trickled from the puncture wounds, and Syrenn felt as the crimson liquid leaked down and onto the floor. Her eyes darted to Ender's, wild and unseeing.

She pushed the memory—the blood—into his mind before Gideon whisked her off to see his healer.

The healer made quick work of her hand, and Syrenn watched as the wound knitted back together seamlessly—the sight reminiscent of Wren. Gideon crooned beside her, whispering reassuring words into her ears.

Syrenn heard none of them. Her heart was pounding out of her chest, and she heard Ender's angry tirade thundering through her mind. How she had all but confirmed Gideon's guilt. How close Gideon had been to her with feigned remorse.

She noticed how the healer studied her, though. Syrenn studied her back. She took in her upturned, copper eyes, her dark hair that was yet again braided elegantly around her head.

"If you're okay, I think I should go and see what Ender was wanting," Gideon's words cut through the silence between the two women.

"I'm okay. Thank you, my prince," Syrenn dismissed. Gideon furrowed his brow.

"Syrenn."

"I'm sorry. *Gideon.* Yes, I'm fine." Syrenn was breathless and annoyed. She just wanted the man to leave her.

He bent down and pressed a kiss into the crown of her head. She cringed but covered it seamlessly with a smile. At least, she thought. "I'll see you for dinner, darling." She flashed him her teeth as he turned and departed from the room.

"Did he hurt you?"

Syrenn started. She peered over at the healer who was still clutching her hand, the injuries now gone.

"No. It was from the thorns." She felt numb.

"I'm not talking about your hand. Has he hurt you in other ways?" The healer gripped her hand tightly, giving it a small shake to try and gain Syrenn's full attention.

"Has he hurt others?" She avoided answering the question again. Syrenn's wounds were far beneath the surface. Syrenn speared her power into the healer's mind. She was met with a wall and was then abruptly shoved away. Syrenn blinked back her surprise.

"Your ability won't work on me, Princess." The healer smirked.

"Don't call me that," she hissed.

"Has he *hurt you*? You need to tell me. I've seen it all and can heal you if he has." She felt the healer's power course through her veins, searching for something to mend. Syrenn couldn't stop the foreign power inside of her, or its discovery of Ender's darkness that still draped itself over her own internal force. "You belong to someone else." She sounded almost sad as she said it, but she wasn't surprised.

Syrenn ripped her hand out of the healer's grip, effectively disconnecting her ability. "You don't know what you're talking about." She clutched her hand to her chest, looking away.

"Yes. I do." She enunciated each word. There was such heartache in her tone, it made Syrenn reassess her.

"You're from Farehail." It wasn't a question, and Syrenn did not expect an answer.

"As are you." The healer blinked back at her.

Syrenn reached out once more with her power, gently. This time she was greeted hesitantly. Syrenn saw a blur of the healer's memories. Not a healer. Assassin. She saw trees, death, and felt such a sorrow—one that had irreversibly cracked something inside of her.

Syrenn pulled back. "No. He hasn't hurt me. Not physically."

"I can heal those wounds too." She held no judgement in the way she looked at her.

"No." Syrenn did not want to forget any atrocity Gideon had bestowed on her.

"He hurts people." The healer confirmed, sounding defeated. "You need to be careful. No matter what platform he puts you on, you are not safe."

"I know," Syrenn breathed.

"Have you seen?" She gestured to Syrenn's head, indicating her ability. Syrenn gave an infinitesimal nod. "So, it's him?" Again, Syrenn nodded as bile rose in her throat. The healer, so attuned to the feelings of others, grasped Syrenn by the back of the neck and soothed her.

She stood above Syrenn as she sent waves of calming into her. The two women stood in silence for a long time. Syrenn tried to breathe evenly but couldn't stop seeing the horrible images from Gideon's head.

It was Iris, and the scene was so like the memory she saw of Scarlett. She felt the spike of morbid delight as he gazed upon the bloody bed, the mutilated corpse. He delighted in her suffering, the girl still sputtering pleas as she lay dying a slow, horrible death. Syrenn could see her insides and the blood pooling out, collecting on the floor. She watched as the light behind the girl's eyes irreversibly dimmed and became unseeing.

"Did she suffer?" The healer kept her voice even, but Syrenn heard the anger behind them.

"Yes." She wept the words. The healer tightened her grip on Syrenn's neck. "Are you going to kill him?" Syrenn asked with such hope.

The healer stilled. "No. That's not why I'm here." Syrenn didn't get a chance to ask her why she was there, if not to enact justice. Daphne burst into the room, interrupting their private conversation. Daphne stilled when she saw Syrenn with the healer.

"I didn't know you would be here. Are you alright, Syrenn?" She hesitated slightly as she stepped further into the room.

"Just a scratch," Syrenn dismissed. "I should leave. Thank you," she said to the healer.

Syrenn stepped past Daphne and hurried to put distance between her and the healer's quarters. She felt as if she were putting space between her and Daphne as well, though she couldn't quite put her finger on why that was.

"I knew it was him."

Ender's voice was full of anguish. His back was pressed against the stone wall of the corridor, his arms crossed delicately over his chest. He had appeared out of nowhere, startling Syrenn.

She glanced behind her, looking for her guards. No one was there.

"I might have a few of them in my pocket." His mouth quirked up on the side.

"Which few?"

"A few." He stared directly into her; his face set in stone. She walked towards him, slipping into the shadows that always seemed to surround him.

"What do we do about it?" Syrenn whispered the question.

"Did you know I once had a sister?" Ender stared up at the ceiling. Syrenn was so taken aback she didn't know how to respond. "She died a long time ago."

How? Her voice was caught in her throat.

"I don't know." He swallowed past a lump in his throat. "It's something that has kept me up most of my life. She was a child—six years old. I was fifteen when it happened. Gideon was eleven." A tear slipped free from his lashes. He brushed it away quickly, then brought his gaze back to Syrenn's.

"I'm so sorry, Ender." Her voice broke.

He smirked at her. "You never say my name." He stepped closer to her, placing a hand on the side of her face. "I think I much prefer *dark, broody Prince.*"

"Tell me what you need from me, my dark, broody Prince." She pushed onto her toes, tilting her chin. She planted a quick kiss onto the side of Ender's mouth, hoping to stave off his sorrow for just a bit. His eyes shuttered closed.

"I want you to stay away from him. I need to think of the best way to handle this." He took a small step back and crossed his arm back over his chest. He let out a long breath. "I had hoped I was wrong."

I know, Syrenn said into him. Ender smiled a sad smile. Syrenn took a moment to do something she hadn't done yet, not since the day of the first murder. She pushed her power towards Ender's mind.

Black, silky hair blew in the wind, long and lovely. Small hands gripped a rock, flinging it into the sea. Soft trills sounded, a giggle bursting from beautiful pouty lips. The splashing of water resounded as the rock sank into its depths. There was a feeling of pure joy and love.

Annalise.

Ender's cheeks were wet when Syrenn pulled herself from his mind. "You loved her." He nodded. "I could tell she loved you too. I have no doubt you were a perfect brother to her." Syrenn felt her own eyes begin to well up.

Thank you. For bringing that memory forth. Ender disappeared from before her.

Syrenn had unwittingly stumbled upon the Queen during her midday tea. She had gone to the parlor to tap out her anguish on the piano yet had found the queen sitting quietly alone instead.

"Beautiful girl, won't you join me?" The Queen Regent asked. Syrenn hesitated for a second too long, drawing a harsh look from the woman.

"Of course, it would be lovely." Syrenn sat across from queen Estia, smoothing her blue skirt over her lap. "It's a beautiful day."

Estia stared wistfully out of the large windows. Syrenn began to squirm with discomfort from the prolonged silence. She almost decided to creep away while the queen was preoccupied, when suddenly she spoke.

"I know you aren't happy about my son's decision." Her hard eyes connected with Syrenn's. "But you will learn to love him. It can be difficult at first, but once the children start coming… Things begin to change. It isn't about love, especially not for your significant other. But about love for your children. It will keep you going."

"I'd never given much thought to children, if I'm being completely honest."

"No, you haven't, have you? You're still so young. Well. Just know that it is what's expected of you. And soon." The queen tipped her cup to her lips and sipped.

Syrenn didn't know what else to do, so she poured herself a cup of tea as well. When she sipped, she realized it was definitely not tea. She sputtered softly, then cleared her throat. The Queen gave her a wry smile.

"You know, Syrenn, when you take my place as queen, you'll realize you can get away with many different things you never thought possible."

"Like not having children?" She was annoyed at the idea of having that decision made for her.

"Not exactly." She thought for a moment before saying, "But you'll have the freedom to find joy in life again. My children are the best thing I've done with my life. You will feel the same, I assure you. They bring you such completeness." She looked unsure for a moment.

"Has it always been happy, then?" Syrenn asked, knowing the answer already.

ery too." Her teacup clattered
back onto the plate. "Did you know my boys were not the only children I
had?"

Syrenn stared at her without answering. She didn't want to be caught
in a lie.

"I had a daughter. She passed at the age of six." The Queen went
back to staring out of the window.

"How?"

"We don't know. One day, she was just gone." Her eyes closed, as if
remembering that day. "Vanished for a bit. But I knew almost instantly
that she had passed on. I could feel it in here." She placed a hand over
her heart. "She was no longer alive. It's strange, that connection a mother
has with her children."

"I'm so sorry, my queen. I can't imagine that pain."

"Well, she wasn't the first child I lost." A sad smile parted her lips. She
began to stand, and Syrenn stood with her, intrigued by this new
admittance.

"What do you mean?" Syrenn was too afraid to try to access the
Queen's mind. She felt the queen would tell her willingly, so she didn't
even try.

"I had a stillbirth. My first child." A tear slipped from her lashes, but
she hurriedly brushed it away as she rounded the table. She gave Syrenn
a hug. "My first boy. He was born sleeping."

Chapter 16

First boy. First *boy.*

Syrenn was panicking, her heart racing. It was thundering so hard she thought she was going to pass out from the surge of blood coursing through her veins.

Ender was the second son of the Southern Kingdom. The rightful heir. What did that make Gideon?

Ender. She forcefully sent the word into the abyss.

Ender! She projected the call into his power that rested inside her. He was ignoring her.

Dark, broody Prince. She tried.

Yes, my violent girl? All of the sorrow that had dug so deeply into him earlier had seemingly disappeared.

I need you. Where are you? Blackness swirled around her and when it cleared, she was once more in the forest. Ender and Asher stood before her.

"How did you just do that?" Syrenn's eyes were wild, almost unbelieving of that movement through space. Ender only glanced at her wrist. She brought it to her face and inspected it closely.

"Are you alright?" Ender roved his gaze over her, checking for obvious injuries.

"No. Can we speak alone?" She threw a pointed look at Asher. "Is he—"

"Mine? Yes. Asher, I'll find you when we're finished here." Asher said nothing, just walked into the nearest tree and vanished. Ender looked speculatively after him.

"You should be King." Syrenn was nearly breathless, as if she had ran all the way into the forest.

"If we figure out how to deal with Gideon, I'm sure that will be expected of me." Ender brushed his hand along his jaw, then turned to look at the trunk of the large tree once more.

"No, Ender, you don't understand." Syrenn darted to him, grabbing his arm and jerking him to her. "You are the second son. The kingdom is supposed to be yours." She was tugging his arm, pleading with him to listen to her. She shoved the memory of the meeting with his mother into his mind.

His eyes glazed over, seeing what she had seen, hearing what she had heard. He blinked once, twice. He cocked his head to the side, thinking. "How did I not know this?" He wasn't looking for an answer. His arm slipped from Syrenn's grasp and he walked away from her, running his fingers through his dark hair.

"I don't know why. I don't understand what they were thinking. You are the rightful heir." Her voice was urgent. "This solves everything."

"No, this solves nothing." He turned back to her, his brow furrowing. "There's a reason my mother kept this from me." He slipped his hands into his pockets, as if unfazed by the new information.

"But it should be you. The second son gets the crown. You are the second son."

"It would appear so, but if even I didn't know about that first baby's existence, I doubt anyone else does. So, in the eyes of the land, of the kingdom, I am the evil firstborn. The people of this kingdom won't believe otherwise. They will likely think it's some trick by the evil Prince if I'm the one to bring this to light." His words had logic, but Syrenn didn't want to see his reason.

"What are you going to do?" Syrenn sounded desperate. She was hopeful that this was her way out.

"Syrenn, calm down. I will handle this." He wrapped his arms around her, crushing her into him. Her breathing slowed; her heart calmed. Darkness stroked along her inner walls, soothing her. "You won't have to endure him much longer. Not now that we know the truth."

"What did you say to him this morning?" Her cheek pressed into his chest, and she inhaled deeply.

"I told him a concerned guard came to me about what's been happening between you two, and how inappropriate it seems. I reminded him that our mother would not condone him taking advantage of his future wife in the way that has been speculated." Syrenn sighed into him.

"Do you think he'll leave me alone, now?"

"No. But he knows I'm watching and I'll keep a closer eye on you. I promise I will step in at the first sign of trouble." Ender breathed the words into her hair. "And don't hesitate to stab him if you feel the need. I will have your back." He chuckled against her.

Syrenn couldn't bring herself to find amusement in the situation. All she could feel was the memory of Gideon atop her. Ender tightened his hold and went rigid. Tilting her head up, he pressed his lips to hers.

I'm so sorry. Anguish laced the words, but there was nothing he could do to rewrite what happened that night. No matter how much he wanted to, no matter how much he tried. *The healer said she could help.*

"I don't want to forget," she whispered.

"I don't want you to hurt," he responded.

"What are you doing out here with Asher?" She was desperate to change the subject.

"I was seeing if he, too, could walk through the trees."

"Of course he can. I told you, if you have power, the trees allow you passage. Have you tried yourself?"

"That's just the thing. I can't do what you and Asher can." His face was serious.

"Really?" Syrenn was astounded.

Ender hummed his confirmation. "I can't quite figure it out."

"Maybe it's because we're from the land with the original tree," Syrenn offered. "Maybe we're special."

"Well, my violent girl, you are special." He fluttered his eyelashes at her. All semblance of sorrow and uncertainty gone. "Can I show you how special I think you are?"

Syrenn felt her cheeks heat from his undertone of menace.

Run.

Her feet moved instantly, and she slipped into the tree, heart full of excitement.

Ender used his power to send Syrenn back to her room. She did not expect to see Daphne sitting on her window seat, staring out her open window. The girl didn't even flinch when Syrenn was suddenly *there.*

"Do you think we're finally safe?" Daphne's voice sounded almost haunted. Hollow.

"What do you mean?" Syrenn walked to her, touching her softly on the arm.

"There hasn't been any new deaths in the past few days."

"Maybe they found who was doing it," Syrenn lied.

Daphne stayed silent for a long time. Syrenn stood with her, rubbing her arm idly.

"Can we skip dinner? Send for someone to bring us food in here?" Her eyes brightened. "You're the future queen. Surely, we can get away with it." A broad smile widened her lips. Syrenn laughed.

"Let's do it."

It was easier than Syrenn thought. Maren went to the kitchens without question, returning nearly an hour later with servants bearing trays of food. There was so much food. She could feel the delight rolling from Daphne when they began placing the trays upon the window seat. Another servant came in bearing a small table, which he set up in the middle of the floor for the girls. Two chairs were brought in as well, and Syrenn didn't have the heart to tell the poor servant that they likely would not use them.

Maren gave the girls a soft smile, telling them she would be just down the stairs in her bedroom should they need anything else. Daphne lunged for the desserts, piling a plate full of macarons, fruits coated in chocolate, and even a slice of cake. She had always had a big sweet tooth. Syrenn chuckled, then plated her own dishes—mostly cheeses and breads.

The girls nestled into Syrenn's bed and began eating. They were silent, but it wasn't the strained silence they had held during the last few days. It felt as if they had settled back into their old ways once more. Syrenn's aching heart calmed, and she felt Daphne's tension drain as well.

"I'm sorry I've been such a jerk to you, lately. I know I've said it once already, but I want you to know I mean it." Daphne spoke between bites, not meeting Syrenn's eyes.

"Daph, it's okay, really. I know you were hurt." Syrenn placed her plate upon her lap and tossed her arm around Daphne's shoulder. She pulled her in and laid her head atop Daphne's brown curls. "I won't let this come between us. He's literally just a boy."

Daphne began laughing, quietly but deeply. "He is, isn't he?" Her voice was strangled from laughter. Syrenn began laughing alongside her. It felt so freeing to laugh like this, even amidst all the death that had been surrounding the castle. Even through the mystery and the unknown, she knew she had Daphne at her side once more, and she couldn't be happier for it.

"It's okay to still have feelings, Daphne," Syrenn said once she stopped laughing. "You've spent your entire life with him, expecting to become his wife one day." Syrenn smoothed the girl's hair beneath her hand. "I'm still holding onto hope I can get out of this."

"I hope so, too. Not for my sake, though. For yours. You'll be miserable." She pushed gently out of Syrenn's grasp and began devouring her sweets once more. "I wish we could eat like this all the time. This is amazing."

"Well, if I do end up stuck with Gideon, I'll be sure to give you dinners like this every night. You'll want for nothing." Syrenn playfully nudged Daphne's shoulder. "It's the least we could do for you." She rolled her own eyes at Gideon's audacity.

"At least I'll live in luxury," Daphne breathed whimsically. It warmed Syrenn's heart to hear, to know the girl would be okay despite it all.

"I love you, Daphne."

"I love you too, Syrenn." They smiled at one another, then busied themselves with more food. Between mouthfuls Daphne asked, "So tell me about Ender."

Syrenn nearly choked on the bread she had shoved into her mouth. She coughed, the sound very unbecoming.

Daphne chuckled, loudly. "How did that even happen? That's so unlike him. I don't think I've ever seen him show the slightest bit of interest in a woman."

"Well," she didn't know where to start. She racked her brain for something that wouldn't condemn Gideon before Ender knew what to do about his brother. "That morning he joined us for breakfast, and he walked me to my room, I think he felt me in his mind." Syrenn thought for a moment longer before continuing. "I thought that memory of Scarlett's murder came from him, so I dug into him when I thought he wouldn't notice."

"But he noticed." Daphne was smirking. "I guess I should have warned you that he's always been very attuned to other people's abilities. You all but screamed into his ear what you could do."

"Yeah, well, we never expected to be around him much, so the warning would have felt unnecessary." Syrenn chewed a bite of cheese thoughtfully. "Then, at dinner that night, he projected his thoughts really loud, as if he wasn't quite sure I'd hear them. But I reacted, and he noticed. Since then, he's been doing much of the same."

"And that led to him crawling into your bed?" Daphne was curious, but not unkind with her question. Syrenn heard no judgement.

"Sort of. He's rather persistent."

"He's rather handsome."

Syrenn blushed. "That too. He isn't what I expected at all. He isn't the evil person the kingdom makes him out to be."

"This kingdom holds a lot of secrets." Daphne's eyes turned inward, and Syrenn wondered what exactly she was referring to.

"I'm beginning to realize that myself." They were silent for a moment. Syrenn couldn't help the next question that left her lips. "Did you know Annalise?" She felt Daphne go rigid beside her. She also felt her slam up that barrier in her mind to keep Syrenn out.

"How did you learn of her?"

"Ender. He still seems extremely broken up about it," Syrenn confided.

"They were really close. They did everything together." Her body was still stiff, her walls still closed around her.

"What happened? I don't feel right asking him about it. I don't want to open those wounds." Syrenn was whispering now. She didn't feel Ender in the room with her, but she couldn't be too careful, considering the shadow locked around her wrist, as well as the piece stuck to her own power. She put up her own wall around those pieces of him, hoping he wouldn't notice.

"They don't know. Some guards doing a routine scouting around the shoreline found her." Daphne's eyes were unseeing. "What was left of her."

Syrenn started. "What do you mean, 'left of her?'"

Daphne's green eyes found Syrenn's brown ones, and they held so much pain and horror. Her voice was barely audible as she said, "She was shriveled up. Broken. Her skin had gone gray—her eyes. They were sunken in. Her body was hollow. They said it was as if her lifeforce had been drained, and only the husk of her remained."

Syrenn's mouth gaped open as she stared at Daphne. Her body began trembling as she processed the information Daphne had laid bare for her. A husk. A husk...

She felt Ender then, slipping into her room beneath the crack in the door. He skittered under her bed, unnoticed by Daphne.

Syrenn straightened. "Let's not talk anymore of this. I think I'll have nightmares."

"We all did. For months afterwards." Daphne tore her macaron to bits. The room was quiet once more for a long time. Syrenn felt Ender's pique of interest within her, but she shoved it down. He relented, but Syrenn knew he would ask her about it later.

"Your parents should be arriving soon. Are you excited?"

Syrenn smiled, "Very. I never thought I would miss them, but here we are."

"I'm glad I didn't have to travel far from home. Even though it's sparse, I still get to see my parents. I couldn't imagine going over a year without them."

"We never had the best relationship to begin with. They always wanted me to become something I wasn't. I loved being immersed within nature; they wanted me to stay in the manor. To wed and have children. But that wasn't the life for me."

"And now look at you," Daphne teased.

"Don't remind me," Syrenn scoffed. "My mother is probably beside herself with glee. I'll be surprised if she arrives by boat and doesn't leap from the deck and swim ahead." Daphne laughed.

"Well, this is every mother's dream. Her daughter marrying a prince?"

"Yes. But it's the wrong Prince." Syrenn regretted the words as soon as they slipped from her tongue. She felt Ender vibrate with pleasure.

It'll be sorted soon, and then I can officially make you mine. Ender purred into her mind.

"Would you marry Ender, then? If you had the option."

"No. I spoke without thinking." Syrenn rolled her eyes.

Liar.

"So, you would just go back home?" Daphne furrowed her brow.

"Yes."

"But I thought Farehail had fallen into disrepair."

"It's true, it has seen better days. But I like how small it is. I like being able to run into the forest and get away. It's so quiet there."

"I guess I could see the appeal." Daphne arose, heading toward the trays of food once more, all her worries seemingly forgotten. The sun was almost set outside, so Syrenn lit the many candles in her room so the girls could see. She idly wished she had Asher's powers, able to light the candles with a single thought.

"Did Annalise have powers?" Syrenn was startled to hear her own voice say the words. She hadn't meant to ask it aloud. Ender's power tensed inside her.

"I know that she did, but no one was told what they were." She continued plating her food—savory bits this time. Syrenn nodded her head, then sat back onto the bed. The candles flickered in the dark, and as the sun finally set beneath the horizon, they cast an ominous glow around the room.

Daphne crossed to the bed, now sipping some wine from a chalice. She handed a second one to Syrenn, who greedily accepted it. She downed the contents, then returned it to Daphne to refill. Her plate clinked onto the side table, returning to gather the entire pitcher of the sweet liquid.

Syrenn's stomach began to warm, and she drank deeply once more. Daphne perched upon the bed, leaning back against the pillows.

"Ouch!" she exclaimed, jumping up and ripping the pillow away. Ender's dagger rested upon the sheets—a bead of ruby now glistening in the firelight. "Why do you have a knife under your pillow?"

"The same reason you had one the other morning." Syrenn chuckled. She gathered the dagger and wiped the blood from the tip. "Are you alright?"

"It's just a prick. It startled me more than anything." She grabbed for the dagger. Syrenn was so caught off guard, Daphne plucked it from her hands easily. Bringing it up to her face, she twisted it within the beam of light. "This is Ender's."

"I nicked it from him."

"And he let you keep it?" She looked aghast. Syrenn shrugged her shoulders and furrowed her brow. "This was his father's. It's probably the only thing he has from him."

"Oh. I didn't know."

"He must like you." Daphne pulled the covers back and snuggled into the bed. She still sat upright, sipping on her wine.

I do.

Heat clawed at Syrenn's cheeks as she nestled below the covers herself. Daphne gave her back the dagger, and she gingerly placed it back under her pillow. The two sipped in silence, pressed closely together beneath the sheets.

Chapter 17

E arly morning rays shone through Syrenn's open window when she finally opened her eyes. Her head pounded from the copious amounts of wine she had consumed the night before. Her tongue was sticking to the roof of her mouth, and she could still taste its stale sweetness. Letting out a groan, she stretched out her arms. Her fingers grazed warm skin next to her, and she smiled as she pictured Ender's sleeping form next to hers.

But then the previous night came crashing down on her when she realized it wasn't Ender in the bed with her. Her and Daphne, tangled in the blankets together. Hot, sweet-smelling breath panting into her mouth. Fingers searching, feeling, drawing out pleasure. Not only hers, but Daphne's as well.

All while Ender lurked somewhere in the room.

Watching. Always watching.

Only because you two said I could.

Syrenn sat up, clutching the sheets to her chest. Daphne was next to her, bare back exposed to the ceiling. She was sprawled out on her stomach and looked so at peace.

Should I wake her? Syrenn asked the abyss.

I'd let her sleep a bit longer. You two had quite the night. There was no jealousy in his tone, only a hint of amusement mixed with intrigue.

Syrenn dropped her face into her palm. What had she done? She never meant to take it this far with Daphne. She had always been so careful in the past, on nights similar to last.

She could imagine Daphne's horror when she awoke, naked, and remembered everything they had done together.

She was very complicit in what transpired. Do not beat yourself up about it.

A little privacy, please? Syrenn tried pushing him out, but he was as much a part of her as the color of her eyes, or the arch of her back. She did, however, see his shadows skitter out of the room upon her command.

Come find me when you get all that sorted.

Her mind went silent, Ender's power nestling back down with her own. She crept from the bed and scooped her dress from the floor. She shimmied it back on, then set to cleaning the remnants of the past night. Their chalices were strewn across the floor, accompanied by spilled food and wine.

The rustling of the covers was near deafening in the silence of the room and the hollow of Syrenn's mind. She could feel rather than see Daphne sit up.

"You slept well, I hope," Syrenn asked, as if nothing had happened between them.

"Better than I have in weeks, actually."

She heard Daphne's feet hit the ground but continued dropping the leftover food onto a tray. The pattering of soft feet against stone grew louder as Daphne closed in on Syrenn. Her heart pounded in her ears, but then she felt soft hands trace around her middle, collecting her in an embrace.

Syrenn turned within Daphne's arms, almost shocked with how relaxed Daphne was acting. Before Syrenn could speak, Daphne leaned forward and caught her lip between her teeth. She sucked on it gently, and Syrenn felt her core tighten. She pressed her own mouth into Daphne's, feeling her warmness.

They moved together for a moment, kissing each other softly—sweetly. Syrenn was keenly aware of the feel of Daphne's fingers gripping her waist, aware of the fact that Daphne was still naked as well. Her arms wrapped around her, and she combed her fingers through her dark curls, winding the tresses around her hand and tugging slightly. Daphne opened her mouth in response, and Syrenn took the opportunity to dip her tongue inside.

Syrenn...

It was Daphne's voice reverberating inside her mind. Her stomach dipped, but she deepened the kiss further. The grip on her waist tightened, and Syrenn pulled Daphne against her, her hard nipples pressing through the fabric of Syrenn's dress. Daphne's breasts were soft pressed against her own. Syrenn moved her hand between their adjoined bodies, cupping Daphne's soft flesh and gliding her finger over a taut point. Daphne groaned deliciously into Syrenn's mouth.

Syrenn clenched her thighs together in an attempt to stifle the heightening need that was forming there. But then Daphne's hand was against her, pulling up her dress and drifting along her skin. Syrenn let her inch between her thighs and brush along her lips. She was so sensitive, and the softness of Daphne's hand was a welcome feeling. She parted her flesh, and it was Syrenn's turn to gasp into Daphne's mouth as her fingers slid along Syrenn's wetness, dipping inside slowly.

Daphne plunged deeper, but at an agonizingly slow pace. She curled them forward, eliciting a moan from Syrenn.

Let's go back to bed, Daphne whispered to Syrenn's power. It pulsed in response. She didn't withdraw her fingers, only began stepping backwards and nearly dragging Syrenn with her. When the back of her knees connected with the bed, she sat down, still gripping Syrenn's waist.

Syrenn tilted Daphne's head up so that their eyes met. "What are you doing?" she whispered.

"Continuing what we started last night." Her eyelashes fluttered innocently. "Unless you don't want this—"

"It's not that. I just didn't think you were attracted to me in that way."

"You never asked." She curled her fingers along Syrenn's inner wall again, then ran her thumb gently over her sensitive nerves. She shuddered in response.

"What about Gideon?" Syrenn breathed.

"What about Ender?" Daphne's voice had become guttural. Syrenn scanned her face for a moment before her lips broke into a devious smile.

"Ender doesn't mind," she said before kissing Daphne once more and grinding her body into Daphne's hand.

"What Gideon doesn't know won't hurt him. It isn't as if he's loyal to me." Daphne quirked an eyebrow then pressed her mouth to Syrenn's again, flicking her finger once more.

She grabbed onto Daphne's wrist as she expertly touched and rubbed her. "I'm sure Ender spied heavily last night, though I can't confirm what he saw."

"If I recall, he did ask permission first." Daphne chuckled, the sound a lovely trill. "Is he here now?" She asked, again curling her fingers inside Syrenn.

"No," she yelped in response.

"So, I get you to myself." She pulled her fingers from Syrenn, and she groaned at how empty that left her. "Get on the bed."

Syrenn was shocked at Daphne's demanding tone, but she complied without hesitation. This was so unlike her, but maybe it was only because she hadn't ever seen this side of Daphne before.

Climbing onto the bed, she wondered if anyone would miss them at breakfast. Then decided she did not care. Daphne pressed her shoulders back, pinning her down, and Syrenn really didn't care who missed them. Her face flushed, but she grabbed her friend by the hair and crashed their mouths together.

Daphne settled a leg between Syrenn's thighs and roamed her hand down the length of her body. She began thrusting her hips against Syrenn, and she felt a pleasure begin with her movements. Syrenn reciprocated, and the two found a rhythm all their own.

Her body was so soft, Syrenn thought. It had been so long since she'd been with another woman, and she forgot how much she craved that feeling. The softness of curves against her own. Greedily, she grabbed and squeezed Daphne everywhere—along her curves and valleys—coming to land on her backside. She encouraged Daphne to keep rolling her hips, to let the sensations build, savoring the whimpers pouring from her luscious mouth.

Abruptly, Daphne pulled away. Syrenn almost thought she was going to bolt for the door when instead, she moved down Syrenn's body. Daphne's mouth sucked a trail along her skin, leaving a wet path as she went. Her hands gripped Syrenn's thighs, parting them so that she could dip her head between them.

Her tongue, hot and wet, licked into Syrenn's own heat. She gasped, arching her back. Again, Daphne licked Syrenn, and it took all her control not to cry out. She continued fervently, and that was when Syrenn lost all control. She clutched at Daphne's hair and rolled her hips forward, meeting each flick of her tongue. She was consumed by pleasure, and as it peaked, she erupted with a small cry. Daphne sucked on her flesh until she came down from that high, eyes transfixed on Syrenn's face the entire time.

Daphne sat up and grinned, wiping her mouth with the back of her hand. Crawling up her body, she planted a kiss on Syrenn's lips before rolling off the bed and to her feet. Between her tremors and panting, Syrenn watched as Daphne pulled her wrinkled dress from the floor and slid it over her head.

"I'll see you at breakfast," she said as she departed from the room. Syrenn sat up, taken aback, but the door clicked shut before she could even think clearly enough to ask Daphne to stay.

Sated? Ender purred into Syrenn as she descended the stairs from the West Wing.

Syrenn tried to keep the blush from the cheeks for fear the guards surrounding her might question it.

I'll take your non-answer as a yes. She felt a shadow caress her fingers. She curled them into a fist.

I don't know what that was, Syrenn replied.

A good time, it felt like. He chuckled the words, and his shadow curled between her fingers. *Don't worry, my violent Syrenn. I know how to share.*

You could feel that? Her thoughts were shrill. She wondered why Ender was so at ease with the fact that Syrenn had been intimate with someone else. Most men would have been irate.

Just because you find pleasure with someone else, doesn't mean they have your heart. She felt that piece of his power curl around what she assumed was her heart, because it fluttered and began to beat rapidly in response. *And yes, I could feel it. The perks of being in your head, I guess, since you kicked me out of the room.*

Does that mean you love me, then? She had meant it as a joke, but her stomach dipped as she awaited his response. When the silence lingered far longer than it should have, she felt fear pulse through her.

She was halfway down the corridor to the dining hall, that place Ender had taken her arm and directed her to her room all those weeks ago, when the darkness culminated before her. Ender formed, and his face was serious. He gave the guards a harsh look and they dispersed and disappeared in opposite directions. The two were alone.

Ender gripped her chin between his thumb and forefinger, tilting her head so that their eyes met.

"My violent, violent girl." He stepped closer, the heat of his body melting into her. She felt her body moving to press into his, her hands flattening onto his chest. "You are the reason my heart beats. The reason that breath fills my lungs." *The reason I must betray my brother.* "I do, in fact, love you. Though the idea completely terrifies me."

Why is that? She pressed the question into him, afraid her voice would wobble if she tried to speak.

My brother has destroyed everything I've ever loved. His fingers brushed along her cheek. Eyes fluttering closed, she lifted to the tips of her toes, intending to plant a kiss upon his lips. Footsteps echoed down the hall, and her body tumbled forward into empty air.

Ender vanished just before Gideon rounded the corner.

Chapter 18

Dishes clanked as the servants placed the many savory foods onto the table. It was dinnertime, and Syrenn was thankful that invites had been extended to both Daphne and Aster. Though Aster was still internally stewing, Syrenn was thankful she didn't have to be alone with her betrothed.

Gideon, however, looked rather perturbed by this. *If only we were alone—*

Syrenn blocked out the images of what Gideon thought he was going to do with her, given the opportunity. Apparently, he hadn't taken Ender's warning seriously.

"My prince, do I need to give input on anything concerning the wedding?" Syrenn felt Gideon's spike of triumph at her seeming acceptance of their impending marriage. "I'm not sure how royal weddings are. Will everything be handled, or do I get to pick out which flowers I desire?" His thoughts turned from him atop Syrenn onto the upcoming nuptials in a snap.

"Well, if you have a preference, I can let the planners know. They will accommodate anything you wish, within reason."

"Reason?"

"Well, yes. I don't think they'd be able to go against Southern tradition. So, as long as it falls in line with those, then I see no problem with you choosing which flowers you prefer, or what food you wish to eat."

"What about the cake? May I choose the flavor?" Syrenn didn't care which flavor of cake they had. She only cared that Gideon saw her continued compliance.

"Of course! How delightful. Which is your favorite?"

Syrenn took a moment to contemplate. "I want a lemon cake made. With buttercream icing, covered in hundreds of pomegranate arils."

Gideon looked at her as if she were insane. "An aril covered cake for a wedding? Are you sure?"

She heard Daphne's giggle from beside her. The girl covered her mouth with her hand, trying as she might to stifle the laugh.

Aster furrowed her brow. *She's got to be joking.*

"Is there something wrong with my choice?" Syrenn asked with feigned innocence.

"Of course not. If that's your favorite, it's no issue. The only thing is that's normally what good intentioned people give to mourners after the passing of a loved one."

"Is it, now?" Syrenn cocked her head to the side, as if she didn't quite believe him.

"Yes. The pomegranate represents death."

"Well, maybe we can view our marriage as a death to loneliness, because after that day we shall forever be in one another's company." Syrenn flashed him an innocent smile. He returned it, a little unsure.

"Right. Lemon with pomegranate on top. Anything for you, my bride." His smile became more genuine as he began eating his dinner. Syrenn felt a flash of a smile radiating from the darkness inside her.

You're funny, Ender said.

I don't know what you're referring to, Syrenn feigned. *In Farehail a pomegranate is just a tasty fruit we enjoy consuming.*

Sure it is, my violent girl, Ender purred, all the while tracing his shadows up her skirt beneath the table. Syrenn shivered from their contact.

Dinner finished while Syrenn had her mind solely on the way Ender dragged his shadows along her skin beneath the table. She didn't know where he was, but that didn't seem to matter anymore. Their connection had grown into something otherworldly. The band around her wrist tightened slightly feeling almost warm against her flesh.

"Will you join me for a walk, Syrenn?" Gideon broke the trance Ender had her under.

"I would love nothing more," she crooned back to him without missing a beat. She was becoming good at playing this game with him.

Gideon stood and held his arm out for her. She looped hers in his, and he guided her from the room. Daphne smirked at her as she passed, causing a flush to spread along her clavicle. She really needed to talk with her, Syrenn thought.

I can't wait to be done with this entire charade, Aster thought mildly. Syrenn agreed with her for once. She couldn't wait to go back home and away from everyone here. Though, that did leave her with the issue of what to do about Ender and Daphne. She was falling in love with Ender, and Daphne was the best friend she had ever had.

Perhaps things in the south would change for the better, and she wouldn't have to leave. Perhaps she would finally be free of the castle. Syrenn could live with that, she thought. She could live in the Southern Kingdom if only she were free to roam the forests and mountains. To swim in the sea. To explore.

Yes. That would be nice, indeed.

Gideon steered them in the direction of the throne room. Syrenn hadn't been here since the night he named her as his betrothed. She felt uneasy, thinking back on that night. She still couldn't believe where her life had taken her.

Guards on either side of the doors opened them with a groan of metal. The room was alighted with fires in the many hearths, as well as candles upon the chandelier looming high above in the center of the room.

"We'll have the ceremony in here." Gideon dropped her arm. He raised his hand out to the sides and twirled in place. "It will be lovely. We'll have an abundance of flowers. We'll take our vows upon the dais. The lords and ladies of the court will bear witness." A broad smile was plastered to his face when he came to a stop before her. "What do you think?"

"It'll be lovely, I'm sure."

He came back toward her, scooping her hands in his. "I want this to be the day you've always dreamed of." His head dipped to her, and he brushed a light kiss to her lips. "I want you to be happy, Syrenn."

She nodded rapidly. Gideon seemed to take it as a good sign, for he wrapped her into an embrace and kissed her deeper. She had to swallow back the bile creeping up her throat as she remembered what he had done to those poor girls. What he had done to her. This man was a monster in so many different ways—one who showed no remorse for his actions.

She pulled back as gracefully as she could manage. She didn't want to offend him, so she fluttered her eyelashes as she stared up into his face.

And it was not a lie that slipped from Syrenn's lips next. "I think I could be happy here."

"How does Ender think he can get you out of this?"

Syrenn didn't expect Daphne to be awaiting her when she returned to her room. The girl was getting good at surprising Syrenn. She closed the door behind her before saying, "I'm not sure, but he said he has to think more on it before he can act." A half-truth, but Daphne didn't need to know what Gideon was quite yet.

"If anyone could pull something like that off, it would be him." She flopped to the bed, resting her head in her arms.

"Can we talk about last night?" Syrenn turned toward the vanity as she removed her jewelry. "And this morning."

"What about it?" Daphne sounded confused.

"Well." Syrenn didn't know how to broach the subject. "It was something new."

"It doesn't have to mean anything more than what it was, Syrenn. I know you have something with Ender. It just is what it is."

"I just wanted to make sure you wouldn't be pining after *me* now," Syrenn jested.

"Oh no, I'm still consumed by all that is Gideon, unfortunately. It would be so much easier if I hated him." Daphne rolled onto her back. "Or was indifferent. But I can't let him go. He has my heart. He always will." She sounded wistful.

"I know it will be hard to move on, but I think it's time. He had the chance to choose you, Daph. But he chose power over your love."

"And the worst part is that if he came groveling, I would take him back in an instant." Her arms dropped to the bed, exasperatedly. "Do you believe in soulmates?"

"I think that there is something to the idea. I believe you can choose who you love. But all in the same breath, I think there can be an undeniable connection to someone that you just can't explain." Syrenn thought about the way her power seemed to call to Ender, and of her different yet true love for Daphne. "I also think you can have both, with different people." Syrenn dropped her necklace to the table. The plinking noise reverberated against the glass tray. "One day it won't hurt as bad, Daphne. I promise."

"Have you been through it?"

"Something similar. I've fallen in love before."

"With whom? And why haven't I heard about this?" Daphne sat up, and Syrenn went to sit beside her.

"I don't like talking about it. In Farehail, we have a… different system of living. I was lucky that I was a part of one of the higher houses. Those who weren't as lucky… Well. They were sent elsewhere. To do the dirty work, essentially."

"So, was the boy you fell in love with sent there? That's so sad." Daphne clutched at Syrenn's arm in sympathy.

"*She* was sent there, yes. I cried for over a month. My parents didn't understand. I never told them. In their eyes, one day, I was just *sad* for no reason." Syrenn remembered those days as a teenager, and her heart still held a pang of hurt for her first love. "That might have been why they started trying to set me up with suitable matches. That also might be why I was so obstinate." Syrenn smiled.

"And then they sent you here when they ran out of options."

"Indeed. I hated them for so long for it. But now? I quite like it here with you."

"And Ender." Daphne bumped her shoulder into Syrenn's.

"Yes. And Ender."

"So even if you get out of this marriage, you'll stay?" Daphne asked innocently.

"I don't know, yet. It's something I've been thinking about. But honestly, I'm not sure."

"Well, it seems we've both got some decisions to make." Daphne dropped onto her back once more.

"Indeed."

Chapter 19

May I have my blade back?"

The voice was directly behind Syrenn, startling her out of the book she was reading. It clattered to the floor. The pages flipped midair, completely losing her place within the story.

"You don't need to sneak up on me like that," she growled.

"But it's so much fun," he taunted, coming to sit next to her.

They were in the enormous main library. It was larger than Gideon's personal one, but not by much. That was one thing Gideon did have going for him—he loved to read. Syrenn, too, enjoyed many different stories.

"What shall I use for protection then?" Syrenn looked about the room, noting the guards had mysteriously disappeared. Ender did have a few tricks up his sleeve.

"Well, I thought you could use this." He pulled a dagger from beneath his jacket. The hilt gleamed in the sunlight that pierced through the open windows. It was encrusted with blue sapphires, and Syrenn sucked in a breath at its beauty. She snatched it from him, turning it over in her hand for inspection.

It, too, had that wave-like pattern through the metal. It was almost identical to his in that aspect, though it was much smaller—made to fit within her palm perfectly. He handed her the sheath to go with it. A loop was attached so that it could be worn around her thigh, underneath her skirts.

"This is beautiful."

"You do like blue, don't you? I thought I heard you say that at one point," Ender mused from beside her.

"It's my favorite color. This is gorgeous, Ender, and it had to have cost a fortune." Her eyes were nearly bulging from her head as she slid her fingers down the sharp edges. A tiny bead of blood spouted from her skin.

"It did. But anything for you, my beautiful, violent girl." He leaned forward and dragged his nose up her neck, inhaling her scent. She shivered beneath his touch as he grumbled into her skin. Hot, wetness seared into her as Ender darted his tongue out to taste her. "I need you, Syrenn," he pleaded into her ear.

Her core tightened as her head knocked back against the couch. He pulled her legs across him, leaning her back slightly as he trailed his finger up her inner thigh.

"Ender, someone is going to walk in," she protested half-heartedly.

"The guards will make up an excuse to deter them." His teeth nipped at her throat, and she gasped. Her legs spread slightly, and he took the moment to dip beneath the fabric separating them. His fingers met her soft flesh, and she pushed into his hand.

He continued his lazy kissing up her neck and around onto her clavicle. Her fingers twined in his hair as her other hand still clung to her new dagger. She held it against his back as he kissed once more up her neck and stopped at her lips.

"Do you think you can keep it down?" There was a hint of a smile in his voice, but Syrenn couldn't see his face. Her eyes were rolled to the back of her head as Ender grazed over her sensitive nerves.

"Yes," she panted into his mouth.

"Good girl."

His mouth crashed into hers, biting and tasting as he bunched her skirts around her hips. With skill, he slid his pants lower and released himself in a swift movement.

Without warning, he was barreling deep inside her. She bit back her scream, not wanting to attract unwanted attention from anyone innocently passing by the library doors. The walls would echo the noise, and she did not want Ender to be interrupted. He moved with a cadence she was beginning to crave. Clinging to his body, she undulated beneath him.

Just when her pleasure started to build, he pulled free. She cried out in protest, but he filled that void with his tongue. Tremors shook her body as Ender licked against her, pulling more pleasure to the surface. She held her dagger against her chest with one hand while the other curled into a fist between her teeth. She bit down to stifle her screams as she erupted against Ender's soft lips.

His flattened tongue licked his fill before he moved back up her body and inserted himself once more. He thrust into her slowly and thoroughly. Her body shook as the remnants of her orgasm still shattered through her.

His groans sank into her mind as he made love to her, dagger still curled in her fist. He kissed her as deeply as he stroked inside her, and she kissed and moved with him until he erupted inside her. Fluttering behind her ribs accompanied the palpitations of her heart as he groaned her name in her ear.

He was hers and she was his. This was something Syrenn knew from the bottom of her soul—from the depths of her power. They were connected not only by their power, but by something more Syrenn couldn't describe.

"So, I can have my dagger back, then?" Ender teased in a breathy, hushed voice. Syrenn laughed and pushed him off her playfully. She pulled Ender's blade from the cushion of the couch behind her. She had tucked it safely there within reach, just in case.

The castle had been too quiet for far too long. Syrenn knew it couldn't be a good sign. Her power had felt unsettled for a few days now. She thought it was due solely to her unwanted betrothal to the Prince.

She was sadly mistaken. Realization of this hit her once those horrid screams started up again. Not just a scream of horror and agony, but that of absolute hatred as well—coming from not one person but from two separate ones.

Syrenn had been descending her steps but launched into a run at the first shrill sound. She ripped her dagger free from its resting place on her thigh and burst through the archway leading into the West Wing.

Aster was atop Daphne, slamming her fists into the girl's face repeatedly.

The guards were nowhere in sight, and Syrenn didn't have time to wonder where they had all gone before she was barreling forward. She lunged into Aster shoulder first, knocking the girl to the floor. She felt Aster's body connect with the stone, tensing upon impact.

Crazy bitch! Aster screamed internally. Syrenn was holding her down, but Aster thrashed against her. Her power was hungrily trying to search Aster's thoughts, but it was cut short as the tether holding Aster's soul into her body abruptly snapped, like a thread being severed.

It took Syrenn a moment to understand what had happened. One moment, her power was latching onto Aster's essence. The next, there was nothing for it to latch onto. It was another moment later that Syrenn finally noticed the slit across Aster's throat, and the dark, crimson blood pulsing from it.

Blood pounded in Syrenn's ears, thundering from her racing heart and spiked panic. Her power retreated back inside her with a snap and a hiss of discontent. Her hands unlatched from Aster, but not before they became coated in Aster's blood. It felt oily against her skin, and Syrenn's stomach lurched. She jumped from the now empty body, clamping her mouth closed so as not to spew the contents of her stomach atop the girl's lifeless body. She fell back onto her haunches, holding a bloody hand over her mouth.

Still on her knees, Daphne loomed over Aster's side. She stared into her vacant face with a look of terror in her own. Blood pooled around the body, encapsulating Daphne's kneeling frame. And that was when Daphne began screaming, life returning to her dead eyes.

Finally, guards came rushing from the doors separating the West Wing from the rest of the castle. Why they hadn't come during the first sounds of distress, Syrenn couldn't understand.

Daphne, what did you do? Syrenn screamed into Daphne's mind. She stayed crouched on the floor, away from the expanding scarlet puddle.

"*She attacked me.*" The words were spoken aloud and projected toward Syrenn's powers. "She was trying to kill me." Daphne was panicking, her chest rising up and down from her rapid intake of breath.

Syrenn was scooped from the ground, and she recognized Asher's power against hers at once. Daphne, too, was collected from the ground and hauled away. Time stood still and sped up all at once. One moment, they were descending the stairs from the West Wing; the next, they were in the tearoom being sat atop a settee.

They were left for only a moment before the Queen Regent appeared before them.

"Speak." There was no greeting, just pure command.

"I don't know what happened, my queen," Syrenn started, tears and panic spilling from her.

"She attacked me." Daphne broke into sobs, and Syrenn placed a hand upon her back, patting gently. Blood smeared across the pale pink fabric of Daphne's dress. It took a long time for the girl to calm enough to speak further. "I think she meant to kill me." Her voice wavered and trailed off.

"What *happened?*" The queen prowled closer, no longer the patient woman Syrenn had come to know.

Daphne only sobbed in response. Syrenn looked at the Queen, perplexed. She didn't know what to tell her, for she had just arrived moments before the death. But Aster had been detained beneath Syrenn when Daphne went for her throat...

"I'll take it from here, Mother." Gideon burst into the room, clearing the space before Daphne in only a few strides. He took a knee before her and collected her hands in his own. "Daph, my love. What happened?" He murmured the words so softly that Syrenn had to strain to hear.

"She meant to kill me," she whispered. She began sobbing once more, and Gideon collected her in his arms and held her tightly.

"You're done here, Mother. They did nothing wrong. Aster is to blame." Gideon shushed the girl lovingly before adding, "I wouldn't be surprised if she was the one at fault for all the other murders. She was so wretched and conniving."

Gideon had a point, though Syrenn knew the truth. She couldn't explain what had transpired between Aster and Daphne. Perhaps it was an argument gone wrong.

"What's happened?" Ender appeared in the tearoom, darkness swirling around him. His eyes found Syrenn instantly, roaming over her body in search of wounds.

"Aster is dead. She attacked Daphne," Gideon said dismissively.

"What?" Ender sounded completely shocked. *What happened?*

Syrenn closed her eyes, recalling the memory and sending it through their connection. She hadn't seen much.

"Daphne, what caused Aster to attack you?" Ender's tone demanded audience. Daphne looked at him, eyes sparkling with tears.

"I don't know. I went to her room to see if she'd walk with me to the dining hall, and she lunged at me. It all happened so fast, I... I..." She didn't finish, only crumpled into a ball of tears once more.

Ender stood with an arm across his torso while his other hand cradled his chin. He was inspecting Daphne.

"Aster was always a bit of a rotten fruit," Ender surmised. He dropped his hand and turned to leave.

You're leaving? Syrenn exclaimed.

I'm not needed here. It's done. Unless you know more?

I showed you everything I saw.

Then, we may never know unless you get a chance to dive into her mind without her knowledge. Though, she's very aware of your ability. If she doesn't want you finding something, she'll do a damn good job at covering it up.

Syrenn didn't like what he implied. Daphne was no murderer. She would talk with her about what happened and get to the bottom of this. It had to be some sort of misunderstanding. Daphne wasn't capable of cruelty. She wouldn't hurt so much as a bug on the garden path. Syrenn would give her time to heal. She looked so fragile, crumpled into Gideon's arms like that.

Chapter 20

The silhouette cursed inwardly.

How many more deaths would there be? Nearly all the girls were gone. It wouldn't stop there, the silhouette knew. Past experiences told it that this was simply the beginning. Once a person turned themselves over to that darkness, there was no coming back.

Only another death could stop this. The death of the culprit.

That was easier said than done. Especially when the silhouette was so helpless. It hated the feeling of being incapable. It didn't want to fall back into that dark place it had tried to eagerly crawl from. Yet here it was.

The cruelty of this kingdom was maddening. The silhouette had come here as a reprieve yet had ended up as a prisoner instead.

The silhouette had yet to get close enough during one of the killings to get any snippets of information. It was always designated to be somewhere else during the heinous acts. It had a feeling this was intentional. That the—

The silhouette couldn't even think the accusation because of those damn bindings. The right words wouldn't even form in its mind. It had tried several times in that girl's presence—hoping she would see into its mind. Hoping that she would get that bit of condemning information for the elder prince to take to the council.

The blindness those on the council seemed to be suffering from was something the silhouette couldn't comprehend. They saw, but they chose not to actually see. The silhouette wanted to eliminate them all. They deserved it. These were innocent people being butchered right under their noses. But if the elder prince could convince them, if he were to show them those snippets, the silhouette was sure that would sway them. And then, these bindings would be lifted.

The silhouette would be set free.

The girl would be free, too.

And the guard, it thought as if in hindsight.

The madman was doing more than just murdering. He was causing so much more damage to those around him. It was never going to stop with just the bloodlust. It had always been about control. At least at its core.

If a man obtains too much power, he goes insane.

The silhouette had heard the fairytales of all the lands. None of which had ended well. Most of these realms were ruled by queens in the beginning, before the men beneath them decided to get too comfortable with power.

Too... out of control.

Perhaps one day, the Wildewood would get it sorted. Perhaps their will would win out in the end.

For now, the silhouette would continue trying. It would give its life to the cause if it needed to.

To protect those that couldn't protect themselves. To guard those whom these monsters inflicted harm unto.

That had always been the silhouette's true motive in life.

Chapter 21

Syrenn looked up into the canopy above her head. Green leaves swayed against the bright blue sky above. Her back was pressed into the dirt of the forest floor. She drew in slow breaths as she listened to Ender and Asher speak.

"What do you think the council will say?" Asher leaned against a tree, his arms casually crossed over his chest. Wind combed through his brown hair, causing it to become even more messy than normal.

"I suspect it will be a lost cause. They don't like being wrong." Ender twirled his dagger, happy to have the blade back in his possession.

"What are you two talking about?" Syrenn sat up on her elbows and loosened her stiff neck.

"Taking our implications to the council. About how I am the rightful heir." Ender threw his dagger. The sound of impact was almost startling.

"You don't think they'll care?" Syrenn rolled to her side, then climbed to her feet. She dusted off her backside. Ender was beside her, assisting in the matter.

"I think they already know. That isn't something my mother and father could have kept secret."

"Then why would they give the throne to Gideon if they knew you were the second born son? It doesn't make any sense."

"It's all about how it looks from the outside. They could have easily covered up a stillbirth from our people. There was no baby to present, so for all anyone else is concerned, I was the firstborn." Ender wrapped an arm around Syrenn's waist.

"What are the fairytales surrounding the third son? If the first is evil, the second the fated ruler who will be fair, then what of the third?" Syrenn pressed closer to him.

"There has never been a third son. Not on record." It was Asher who answered. "I've checked. I have found nothing."

"So, then the third son could be the most heinous of them all."

"It would seem that way," Asher commended.

"If there were no stories on it, then the council had no way of knowing. My parents had no way of knowing. They probably assumed their baby who died was a terrible person, and it was for the best." Ender's logic was solid, and he did know his parents best.

"So, it seems they just wanted to keep up tradition and put Gideon in a place of power since you looked like the firstborn to everyone else." Syrenn was still annoyed with the King and Queen for their decision. Ender was obviously more worthy of the position by his character alone.

"All we can do is hope they hear me out. If they refuse my suggestion, then I will bring forth what we know about the murders. He's tried to pin them on Aster, but maybe I can show them otherwise."

"Why not tell them what I saw in his mind? It would be a closed case then, and with them on our side, I would be protected."

"Absolutely not." Ender dropped his arm and took a step back. His eyes had hardened. "I don't want you to be involved at all. There is no such thing as safety when it involves my brother, or have you not figured that out yet?"

His words stung, but Syrenn would not show how they affected her. "But if it will persuade them—"

"I will not risk you for my own gain. I won't hear any more about it either." Syrenn knew the conversation was over, but she still wanted to argue. She chose to bite her tongue instead. She chose to change the subject.

"Asher, did you know Gideon's healer in Farehail?" Syrenn had been curious for a while.

"Yes, actually. We were good friends."

"Are the two of you together?" Syrenn knew it was an invasive question, but she wanted to know more about the girl who had healed her so perfectly and often. The girl who had reached out, even though Syrenn did not want her help.

Asher looked affronted and did not answer. Instead, he said, "She came here before me and she wasn't happy to see me when I arrived."

"Why are you here? Why did you leave Farehail?" If he had powers and lived on the island, he, too, had to have been a part of the guild. Unless he had evaded being sent away, just as she had.

"We each had our own reasons." Syrenn waited, but Asher didn't continue.

"You work for Ender, though."

"Ender is a good man." Asher nodded to Ender, who had gone to retrieve his dagger from the poor tree. Then, Ender had to know the secrets of their land. Or at least some of them.

"Does the healer work for Ender?"

"No. She works for Gideon."

"But she doesn't like him."

"No."

Ender sauntered back through the trees, sheathing his dagger into his belt. "Let's get you back to the castle. Did you get enough fresh air?"

"Yes. I did." Syrenn walked into Ender's embrace. Asher placed a palm on Ender's shoulder, and then blackness swirled around them all consecutively.

Syrenn was dumped in her tower before the two men abruptly disappeared once more. She hated being locked in her tower, though Gideon had dismissed the extra guards since Aster's death.

Everyone was going on with their lives, assuming the threat was extinguished. Syrenn knew better, and she didn't understand how others couldn't feel it too. How had no one noticed Gideon's madness?

She descended the steps and went directly to Daphne's room.

She was gone. Syrenn paused, trying to decide where Daphne would go after such a terrible occurrence. Yes, it had been a few days, but she could still tell that Daph was rattled by it. There was something more going on, and Syrenn could tell by that continuous vacant look in Daphne's eyes.

She searched the halls, popping into the libraries, tearooms, and offices as she went, but she came up empty handed. She made it to the garden, again getting plagued by the images of Gideon and Aster on the stone bench.

She felt sad, remembering Gideon's memory. Was he upset about Aster's passing? He hadn't killed her, so it was likely he didn't intend to do away with her. However, Syrenn was confident he would have rather Daphne walk away from that fight than Aster.

She roamed through the flowers and along the paths. There was no sign of Daphne. She left, feeling a bit of unease start to creep back in on her.

It dawned on her then. Perhaps she was with the healer.

That was where Syrenn started toward next. It would make sense for Daphne to seek out the healer to assist in relieving her remorse or even search for something to help her sleep. Syrenn herself was having trouble sleeping after witnessing the murder.

No, not murder, Syrenn corrected herself. Death.

She knocked once before entering the healer's ward. She didn't pause long enough to wait for an answer. If she were to become queen of this castle, as everyone expected, she would need to start acting like it.

Daphne lay on a platform, raised to about the healer's waist. The healer had her hands upon Daphne's head, a far-off look in her eyes. Neither stirred when Syrenn entered the room, so she perched on a chair and waited for them to come to.

Apparently, the healer was hard at work. After nearly an hour in the same place, Syrenn almost gave up waiting.

What are you doing? Ender's voice floated into her mind.

I need to know what happened with Daphne and Aster.

The healer is working on her?

It seems so. I'm not sure what they're doing, though.

"Why are you here?" Syrenn flinched. Daphne had sat up on the table, and she was angry.

"I need to speak with you."

"About what, Syrenn? This is very invasive." She swung her legs over the ledge and dropped to her feet.

"You're avoiding me."

"I'm avoiding everyone, Syrenn. Not everything is about you." She stomped to the door. "I have nothing to say about it, okay? I don't want to talk about it. I'm actually doing my best to forget about it."

"I'm sorry, it just seemed—"

"Just *stop.*"

Syrenn's power leapt out and clashed into Daphne's walls. It clawed, trying to force its way in. Syrenn was taken aback by its force and tried to reel it back in. But the deed was done.

Daphne looked at Syrenn like she had struck her.

"I can't believe you. I thought we trusted each other." Her face dropped. She shook her head, then left the room without another word, slamming the door behind her.

The healer watched Syrenn with a guarded expression. She was studying her, and Syrenn felt uncomfortable under her steady, knowing gaze.

"You care about her," the healer stated.

"Of course, I do. She's my best friend."

"It goes a bit deeper than that." Syrenn didn't know how the healer had figured it out, and she didn't question it, not wanting to draw attention to their relationship. "She's dealing with something I can't quite figure out," the healer went on. "She has gaps in her memory, and we're trying to figure out what's causing it."

"Why doesn't she just tell me, then?"

"I think she's afraid of what she's doing during those gaps." The healer leveled a glance at her.

"What are you implying?" Syrenn felt dread coil in her gut.

"We've discovered the gaps happen when she's with the Prince. I suspect that the Prince is doing something to her that she feels she needs to block out."

"You think he's hurting her?"

"Yes. But she shows no signs of trauma. There's something, though. For her mind to shield itself like that and have such long blocks of memory loss?" The healer didn't go on. Syrenn had heard of people blocking out things like tragedy, the death of someone close to them, abuse.

"Maybe I can get into her mind and uncover what it is—"

"No. Her mind is in such a delicate state, something like your power could shatter the parts that aren't broken. There's no telling if she would be able to handle that intrusion." The healer was pacing the floor of the infirmary, idly picking at the sleeve of her dress.

"I'll dig into the Prince's mind, then. If he's hurting her, I need to know."

"And do what about it? He'll do worse to you if he thinks you're spying on him."

"I've been spying on him for weeks, and he hasn't noticed yet." Syrenn's eyes widened as she realized what she had just divulged to the healer. "I mean—"

"I won't say a word," the healer whispered to Syrenn. "If you're searching for a way to keep him from the throne, just know you have my complete support. And if I can help in any way, *any* way, come and find me." She had closed in on Syrenn and gripped her arms, hoisting her from her chair. "But be careful, Syrenn."

"I have been. As I said, he isn't wise to it," Syrenn whispered in confidence. Syrenn could feel the trust between them growing as if there were a physical bridge connecting them. Perhaps it was simply because they were from the same land. Maybe it was because she knew the healer genuinely cared for her wellbeing. Whatever it was, Syrenn knew she had found a true friend within the woman. "I've never asked your name." Her eyes fluttered up to meet the healer's.

"It isn't important." She sounded sad but wouldn't continue, only shook her head. She guided Syrenn to the door and ushered her from the room. Before Syrenn could turn back or make any sort of objection, the healer was shutting the door in her face.

She stood there for a moment, contemplating shoving her way back in. She raised a hand, then lowered it once more. The healer was putting distance between them, but Syrenn, for the life of her, could not fathom why that would be.

Syrenn left without trying to pry any more information from the kind woman.

Chapter 22

Syrenn wasn't sure how she ended up here.

She was currently wedged between Gideon and the wall that connected his room with his library. His hands roamed up and down her body in such a claiming way. He whispered sweet nothings into her ears as he nibbled on her skin.

Her eyes remained closed as she tried to force her power deep inside herself. The last thing she wanted was to see any more of his loose memories of those murders. Alas, her power slipped through her grasp and into his mind. She became less aware of what was happening to her body and more aware of the memories barreling into her.

Gideon kissed Iris fervently, hand roving over her body in a greedy manner. Not unlike how he had been caressing Syrenn. A creak of a door, then a shocked gasp filled the room. Gideon broke free of Iris and looked at the intruder.

Daphne stood in the doorway, a second away from tears.

"Darling, it's not what it seems," Gideon began. He shoved Iris off him—indifferent to her cries—then rose to collect Daphne from the doorway. "It doesn't mean anything. She offered me a kiss, and I couldn't offend her. I couldn't hurt her feelings like that." Gideon murmured sweetly as he pulled Daphne closer.

Her eyes darted between Gideon and Iris, who was now fixing her dress and making to leave. After she was gone, Daphne's focus returned to Gideon. "It's okay. I know you don't care for her. It's fine." Daphne's lip trembled as she spoke, but she tried her best to smile. Syrenn wanted to leap forward and throttle the man, but the memory shifted.

Young Gideon with Daphne in the forest. Sprawled out beside one another on a bed of grass, both wistfully staring into the canopy of trees above them.

"It'll be okay. I promise." Gideon said.

"How do you know you aren't going to hurt her?" Daphne's voice sounded childlike, though sternly angry.

"I swear it won't hurt her. I just want to see what all she can do."

"Why don't you just wait for them to completely manifest then? She's still so young." Daphne laced her fingers in Gideon's. Syrenn could feel how that sent his heart fluttering.

"I'm just curious." It seemed his feigned innocence appeased Daphne, for she said nothing more on the matter—whatever it was they were talking about. It was becoming very clear to Syrenn that Daphne had always been an unquestioning follower in her relationship with Gideon. Ever since the beginning of it, apparently, because the two within this memory were only around age eleven.

Syrenn found herself in another memory. The waves crashed along the shore. Thunder rumbled above, the dark and stormy clouds swirling ominously. She saw a flash of long, dark hair. She remembered that dark hair from Ender's memories.

The scream that came directly after had Syrenn's blood chilling in her veins. Gideon's power surged. It was unlike anything Syrenn had ever felt before. She could feel her own powers writhe against it. It thrashed about, nearly tearing the memory to shreds within Gideon's mind.

Syrenn felt something sting across her face, affectively forcing her power from Gideon's mind. Her head knocked back against the stone wall, causing her vision to go black for a moment.

"You bitch." The words were hissed into her face through rows of clenched teeth. She felt the splatter of saliva as it hit her skin. She flinched away from him, hands coming to block her face from his attack.

When her vision cleared, she could see flashes of the utter rage that clung to Gideon's face.

"Are you seriously prying into my mind?" His hand was gripping her throat so hard she almost couldn't breathe. Her nails dug into his flesh, but he gave no inclination that it affected him.

"Gideon, please," she choked, panting down small breaths. Her voice was so low and broken she wasn't sure he could hear her. "It wasn't on purpose. Sometimes." She tried to suck in a shallow breath. "Sometimes my power just leaches out." *Please, Gideon.*

He dropped his hold, and Syrenn began rubbing at the tenderness he left behind. She took a step to the side, hoping to put a bit of distance between them.

She heard the sound of something snapping before she registered the pain in her nose. Hot liquid began pouring down her face. A moan escaped her without her volition as she clutched at the wound, blinking back the tears that stung so painfully in her eyes.

"Bullshit. What all have you seen?" He was on her, pinning her into the wall, his hand wrapped aggressively around one of her wrists. She whimpered and cowered down.

Syrenn was in a lot of pain, but she was still completely aware of the danger she was now in. If Gideon suspected that she figured out he was the one killing the girls, he could very well kill her right now just to cover it up. To keep her from talking. As she was cowering away from him, she reached into the pocket of her skirt with her free hand and pulled out her dagger.

In a flash, she had it pressed to his throat. He made no move to step back, only pressed further into her blade.

"And where did you get *this,* Syrenn?" His hand wrapped around hers, gripping her fingers so tightly she almost dropped the blade.

"I have it for protection. Or did you forget women are being murdered in this castle?" She seethed through clenched teeth, her anger replacing the fear from only moments ago. Her stare hardened, and she refused to acknowledge the pain in her hand. Gideon gripped even tighter, and she hissed but did not release her grip.

"If you're going to do it, then please go ahead," he challenged.

Neither one moved. If Syrenn harmed the Prince, she would be killed. She knew that.

Where were his guards? Where were Ender's guards. Hell, where was *Ender?*

"I didn't kill those girls, Syrenn. That's what you're thinking, right? I can see it written across your pretty little face. So, there's no reason you should have this blade to my throat right now." His face softened with sincerity. Or was he manipulating her?

"What did you do to your sister?" she breathed.

Gideon stilled as if frozen in place. She wasn't even sure he was breathing.

"What are you accusing me of?" His head cocked to the side, outright scaring Syrenn with the ease with which he spoke. His eyes were lethal.

"She died." Syrenn almost whispered the words.

"That she did. And what a horrible accident it was." He jerked her knife hand forward, causing her to hit herself across the cheek. Her body whirled. His hand gripped into her hair and slammed her face against the wall.

She screamed as her teeth sang with the impact.

One moment, Gideon was against her; the next, she was alone, barely able to steady herself. She wouldn't fall. She wouldn't show him weakness.

She heard a crash, but it took her a moment to orient herself. Her head pulsed, and stars swam in her vision.

"Touch her again, and I will slaughter you." There was so much venom in Ender's words; it even had Syrenn quaking where she stood.

Gideon was on the floor, and it looked as if he had been thrown over the hall table. Candles were strewn everywhere. Wax splattered the walls and floor around him, solidifying where it had landed.

Gideon began to laugh. "Oh, I get it. The two of you are fucking."

"No," Ender all out lied to his brother's face, without batting an eye or missing a beat." I don't approve of you treating *anyone* in the manner you treat her. She is not an object or a toy. She is to be your *wife.* But you abuse and take advantage of her."

"She was in my head." Gideon whined, sounding like a child arguing for another slice of cake after dinner.

"Accidents happen. As she clarified." Ender turned from his brother and collected Syrenn. He turned his head over his shoulder and asked, "Do you have something you're hiding, brother? Is there something you don't wish for Miss Syrenn to see?" He said it like a threat, implying that he already knew. *Are you alright, my love?*

Syrenn gave a slight nod toward Ender.

"Asher, take Miss Syrenn here back to her rooms."

"Does it make you angry, *brother*, that I get everything you can't have?" Gideon bared his teeth at Ender as he rose from the ground. "Is that why your shadows spy on me? She's beautiful, isn't she? And soon, she will be mine to do whatever I wish. Once I'm King, you won't be able to intervene anymore." The look Gideon gave Syrenn was ugly. His lip was curled up in a snarl, and Syrenn blanched.

"Asher. Take Syrenn to her room *now*. The healer will be there shortly." Ender did not remove his eyes from his brother.

Asher grabbed Syrenn by the arm and delicately dragged her from the room. She was thankful to have him to lean on, for her head was still spinning and throbbing.

"I will talk to the council about this," Ender began to lecture. But Syrenn didn't hear the rest of what he said. The door closed behind them, and two guards took up posts in front. Her head was in too much pain to try and listen through her connection with Ender.

Her power still writhed in her gut from the memory of Annalise's scream.

Syrenn was sitting upon her window seat when the healer appeared. The woman paused as she entered the room as if Syrenn's injuries jostled her. She let the door fall closed behind her, coming to a crouch on the floor before Syrenn.

As was this woman's way, she said nothing as she took Syrenn's hand. Syrenn felt a soothing calm almost instantly as the healer's power coursed through her. She stood a moment later, then pressed her fingers gingerly to Syrenn's crushed nose. Syrenn jolted back slightly from the pain there.

A moment later, Syrenn felt nothing. Her nose no longer stung or felt crooked.

Next, the healer's palm flattened against her forehead. More waves of mollifying power leached into Syrenn. She felt her own power dance in the healer's presence.

Friend, it seemed to say.

"Did you know a girl by the name of Wren?" Syrenn asked, breaking the silence that stood between them. Her voice was low and sorrowful, and she felt the healer go still.

"Why do you ask?" Her tone was flat—unfeeling. A mask.

"I knew her. A long time ago." Syrenn paused, thinking back. "We were close. But then... Then she was taken away."

"She had powers."

Syrenn nodded against the healer's hand, which was still pressed into her head. She leaned into the woman's touch.

"I know her very well, actually. She is a friend of my brother." The healer continued brushing her healing touch along Syrenn's clammy skin.

"Is she happy?" Syrenn felt a single tear slip down her cheek.

"As happy as you, I would gather. Though it's been some time since I've been home." She finally removed her hand, then sank to her knees in front of Syrenn. "I think she is smitten with my brother, though." The healer smirked to herself, yet a sadness crept over her expression.

Syrenn startled herself when she laughed through her tears. "Is your brother quite handsome?" She smiled at the woman.

"Very. We aren't blood-related. None of us are. We tend to make our own families." She thought for a moment before adding, "Being taken isn't as bad as you outsiders may think, though I wonder how you managed to avoid it."

"Syrenn."

Ender appeared in the middle of the room, just behind the healer. He did not pause but headed directly for her. His hand cupped her cheek as he inspected the healer's work.

"I'll leave the two of you in peace." The healer gave Syrenn a knowing smile before standing and departing from the room. She couldn't help smiling back.

"She is powerful," Syrenn said in lieu of a greeting.

"That's why she's here. My brother has a way of… ensuring people don't return home."

"She's here against her will?" Syrenn asked, bewildered.

"Yes. As is Asher. There are others as well."

"How does he do it? Does he have something on them?"

"I have no idea, honestly. It must be that. He keeps them here, though as you have guessed, not all of them are loyal to him." Ender coaxed Syrenn up, then lifted her. He carried her the handful of steps to her bed and placed her atop it, gingerly. "Just like I have my secrets, so does Gideon. Though his seem more sinister than mine."

"He's never going to trust me again." Syrenn curled beneath her blanket.

"I think he believes it wasn't intentional, though he will be sure to have his guard up around you from now on." Ender tucked the blanket around her body, then pressed a kiss to her forehead. "We have what we need. You don't need to risk yourself anymore, my violent girl."

"What do you plan to do about it?" Her eyes were growing heavy. Her body was exhausted from the healing work that had been done to her.

"I need to tell the council what I've learned. And what just transpired. It will ultimately be up to them." Ender sounded unsure about this.

"Do you think they'll overthrow him?"

"No."

Syrenn closed her eyes completely, trying to fight the nausea roiling in her gut. "Ender?"

"Yes?"

"I think he killed your sister."

Ender was silent for so long, Syrenn thought he had left. But then she felt his body press into the bed next to her. His arm curled protectively over her body, tucking her further into him. "I have no doubt in my mind that's what happened to her." His words were soft, but the agony was palpable. Syrenn's heart cracked.

"I think he's doing something to Daphne as well. Maybe even the same thing he did to Annalise." She felt a tear slip from her closed eye.

"We'll stop him, my violent girl. One way or another."

Syrenn awoke to pure darkness. She could tell she was alone, though she couldn't see a thing.

She could also tell she was no longer in her own room. Panicking, she felt around herself for something, *anything,* to light the room. Her hands fumbled across the table next to the bed, far out of reach from where she had awoken.

This bed is huge, Syrenn thought as her hand landed upon a candle. She brushed her hand gently over the smooth surface of the table, feeling for some matches. *To have Asher's power right about now...* Syrenn lamented to herself. When she found them, she struck one and felt for the candle wick. The tiny flame illuminated just enough for Syrenn to make out the shadows of furniture.

The bed *was* huge. The entire room was huge, and beautifully decorated from what little bit Syrenn could make out. She hadn't been in this room before, though she knew instantly it was Ender's private bedroom.

She could smell his lingering scent in the air. She laid back down, nestling into the pillow beside her and smashing her face into the fabric— she inhaled deeply. The pine scent clung to the fabric and caused Syrenn's stomach to tighten.

Where was Ender? She called out for him within her mind, dancing her power with his darkness.

Shadows swirled beside the bed in response, and Ender appeared a second later.

"I was with the council." His voice sounded dull, and Syrenn tried to study his face in the dimness of the room.

"What did they say?"

"They didn't care and paid my qualms no mind."

"You told them of your suspicions?"

"Yes, Syrenn. They told me bringing forth such issues is treasonous, though it appeared as if they had already suspected as much." Ender shook his head and looked away. "They were complacent and will be no help in handling him."

"So, they'll just let him continue murdering people just because they think he should be king? That's absurd! Did you tell them what I learned from your mother?"

"They were already aware." He turned back to Syrenn then. "It's all about how it looks to the people, as I suspected. The people of this kingdom are unaware of my mother's stillbirth, so in their eyes I am the oldest son. They will never willingly accept me as their king." Ender sounded solemn as he spoke the truth.

"Surely, we can change their minds? We can tell them the truth. We can persuade them, make them believe."

"Syrenn, it's a lost cause."

"It can't be!"

"Syrenn."

Syrenn was no longer listening to Ender. She was on her knees, clambering towards him. She grabbed him by the forearms, yanking him toward her. "I will not marry him. You promised me you'd get me out. You *promised!*"

Syrenn. His voice sounded in her mind, commanding her full attention. "I will find a way. There must be another way; just trust me to find it." His hands were on her, brushing soothing strokes along her skin.

He pierced his gaze into hers, leveling a look so sincere that Syrenn had to blink back her surprise.

"I want to believe you—"

"Then believe me," he said with finality. Syrenn nodded in response, swallowing her reply. She still held a fear that there was nothing Ender could do for her—short of killing Gideon—to get her out of this betrothal.

Chapter 23

Syrenn stayed in Ender's room for the entirety of the night. She didn't want to be alone in fear of Gideon's retaliation. In theory, she should be safe from any repercussions. However, she knew better than to trust anything she thought she knew about the Prince.

She skipped breakfast, not wanting to face the Prince even now. Not after last night and his accusations, and especially not after Ender went to the council about him. She knew they would have relayed the details of that meeting to him. Would even Ender be safe from his wrath?

There were no more girls left for him to take his anger out on. He wouldn't dare hurt Daphne, Syrenn knew. She herself was supposedly off limits as well. Though, with her out of the way, Gideon could finally have what he truly wanted.

Daphne.

What would the Prince do if he discovered Syrenn's tryst with Daphne, she wondered? Would he dispose of Syrenn, then? Perhaps she would let that information slip the next time she saw him.

Enough. The voice in her mind was shrouded in darkness. Syrenn closed her eyes and smiled to herself. *I will not condone any plans of putting yourself into harm's way.*

Well, if he tries to off his future bride, won't the council be compelled to listen? Syrenn teased.

Yes, but then you would be dead, and I might have a problem with that, came Ender's reply.

You're no fun, Syrenn sulked. She was tired of waiting on Ender to fulfill his promise. Perhaps he was stalling, knowing that once she was free of Gideon, she would go home. She would leave him.

Though, if Gideon were dead, that wouldn't be an issue. She could stay. She *would* stay.

"My dear, your parents have just arrived." The Queen's voice cut through Syrenn like a knife. It took a moment for the words to register.

"My parents?" Syrenn asked, wondering what in the world the Queen was on about.

"Yes, Syrenn. My son told you that he sent for them. For the wedding. They've arrived with a week to spare." A week. Syrenn hadn't been keeping track of the days. Had it nearly been a month already?

"Where are they?" Syrenn was suddenly beside herself with terror. How could he have brought her parents here? They wouldn't be safe, not now that she'd thoroughly pissed off the Prince.

"They're getting settled. They had a rough journey, it seems. I think it best we let them rest before visiting." Queen Estia said it like a suggestion, though Syrenn could tell it was an order.

"When will I be allowed to visit with them?" She couldn't keep her voice from wobbling.

"They'll be at dinner. We'll make a party out of it. I can't wait to meet them formally." Estia smiled genuinely at Syrenn, and she wondered how the Queen had birthed such an odious man as Gideon. Maybe there really was something to these fairytales.

Syrenn decided to let the issue rest for now. Her parents had only just arrived, and surely Gideon wouldn't go straight to killing them just to spite her. She would have to warn them as well—though discreetly. And she would have to assure them they needn't worry about her.

It took a lot to keep Syrenn's mind busy that day. She had this horrible feeling gnawing at her. Something was off, but she couldn't figure out what.

She hadn't seen Gideon. Or Daphne. Or even Ender, for that matter. She knew Ender was around, he had broken up her train of thought on multiple occasions.

The castle was quiet, but it wasn't a peaceful sort of quiet.

She spent the morning playing the piano in the parlor. She took tea and a light lunch directly after. She had read for hours, and yet dinner seemed a far time off.

It was finally an acceptable time for Syrenn to dress for dinner, so she went to her rooms for the first time since last night, followed closely by Maren. When they arrived in the tower, however, Syrenn was shaken by what she found.

Her room was in total disarray. Belongings were thrown about. Her oils were all shattered upon the floor, pooling into a sickly mix of different scents. Her dresses were in ribbons. Even her bed was toppled over as if someone had been searching for something.

There was nothing to find, so Syrenn couldn't fathom what the reason was behind the mess.

It wasn't until Syrenn saw the dress Ender had gifted her, shredded and half burned, that the terror fully took hold. Gideon had done this, she thought. Gideon knew the truth, as he accused her of last night.

"My lady, come. You shouldn't see this." Maren stepped before Syrenn, her blond hair blocking the view. The maid abruptly pushed Syrenn from the room and closed the door behind them. "I'll send someone straight away to clean this up."

Syrenn didn't argue with Maren as she took her hand and practically dragged her down the tower stairs. Her mind and heart were still, dread pulling deep in her belly as she recognized what the violation meant.

He had come looking for her, and when she wasn't there and didn't return, he took his rage out upon her things.

He had meant to kill her.

"I'll send out to one of the shops for a gown for the evening. Something new and lovely for your parents to see you in. The future queen." Maren was rambling, probably to keep them both calm, Syrenn presumed. "We'll get something red for the—"

"*No*," Syrenn growled.

Maren stopped mid-stride, turning wide eyes onto Syrenn. She had never taken such a terse tone with her maid and immediately felt guilty for her harshness.

"I mean, no. My apologies, Maren. I'm just really shaken right now." Syrenn hoped the apology sounded as genuine as she meant it.

"It's alright, my lady. You've had quite the fright. We both have." She rubbed soothing lines down Syrenn's arm.

"I would prefer a gray gown if you can find one. One similar to the gown the Prince gifted me." Syrenn's words were calmer than she felt.

"What a lovely idea." Maren's mood brightened immensely.

"Thank you, Maren." The maid beamed at Syrenn as she directed her into the bathing room.

"How about a long bath while they fetch your gown, hmm? That will be soothing." She ushered her into the bathing room, then went to fetch a guard about the dress. She returned almost immediately, drawing the warm water and pouring salts and oils into its depths. She undressed Syrenn and urged her into the water's embrace. Syrenn gladly complied. As she soaked, she began to doze, forcefully pushing all terror and dread from her body.

The gown was beautiful, though nothing like the one Ender had given her. It was indeed a stormy gray, but it didn't glitter in the light like the other one had. And it was much more modest. The fabric was lovely, regardless.

The skirts swished around Syrenn as she walked through the corridors and into the dining hall. Somehow, she was the last to arrive. Perhaps this was intentional, a plan devised by Maren in order for Syrenn to have a big entrance.

As soon as she was through the doorway that led into the dining hall, her eyes landed on her mother.

Syrenn did not expect the cascade of emotions that rammed into her at the sight of her parents. She felt tears prick at her eyes only seconds before the sobs broke free. Before she knew it, she was running, landing straight into her mother's arms, her father wrapping himself about the pair as they embraced.

Her mother murmured soothing words into Syrenn's hair as she clung to her, gripping her back. Her hold was just as tight, if not tighter than Syrenn's. Encased in her father's embrace, she felt safer than she had in a long, long time.

"My sweet girl. My baby," her mother whispered. Syrenn cried harder than she ever had as a child. She couldn't decide if it was because she missed her parents or because of everything she had been through this past year. Even though she was still angry with them for sending her to the Southern Kingdom, she was so glad to have them within arm's reach once more.

"Have you heard?" Syrenn whispered into her mother's neck. Her mother's fingers dug into her in response.

So, they're aware, Syrenn thought towards Ender. She squeezed her arms tight and sunk into her mother once more before finally pulling herself free from her parents' embrace. Her father planted a kiss on the top of her head before backing away. The two women disentangled themselves. Syrenn wiped a few stray tears from her eyes before turning towards Prince Gideon.

They were filled in during their travels.

"Thank you for having them brought here," she said with a slight bow of her head. Gideon smirked at her.

"Of course. I knew you would want them present for our wedding. What daughter wouldn't want her father to walk her down the aisle on her big day?" He almost sounded mocking, and Syrenn had to bite back her retort.

She still wanted to slice into him after what had happened between them. How he had tried to kill her. He probably would have killed her had Ender not intervened. Had she been in her tower when he had come searching for her.

"Let's take our seats, shall we?" Gideon gestured to the table and pulled out his own chair. The room waited for him to sit before anyone else took their seats. Syrenn watched out of the corner of her eye as Ender pulled back a chair for Queen Estia before moving to her right and taking his place next to her.

Syrenn eyed the seat next to Gideon, not wanting to step any closer to the Prince than she had to. Though, she supposed she still needed to keep up pretenses, especially now that her parents were here. She wouldn't let Gideon take out his wrath on them, not for her own shortcomings.

Syrenn watched as her father gingerly pulled back that exact chair, then motioned for her to sit. She smiled at him, blinking back the tears stinging her eyes. If only her father knew the truth of the Prince. He would be lifting that chair into the air just to send it crashing down over Gideon's head.

Taking her seat like the good little bride she was to be in just a short week, she paid no more mind to the Prince next to her. Her stomach plummeted, though. Only a week left until her life was tied to a murderer. She hated to think it, but she was beginning to doubt Ender's ability to set her free.

She could feel Ender's anger peak as she realized he felt every bit of that doubt. She chewed the inside of her lip, not at all sorry for thinking it. Syrenn could see no way out of this mess. At least, not an honest way out of it.

"Daphne, is it?" Syrenn's mother said from the seat beside her. "I'm Madge. Syrenn has told me so much about you in her letters. Thank you for being such a wonderful friend to my daughter."

Daphne blushed, her head dipping slightly. "She's been a wonderful friend in return. It's been a long year, and it's been nice having each other to lean on. Especially here lately—"

"Yes, it's been a bit frightening. Though, we've taken care of the problem. There seems to have been an intruder hiding in the maids' ranks. She has been dealt with. Our girls are safe." Gideon speared some food and flashed a grin towards Madge. Syrenn stared at him, wondering who he thought he was fooling with this nonsense.

"That's a relief. You have no idea how terrified we were to learn on the journey over here that there had been murders happening. Those poor girls. I couldn't imagine what their mothers are going through." Madge's hand trembled slightly, and Syrenn grasped it in her own. She gave it a slight squeeze.

"I was unaware that a culprit had been caught," Ender drawled from beside Estia.

"Ah, yes. The council must have forgotten to fill you in last night when you met with them." Gideon shot a fearsome look toward his brother.

They told him, Syrenn said to Ender.

Of course they did. He's to be king. They'll be licking his boots any chance they get. Ender rubbed his jaw, returning Gideon's look with one of amusement.

"Well, I'm glad our Daphne and Syrenn will be safe once more."

"How about we talk of the wedding?" Estia chimed in. "Madge, Cairn, would you like to see the throne room after dinner? That's where we'll be holding the ceremony and celebration. Directly after, Gideon will be crowned King."

"All in the same night?" Cairn asked, looking toward his daughter. Syrenn knew her father was only concerned about the focus being stolen away from Syrenn on her own wedding day.

"That was my late husband's wish. That we uphold tradition. A new king is only crowned once he is wed, and many of the men in our family are… eager to be crowned as soon as possible. So, we do the coronation and wedding in one fell swoop."

"Yes, and that way, we don't have to fill the castle with guests more than once in such a short span," Gideon said, swirling his glass of wine. "I like parties, but sometimes the aristocrats of this realm can be quite… annoying."

Estia chuckled quietly, and both Madge and Cairn offered a polite smile of their own. Syrenn's parents were no strangers to upper society. With them being well off in Farehail, they were invited or hosted their fair share of lavish dinners.

"Well, it sounds like it will be a night to remember," Madge commended. Syrenn sank lower in her seat and watched as Daphne did the same from across the table.

Chapter 24

After taking her parents on a tour of the throne room, the garden, the library, and just about everywhere else in the castle Syrenn dropped them off at their assigned room. They would be staying in the main castle, on the lower levels of the east wing.

They couldn't be farther from their daughter, Syrenn mused as she listened to the echoing of her footfalls. She wandered out of the wing and down the corridor, making her way to the garden.

There is no way I'm sleeping in my own room tonight, she speared towards Ender.

I'll collect you once I'm done.

What are you doing? Syrenn smiled to herself, hanging on to the notes of Ender's voice as they rang through her mind.

Business, came his short reply.

Syrenn scrunched her brow, wondering what sort of business he could be conducting this late at night. Changing course, Syrenn began walking toward the large main study. The council normally met there, and she wondered if Ender wasn't speaking with them once more. Perhaps she could listen in for herself.

The door came into view, and Syrenn slowed her steps. The door was slightly ajar, so she would have to creep quietly in order to go undetected.

Asher stood in the hall, the only guard within sight. She knew he wouldn't say a word about her eavesdropping because he was probably doing exactly that himself. Their eyes connected as she backed against the stone wall, and he flashed her a smirk.

Exactly what she thought.

"That's why we haven't been receiving any shipments?" Ender's bewildered question seeped through the opening, piquing Syrenn's interest.

"Unfortunately, though, we do intend to start up a trade once more." Syrenn had never heard that voice before. The man in the room with Ender was not from the castle. She craned her neck, not wanting to miss a word exchanged between the two. "Once everything settles, and we get back onto our feet. It won't be the same as before, probably much smaller quantities—"

"Of course. There's nothing you need to worry about. And if there's anything we can do to assist the rebuild, we would be happy to." Ender's voice held so much compassion for whatever it was the man had shared with him.

"We wouldn't be opposed to a loan of sorts. We could really use some supplies to get back on our feet. We're doing everything we can, but I don't want our people to go without because of something they've suffered through." The stranger's voice was strong, though Syrenn could detect heartache in his words. She leaned closer to the door, her shoulder brushing against it.

It creaked, and Asher stifled a laugh.

The door was suddenly pulled open, causing Syrenn to stumble inside. She straightened herself, then took in the man seated at the table.

He had long blond hair, eyes of a beautiful sage, and held a look of... amusement. He blinked, staring at Syrenn as if she had something on her face.

"Hello," Syrenn said to the man.

"Who is this?" he asked Ender, not taking his eyes off Syrenn.

"This is my brother's betrothed, Miss Syrenn." Ender placed a hand on Syrenn's upper arm. "Syrenn, this is Tiernan. He's here from the North."

"You're from Kahnan?"

"Yes. I felt I owed your kingdom an explanation for the lack of trade as of late. And an apology for the last one you received." Tiernan stood, rounding the table and offering a hand to Syrenn. She reached out, grasping it in her own. Tiernan lowered his head over their joined hands and kissed the back of Syrenn's.

Syrenn's power flung out toward the stranger. It was inside his mind before she could reel it back in. Fire flashed, so hot and all-consuming Syrenn couldn't breathe. She yanked back, her power snapping free of its hold.

Tiernan cocked his head to one side, then dropped Syrenn's hand.

"I think I like you." The corner of his mouth quirked up. "You have the North's congratulations on your upcoming marriage. I have no doubt you'll make a perfect queen." Tiernan looked from Syrenn to Ender, then back again. Something like understanding flashed across his pupils before he stepped from the room. Turning back, he said, "I'll be on the first ship in the morning. Thank you for hearing me out, Prince Ender."

"I'll assure that your supplies are loaded. If your kingdom needs anything else, don't hesitate to send word our way."

Tiernan inclined his head towards Ender, then set off down the corridor once more.

"I told you I would collect you when I was finished," Ender scolded halfheartedly.

"I was curious." Syrenn looked up into Ender's face and fluttered her lashes. "But please, don't let me stop you from collecting me now."

Shadows swirled as Ender stared into Syrenn's eyes. His arms closed around her, pressing her into the heat of his body. He released her almost instantly and stepped away. Crouching down, he lit the hearth in his room with a long match. It took a moment for the flames to catch, but Syrenn watched him as he worked.

"I do hope my room is to your liking because you won't be sleeping elsewhere for as long as my heart is beating." His voice was low, the words a growl as he stood and came back to face Syrenn.

Her heart skittered as he backed her into his bed, tucking her into his body. Their mouths crashed together; hands searched one another until they were both clinging tightly to each other's clothes—tugging and pulling at the fabric. Syrenn drank Ender in, pressing her lips harder into his mouth.

I love you, the words reverberated through Syrenn's mind, and her breath shuddered. *You are mine. He will never have you.*

Syrenn bit Ender's lip, and he abruptly stopped his proclamations.

"Just get on the bed. We can discuss this later," Syrenn breathed into his mouth. She felt his lips curve into a smile against hers.

"As you wish, my violent girl." Ripping his jacket off and throwing it to the ground, Ender flung himself backwards onto the bed. He kicked his shoes off one at a time, shuffling backwards so that his shoulders were braced against the headboard. "Is this what you want?" He taunted, unbuttoning his shirt without breaking eye contact.

Syrenn untied the belt around her waist and balled it up into her palm. She pulled the sleeves of her dress down her shoulder, letting gravity do its work. The fabric slipped down the length of her body, revealing her nearly see-through slip beneath. Ender's eyes darkened as he took her in, his eyes snagging on her breasts. Bumps broke out along her skin at the weight of his gaze.

Stepping out of her own slippers, she crawled onto the bed. Moving on her knees, she made her way up Ender's body. His hands roamed lightly from her upper thighs onto her ribcage. His lips parted, and his eyelids drooped as he felt her through the thin fabric.

Syrenn let her belt drop from her palm, catching it between her fingers. It dangled between them, and Ender finally noticed it. His eyes caught Syrenn's, and she flashed him a wicked smile.

Before Ender could realize what she was doing, she grabbed his wrists and dragged them above his head. Ender's eyes flashed with excitement as Syrenn began wrapping the fabric of the belt around his wrists, securing it tightly to the headboard behind him. A sigh of contentment rumbled deep in his throat as he smiled up at her.

She tugged the belt as tightly as she could, tying it into a knot between his hands.

"Don't move," she whispered as she lowered her head to his. He tilted his chin, trying to catch her kiss, but she moved her mouth onto his upper chest instead. He groaned in annoyance.

"Do you like your men helpless, Syrenn?" He bit his lip, trying to stifle a groan as Syrenn licked down his chest, making quick work of the buttons still holding his shirt in place. When the last one was free, she ripped the fabric to each side and skimmed her fingers down the ridges of his torso.

His body trembled slightly below her touch, and Syrenn's body heated in response.

"I like *you* helpless beneath me." He was anything but helpless, for he could shadow himself away at any time he wished. But Syrenn knew he didn't wish to be anywhere but beneath her body. She bit into his flesh just above his hip. He grunted but pushed up into the pain.

"You're going to be the death of me," he mused. Syrenn ignored the truth of his words. Instead, she focused on the hair poking just above where his pants rested across his hips. She moved her mouth in that direction, her eyes peering up into Ender's face. He watched as her tongue broke between her lips and licked forcefully across the center of his lower abdomen. His jaw flexed, his throat bobbing as he swallowed.

Her hands joined her mouth, and she flicked open the buttons of his pants. Gripping the top of the fabric, she slowly, slowly moved them down his legs. When they were around his ankles, he kicked them free.

Come here, he growled into her mind. She smiled at him but shook her head. She straddled his upper thighs, letting the heat of his skin against her inner thighs spike her arousal. *Please,* he begged.

Syrenn grasped his hardness and began moving her hand along his shaft at an agonizingly slow pace. His hips flexed beneath her, but with her position, he couldn't push himself into her grip any more than she was allowing.

Syrenn could feel the brush of his shadows across her skin. She looked down her body, seeing them skate across her thighs, then up to her breasts. They flitted across her nipples, pulling a soft moan from her lips. They curled under her backside, then between her legs.

A cry bursts from her throat as a shadow slithered against the sensitive flesh between her thighs. She rocked forward against it, craving a friction she knew the shadows could not provide.

Two can play this game, came Ender's response. She looked at him, but his head was tilted so far back she could only see the underside of his chin. He still tried unsuccessfully to thrust his hips upwards. She tightened her grip around him eliciting a shudder. *Syrenn...*

Another flick against her flesh had her pressing down into Ender. She felt the heat of him against her core, and she moved against his thigh in search of that friction. Ender moaned, his chest heaving up and down quickly.

"Fuck you," he bit out. Syrenn huffed a small laugh and dragged her wetness against him once more. He lifted his leg higher, allowing her more pressure. She stroked him in thanks.

The hair of his thighs prickled against her as she rubbed her core onto him. Her body pulsed with need for him. She pulled back long enough to move farther up his body, angling herself over him. Pressing both hands into his chest, she watched as he looked at her with such an undeniable need.

She positioned him at her entrance but didn't push down onto him. His head fell back once more in defeat, but she grabbed hold of his neck, squeezing slightly. "Look at me," she commanded.

He obeyed.

She slid down his length slowly, and Ender didn't take his eyes from her the entire way down. When she was finally seated herself all the way, she let out a sigh of contentment and lolled her head back. Syrenn rocked her hips into him, feeling his reach deepen.

Ender flexed beneath her, and she looked at him once more. With her hand still at his throat, his eyes still on hers, she felt a flush pour over her chest. Holding his eye contact, she thrust against him—slowly at first, then harder and faster as she felt her orgasm already beginning to build. It crashed into her so quickly she was caught off guard, yelling his name in euphoria.

Still, his eyes remained on her.

She stilled above him, panting, then laid her head against his chest. His heart pounded in time with hers, and she felt him tug against his restraints to no avail.

After sitting up, she lifted herself off him.

"Syrenn," he protested. She gave him a devious smile before sliding down his body and enveloping him in her mouth. The groan that followed was so feral she sucked harder and wrapped her hand around his base.

She moved her mouth up and down in unison with her hand, flicking her tongue along his tip. She tasted him, and herself, as she worked him into oblivion.

His hips bucked against her as he panted her name over and over again. She hastened her pace, bringing him further into her mouth and feeling him against the back of her throat. She could feel him losing control, so she ran her tongue along the underside of him, causing him to stiffen and shudder.

"Syrenn..." he moaned, his body shaking as he came into her. She watched as he pulled at the restraints but then gave up. Their eyes met a moment later, and Syrenn broke her connection with him before swallowing and flashing him a grin. "You're evil," he breathed.

"You love it," she teased.

Darkness swirled around his arms, and then he was curling forward to pull her up against him. He kissed her deeply, tangling his now free fingers into her hair. Their kisses slowed, turning languid as they both drifted off to sleep, still wrapped tightly in each other's arms.

Chapter 25

The constriction around Syrenn's rib cage was starting to cause her to see spots. Her head felt light, and she swayed slightly on her feet. She couldn't seem to draw in enough air with each breath, which was causing her to pant and sweat to form along her upper lip.

"I think it's a bit tight," she gritted out between clenched teeth. Smoothing her hands over her bodice, her palms snagged on the hundreds of jewels encrusting the white fabric strapped firmly around her middle.

"We want to highlight your silhouette," Estia chastised from where she lounged on her settee. She and Madge sat drinking tea as Daphne fidgeted in a wingback chair beside them. The Queen Regent had asked them all to her chambers for Syrenn's fitting. With only five days now until the wedding, Syrenn knew it was a matter of time before she was asked to put on a wedding dress. She hadn't been looking forward to the occasion.

Maren tugged the ties at Syrenn's back tighter, causing a sharp pain to lance through her lungs. Syrenn hated the dress. It was gaudy and huge—nothing like the dress she envisioned as a girl.

It's hideous, Ender's thought permeated through her—reflecting her own feelings.

Perhaps Asher could incinerate it for me.

"I think if we highlight it anymore, my ribcage will collapse, and we'll have an entirely different issue on our hands," Syrenn ground out. She was sweating profusely now. "And if you don't get this thing off me right now, I'm going to pass out."

Maren began hurriedly ripping at the laces that wove across Syrenn's back. The loosening of the dress was met with a sigh of relief from Syrenn. Her head tilted towards the ceiling as she breathed in the first deep breath in the last twenty minutes. How was she expected to wear this for an entire evening?

"We can make a few adjustments before the ceremony," Estia promised, biting into a scone. "It really is lovely on you, my sweet girl." She flashed Syrenn a heartwarming smile that almost had her feeling bad about her hate for her son. The Queen Regent was a nice woman, even if her youngest son was a complete tyrant.

"I have to agree. You look just as I always imagined you would, Syrenn," Madge said, smiling sweetly at her daughter. Her eyes glimmered with a few unshed tears, and Syrenn had to look away. Her stomach churned.

"What do you think, Daphne?" The Queen Regent looked at Daphne expectantly and with her full attention. Daphne fidgeted, not wanting to be caught in a lie.

"It's… not what I pictured her in. Syrenn usually wears things a bit more… subtle." Daphne blushed and planted her eyes on the bottom of Syrenn's dress.

"We can't have subtle for a royal wedding." Estia blatantly dismissed her. Syrenn had to stop herself from rolling her eyes so as not to offend the Queen Regent. She did note that Estia didn't ask for her own opinion on the matter. She seethed inwardly, annoyed that she was being forced to wear a dress she loathed, let alone marry a man she loathed even more.

Estia rose from her seat, Madge and Daphne following suit. She glided across the floor of her room, then stopped just before Syrenn. Placing a hand on her cheek, she said, "I cannot wait to call you my daughter. You are very special indeed, and my son is lucky to have found you." Her fingers stroked across Syrenn's skin, which heated under her gaze.

"Thank you, Queen Estia. Your words mean so much," Syrenn blinked back tears. She didn't deserve this woman's love. Not when she planned to—

Estia cut Syrenn off mid-thought. "I need to head to my son's room. He is trying on his attire today as well, and I want to ensure it's to my liking." Estia departed with Maren in tow, leaving the three women alone in her private chambers.

"I can tell you aren't happy," Madge said as soon as they could no longer hear the clicking of the Queen's shoes upon the stone corridor.

"You shipped me off to be married, which is the one thing in the world I didn't want to do. So no, mother, I am not happy." Syrenn let the gown fall to the floor. She stepped over the mountain of white fabric and to the chair in which her day dress was draped. Pulling it over her head, she said, "And I am not a fan of the Prince in the slightest. So, because of you and father, I am to not only marry but marry a man I absolutely loathe."

Her mother sat back down in her seat; attention turned inward as she thought of what to say next.

"Gideon isn't that bad, Syrenn. Surely, you two will come to some sort of common ground where you can both find happiness." Daphne spoke softly—lovingly—toward Syrenn. "He isn't too keen on the marriage either."

Their eyes met, and Syrenn felt a terrible guilt rise within her. She loved Daphne so dearly, and she knew this situation was hurting her too. But Daphne didn't know about Gideon's darker side. Or so Syrenn thought. She revisited the new memory she gathered from Gideon, where Daphne had been cautioning him of something right before his sister's death...

Did she know Gideon was at fault for the death of Annalise?

"Right. Perhaps we can come to some sort of agreement," Syrenn nearly choked on the words.

"Do you want to talk about anything, honey?" Madge asked. "What is it that's so horrible about the Prince?"

Syrenn wanted to come clean to her mother. She had always been honest with her, but she couldn't say anything with Daphne in the room. Or with the potential of the guards overhearing.

"He's just a bit full of himself, is all."

"Oh, he's still young, my girl. Men grow out of that." She offered Syrenn an amused smile. "Especially after the wedding night." She chuckled to herself, then looked slightly alarmed. "Would you like to talk about what will be expected from you?"

Syrenn locked her jaw to keep her mouth from gaping open. Was her mother really asking her about this?

Syrenn cleared her throat, "I think I'll be alright."

"Are you sure? It's okay to be nervous, Syrenn—"

"Mother." Syrenn's voice came out shrill. "Please stop talking." She could feel heat rising to her cheeks.

Her mother pursed her lips but didn't continue. Daphne stifled a laugh, and Syrenn shot her a heated glare.

"Since we're finished, I best go find your father." Madge rose, then pecked a kiss upon her daughter's cheek before leaving the chamber.

"We should probably leave the Queen's room as well." Daphne closed the distance between her and Syrenn. She brought her hand to Syrenn's cheek, grazing it lovingly. Raising onto her toes, she pressed her lips to Syrenn's. Their warmth melted into Syrenn, and she leaned into Daphne.

Pulling away, Daphne said, "I love you. But the dress is hideous."

Syrenn laughed and looped her arm through Daphne's. They left the room, not sparing a glance to the heap of white fabric abandoned on the floor.

"She's right. The dress is atrocious."

Ender leaned against the mantle in his room, one foot crossed over the other. He looked to have been waiting for her. She tossed her book atop the chair, then crossed to where Ender stood. Draping her arms over his shoulders, she tilted her face up to meet his.

"Any luck?" Syrenn asked him.

"With?"

"Finding me a way out of this?" She backed away, twining her fingers into the fabric at her back. She popped a few buttons free. Shadows made quick work of the last few that were just out of her reach. She dropped the dress to the floor, then pulled on her robe that she had left from the previous nights.

"I'm tossing around a few ideas."

"Are you willing to share them with me, or shall it be a surprise?"

Ender pushed away from the mantle, coming to a stop in front of her. He crossed his arms over his chest before saying, "If I told you, you would look complicit." He brushed a stray hair from her face. "I want you as innocent in this as possible, my violent girl. I won't give them a reason to harm you."

"Well, you best hurry with your little plans, or else I'll take care of it myself."

"I know, Syrenn. I wouldn't put it past you to stab him the next time you two are alone." The corner of his mouth tugged up. "But for that very reason, I want you in my rooms every night. I don't want to chance him thinking he can try anything for which he will find himself at the wrong end of your blade."

"I've already talked to Maren. I told her that ever since the incident with my room being trashed, I no longer feel comfortable in there."

"And where did you tell her you'd be sleeping?" His eyes took on a mischievous twinkle.

"With my parents, of course." Syrenn batted her lashes innocently back at him. "She assured me she would stay in my place. So that if anyone were to come knocking, she could tell them they've just missed me."

"Do you really think that will work?" Ender quirked an eyebrow.

"Are they going to accuse me of lying? Then Gideon will have to explain why he thought it a good idea to visit his intended in her chambers in the middle of the night." Syrenn crossed her arm over her chest. "That isn't a good show of propriety on his part. What other motive might he have than trying to have his way with me before the wedding night?"

"You're right. My mother would be beside herself to learn her son was being dishonorable." Ender lowered his head and planted a soft kiss along Syrenn's lips. "Clever girl. Though you're just going to anger my little brother more."

"As you said, he'll just find himself at the wrong end of my blade."

Chapter 26

Y ou weren't in your room last night," Daphne whispered as she and Syrenn wove through the gardens, selecting the flowers for the wedding ceremony. Two maids were tying ribbons loosely around the stems of the flowers both Syrenn and Daph selected. In four days' time, someone would come to cut each one for the arrangements.

"I was not." Syrenn said softly.

"Nor were you the previous night." It wasn't a question, and Syrenn didn't bother commenting on it. "Or the one before that."

"Have you come searching for me, Daphne?" Syrenn looked upon her dearest friend. Daphne kept her eyes forward, her delicate fingers brushing the petal of a purple flower. One of the maids hurried forward, tying a ribbon around its stem. Daphne, oblivious to the maid's actions, plucked a petal and crumpled it between her fingers, letting the ball of flesh fall to the ground.

"I'm just worried for you, Syrenn." She turned, bringing sad eyes upon her face. "What you're doing is dangerous. If Gideon finds out…"

"What will he do to me, Daphne?" Syrenn flicked her hand, signaling for the maids to leave them to their conversation. The two girls scurried off; faces tilted toward the floor. "He's forcing me to marry him against my will. He's taken advantage of me. He's hurt me. What more could he do?" There was challenge in her voice, begging Daphne to see the truth.

Her eyes welled with tears, and she worried her lip between her teeth. "Syrenn, I think something is happening—"

"Ladies! You've started without me," Gideon called, weaving through the maze of flowers. "What is the color scheme?" he asked them as he approached. He flashed them each a smile. It faltered slightly when he took in Daphne's state, but he didn't question her.

"Purple. Various shades." Syrenn dismissed him, not even sparing him a glance as she focused on Daphne and what she was about to say. She had kept her distance from him since the night he had struck her so violently. Syrenn stretched out her power, reaching for Daphne, but Daphne threw up a wall, effectively blocking Syrenn from her mind completely.

Daphne shook her head, as if clearing her thoughts. She smiled up at Gideon, collecting herself. "Syrenn seems to like the darker shades more, but we've been adding in some light purple and white ones to make them pop." She fluttered her lashes, no longer the forlorn girl of only moments ago. She skipped off, disappearing around a bend in the walkway, trailing after the two maids.

"Purple?" Gideon quirked an eyebrow at her.

She glared through him. He looked nervous, which Syrenn scoffed at. She turned, walking after Daphne and paying no mind to any of the flowers as she passed them.

"Syrenn, wait." Gideon's hurried footsteps sounded against the stone pathway. His hand landed on her shoulder, and she violently shook it off. "Syrenn, please. I'm trying to apologize."

She halted so quickly he ran into her back. Whirling on him, she shoved a finger toward his face. "You want to apologize? Seriously? You could have killed me, Gideon. Do you really think a simple 'I'm sorry' will fix that?" Her voice had gone shrill, and he blanched with every strike of her words. She hadn't realized she was so angry with him about it.

"Syrenn. I am sorry." He relinquished a step. "Truly." He placed a hand over his heart.

Face set in stone, she turned from him and stomped down the path.

"I realize it was unintentional. And I didn't mean what I accused you of. I was just lashing out." He was only a step behind her. "Syrenn, would you just talk to me, please? I don't want to start our marriage—"

"Gideon, I don't want to start our marriage, period." She turned, bracing her arms for the impact of his body. She shoved hard into his chest. "If you want me to accept your apology," she loomed closer, putting every bit of acid into her words as she continued, "You would let. Me. Leave."

Gideon stared at her as if she had slapped him. When he regained himself, his brow furrowed. "I can't do that, and you know it." His face took on a wounded expression.

"You can't, or you won't?" she spat at him.

"Can't." He stepped closer, hardening his features. "If I could get rid of you, Syrenn, I *would*. As I'm sure you've *accidentally* seen, I have one woman who owns my heart. It is not and will never be *you*, Syrenn." His face was inches from hers now, and a bit of terror began clawing its way into her throat.

"Then leave me alone. If I have to go through with this, I will. But don't act like some doting husband or expect me to be some simpering wife when it's obvious we're both in love with other people."

Gideon drew back, regarding Syrenn. His head tilted to one side, and he smiled just as she realized what she had said. He chuckled incredulously. "Right." He shook his head and laughed softly to himself. "Do have fun with your flowers, Syrenn. I'll see you on our wedding night."

With that, Gideon strode off without a care in the world, leaving Syrenn stewing on her own.

"I feel like we just keep going around in circles," Syrenn quipped to Ender as they walked along the beach. The stars twinkled overhead, and the cool air whipped through Syrenn's hair, tangling the tresses behind her.

Ender tightened his arm around hers, tucking her closer into his body. Asher walked a few paces behind them, taking up the rear on the off chance that someone were to spot them together.

"We've been heading in a straight line this entire time," Ender mused.

"That's not what I mean, and you know it."

Ender was quiet for a moment before he said, "I have found an ally in the council. He's working on swaying the others."

"Swaying them to what?" Syrenn leaned her head onto Ender's shoulder, breathing in his fresh scent. Her power fluttered in response to their proximity.

"To either let you break your arrangement with him," Ender leaned his cheek against the top of Syrenn's head. "Or, to overthrow him as heir to the throne."

Syrenn gasped and stopped in her tracks, dropping her arm from Ender's. He looked down at her with a grin she could barely see in the starlight. She reached into his mind, searching for the information.

"You're serious." Syrenn couldn't believe what she was hearing. She had a chance.

"Give him another day or two, but I think we have a chance." He held her chin between his thumb and forefinger, angling her face up so he could plant a kiss on her. "I told you I would get you out, Syrenn. One way or another."

"Asher, could you go take a walk?" Syrenn smiled as she breathed the words against Ender's lips. They heard the quiet footfalls of Asher's retreating form. Alone, Syrenn showed Ender just how appreciative she was of him.

Chapter 27

There was a darkness to this memory, one that Syrenn knew and loved more than anything. A darkness that hadn't been there when this moment had originally played out.

Syrenn careened into her past once more, her power manipulating her dream—memory—showing her something it felt she needed to remember. *The night sky glittering above her head usually brought her joy. But tonight, it was anything but magical.*

Syrenn was being sent away. To the Southern Kingdom. Her parents were shipping her away in the hopes that she would be married off. Syrenn did not want to be queen. Syrenn did not even want to be a wife.

Her parents had betrayed her, and she didn't think she could ever forgive them.

Not that there was anything in Farehail for her, not anymore. Wren had long since been stationed far, far away from her, their relationship dwindling into ashes with the distance that was put between them. Darkness brushed along her hand, twisting between her fingers in an embrace as Syrenn looked upon her past self with sorrow.

It seemed her power had brought Ender along as well.

Footsteps swept over the forest floor as someone crept up behind Syrenn. "It's really for the best." Her mother's voice was soothing, and

Syrenn was bitter because that voice calmed her—even as it was sending her away.

"This isn't what I want."

"The South demanded we send someone from the island. It makes sense for it to be you."

"Because I have no power?" Syrenn asked. "Because I can keep our secrets?"

"Yes, Syrenn." Her mother grabbed Syrenn's hand, pulling her so that her head rested upon her shoulder. "He won't choose you. Our sources say he has someone in mind already. But be wary."

"Why?" Syrenn asked, confused as to why her mother would send her somewhere she needed to be on her guard.

"I've heard that the Prince is greedy for power." Her mom rubbed soothing circles along her arm before continuing. "They found a husk on the shore near the castle a decade and a half ago. The people Farehail has stationed there believe it was the elder Prince who created it."

Syrenn's past self stilled, heart stopping as she recalled what that meant.

"Then why are you sending me there?" She ripped from her mother's grasp, whirling on her.

"Because if we don't send someone, they will come and take someone. We do not want anyone from the South on our island if we can help it." Madge, always the protector. Though, Syrenn believed she should put her before the well-being of the island. That was never the case with her parents, though. It never would be.

"Trust me, mother," Syrenn began. She stepped into Madge's awaiting arms. "I will steer clear of both princes, especially the elder Prince if I can help it."

Chapter 28

Piercing light stabbed into Syrenn's eyes. She groaned and rolled to the side. The ground beneath her shifted, causing Syrenn's heart to leap with the feeling of falling. She bolted upright, her eyes flying open to an expanse of blue.

The waves of the ocean licked at her feet. Ender lay beside her, still sleeping regardless of the sun's violent rays. She shoved against him hard.

Grunting, he thrust himself into a sitting position.

"Shit," he mumbled when he realized where they were.

"You need to get me back to my room." Syrenn scrubbed her hand over her face. "I need clean clothes and a bath." She tried to swallow. "And some water."

"I didn't mean for us to sleep out here. I wonder why Asher didn't wake us." Ender looked behind them and towards the forest. Asher wasn't within sight.

"He probably fell asleep too," Syrenn said, getting to her feet. She brushed the sand from her dress and reached a hand down for Ender.

Accepting it, he said, "I'll check in with the council after I drop you off. See if they had a change of heart yet." Now on his feet, he folded Syrenn into his arms. She kissed him as his darkness swirled around them— floating them through emptiness and back into her tower room.

The world solidified beneath her feet, but she savored their kiss for a moment longer. They parted, and Syrenn watched as Ender ran his tongue over his lips, tasting her. His eyes were glued to hers as she gazed up into him. Something sparked within his dark irises before they shot to the side—just above Syrenn's head.

His jaw slacked, a look of utter surprise and disbelief contorting his face. Syrenn turned, but Ender grabbed her before she could and slammed her head into his chest.

"Don't look," he hissed. His fingers dug into her scalp, his grip vice like. She couldn't move even if she were to thrash against him.

"Ender, what—"

"We have to leave. Now." Darkness whirled around them before Syrenn could object or demand an answer from him. She threw her power into his mind. He wasn't ready, for she saw everything.

Her bed—the sheets shredded to pieces and no longer white, but red. Crimson dripped onto the floor in a heavy pool, the morning light glimmering along its surface. The body prostrate atop the blankets and pillows, mutilated almost beyond recognition.

Almost.

That had been Maren's golden hair—now drenched in blood—splayed out across the pillows. That had been Maren's face, now hollow and pale with unseeing eyes, her skin drained of all life.

Maren. Maren… *Maren.*

Syrenn pulled her power from Ender and shoved away from his embrace. She collapsed to the floor, a sob breaking from her throat.

She screamed; the sound almost animalistic. Ender bent down, placing a palm on Syrenn's back in comfort.

"You weren't supposed to see," Ender whispered, the words breaking. "I'm so sorry, Syrenn."

Syrenn shucked Ender's hand off her back, another guttural cry ripping from her chest. She pounded her fists against the floor of Ender's room. He backed into his bed, then sat, letting his head fall into his hands.

"This is my fault. I should have had someone watching her," Ender agonized.

"It should have been *me*," Syrenn yelled toward the floor. "*Me*. *I* was the target. *I'm* the one who should be dead." Her head fell into her own hands as she sobbed. "She's dead because of me."

"None of this is your fault, Syrenn," Ender's voice was so low she almost couldn't hear it over her own sobbing.

"He mistook her for me because I sent her there in my place."

Their eyes met. Ender looked at a loss of what else to say to calm Syrenn. She wouldn't hear anything regardless, not in her current state. He closed his eyes and hung his head.

"We need to tell someone," Ender said.

"How do we explain this? Her dead in my place? How do I explain my not being there and only finding out this morning?"

"We lie." Ender stood, his face becoming hard. "You were with your parents, remember? It's early. I'm sure they're still in their bed chamber." Ender grasped Syrenn by the arm and yanked her from the floor. He turned her so that she was facing him, then shook her slightly. "I'm going to take you to them. And then you're going to walk to your tower room for a new set of clothes like you have no idea what will be waiting up there for you. Do you understand?" His eyes searched her face for comprehension. Upon finding none, he shook her a bit more aggressively. "*Syrenn*! Do you understand me?"

"*Yes*." She bit out between clenched teeth before repeating more softly, "Yes. I understand."

"Good," was all he said before blackness consumed them once more. Before Syrenn could even blink, they were standing in the middle of a new bedchamber. She heard a small scream followed by a gasp.

"You both need to listen," Ender's voice had become a threatening murmur as he confronted Syrenn's parents. He dropped his grip on Syrenn and took a step back toward the wall, opening the room for Syrenn to take the lead.

"He's killing them," she said too quietly. "Me. He's trying to kill me. You have to pretend I was here with you all night—"

"Syrenn, what's going on?" Madge's tone was panicked. She started for her daughter but stopped after receiving a deadly look from Ender.

"Listen," he growled at them again.

Syrenn closed her eyes and steadied her breathing. She took a moment before continuing, trying to stave off the wobbling in her voice. "Prince Gideon. He is the one who has been killing the girls. And now he is after me." She opened her eyes and planted them directly onto her mother's.

"What you're accusing the Prince of will get you killed. It will get us all killed—"

"He's already trying to kill me," Syrenn cut her father off before he could finish. "That's what I'm trying to explain. He killed them."

"What do you mean?" her mother pleaded, sending a questioning look towards Ender.

Syrenn dared a glance at Ender as well, who looked back at her with a calm she could not herself command. He nodded once. *You need to tell them.*

"I saw it in his memories."

Madge and Cairn gaped at their daughter as if seeing her for the first time. They shared a glance, and then Cairn clarified, "Memories?"

"Yes. I have power. I never told you because I didn't want to be sent away. But that is why the Prince chose me as his wife. He discovered what I was hiding, and it was decided that I would be his wife." She watched her parents absorb the information.

"And you saw these murders in his memories?" Cairn whispered incredulously. He had taken a step closer to his daughter, ignoring the shadows that leaked from Ender in response.

"Yes. Pieces. It was too much for me to linger that long in his mind."

"Okay. So, is that why he is here? Did you confide in him?" Madge gestured to Ender while finally closing the distance between her and her daughter. She grasped Syrenn's arm lightly, trying to gain the girl's full attention.

"He asked me to help uncover the truth. In exchange he would get me away from here." Syrenn watched her father's face take on a deathly edge. He whipped his attention to Ender.

"You've risked my daughter for your games?" he nearly shouted.

"Cairn, be quiet. If they're in some kind of trouble we don't want to let anyone know where they are," Madge reprimanded. His face had gone red, but he heeded his wife's warning. "And you're sure it was Gideon you saw these memories come from?" She glanced quickly at Ender, silently communicating to her daughter.

"Yes." There was a finality to Syrenn's response, and her mother didn't question her further.

"I chose to do it, father. He needs to be brought to justice. He's killed so many innocent..." Syrenn couldn't form the words. She swallowed past the lump in her throat before continuing. "He killed my maid. She was in my room overnight covering for me, and when I returned..." Syrenn couldn't say more.

"You need us to say you were with us all night? It's done." Cairn didn't question where exactly his daughter had actually been, though he kept his deadly gaze on Ender as he spoke. "But I can't vouch for this one. He's on his own."

"I don't need your protection, sir. Only for your daughter." Ender's voice was calm. Syrenn looked at him, noting that he was lost within his own thoughts.

What is it? she asked him.

His eyes flicked to hers. *I need to go. I need to find out where Asher went.*

"Thank you, Ender," Syrenn whispered aloud, effectively dismissing the elder Prince. Darkness swirled and then caved in on itself, leaving no trace of the man behind. The dark band around Syrenn's wrist tightened slightly as if in a caress.

"What kind of mess did you get into?" Cairn asked, scooping Syrenn into a hug.

"The one you sent me to," Syrenn responded blandly. Her father's arms tightened around her.

"What else do we need to do?" Madge asked wearily.

"Nothing. Just walk me out of here and tell me you'll see me at breakfast after I head to my room to change." Syrenn pulled out of her father's embrace. "I have to go and discover the body."

"What?" her mother gasped. "You can't be serious."

"I am. No one knows Maren is dead. I have to sound the alarm." Syrenn scrubbed at her face, trying to fix the mess she knew it held. "I don't know how Gideon is going to cover this one up, seeing how he pinned the murders on some rogue maid already."

"It's really him? You're sure?" Cairn asked.

"Without a doubt."

After Madge fixed Syrenn's hair and helped her to splash some cool water on her face, the three departed the room. Both parents hugged their daughter and bid her farewell until breakfast. Syrenn parted from them with what felt like a boulder in her gut. The closer she came to the West Wing, the heavier that feeling became.

She passed guards and maids alike on her journey, many of them bowing their heads at her passing. Just like her, they were still getting accustomed to her soon-to-be title. She tried her hardest not to let her carefully crafted mask falter as she reached the doors to the West Wing. The guards opened them for her without hesitation, and Syrenn inclined her head in thanks.

The wing was mostly empty, save for the guards outside Daphne's room and a couple of maids flitting around, dusting and cleaning. They all focused on her as she entered, lowering their heads in a slight bow. Syrenn did not acknowledge them, too focused on her target.

The steps to the tower were straight ahead, and Syrenn careened toward them. Trying not to all-out run, she focused on controlling her steps so they were a normal pace for someone going to change for breakfast. Not for someone going to discover a dead body. With her attention fully on controlling her own movements and expressions, as well as keeping her breathing even, she barely heard the creaking of a door being opened. It wasn't until she heard a small, startled intake of breath that her head snapped to the side.

"Syrenn."

Daphne stood in her doorway, grasping the frame as if it were the only thing holding her upright. Shock plastered her face as if she were seeing a ghost.

Syrenn's stomach dropped.

Controlling her features and steadying her voice, she said, "Yes, Daphne?"

Daphne's mouth opened and shut, at a loss for the right words, it seemed. She licked her lips then said, "Where were you last night?"

Syrenn stared at her friend—her lover—before answering, "I stayed with my parents. Ever since my room was ransacked the other day, I don't feel comfortable staying there. I swear I've mentioned that to you." She could feel her brow knitting together in disdain and tried her best to soften it into a look of innocence. Because that *was* shock plastered across Daphne's face.

Shock at seeing *her.*

"Right. You did. It must have slipped my mind." Daphne's hand fell from the frame, coming to hang loose at her side. "I've been losing gaps of time, it seems. The healer is trying to help me with that." Daphne planted innocent eyes on Syrenn. It took everything for Syrenn not to scoff at her. Not to scream, or thrash about, or cry.

She could feel anger boiling inside her and had to get away from the girl before she burst. "I need to change before breakfast. I didn't bring anything when I went to my parent's chamber last night." Syrenn turned to go, but Daphne grabbed her arm and pulled her back before she could.

"Why not let one of the maids fetch it for you?" Syrenn could feel Daphne's hand trembling where they were connected. She felt sick at her touch against her skin.

"I can get it myself, thank you." Shaking Daphne off, she continued to the tower steps. Daphne did not follow.

As her foot connected with the bottom step, Syrenn's stomach bottomed out. She focused only on putting one foot in front of the other as she ascended. She would not think about Daphne. Nor the fact that her best friend was surprised to see her this morning.

No. She simply took the steps one at a time until there were no more steps left to take. Her hand extended towards the knob, and Syrenn watched as it shook uncontrollably. Flexing her fingers, she placed them onto the cold, hard brass. Twisting it, she heard the telltale click of the door snicking free. She let it swing inward, then took another step.

The unmistakable tang of blood filled the room. Unseeing, she turned her head towards the bed. Her eyes remained unfocused, but she could still make out the crimson of the blood.

She did not have to fake her scream.

Chapter 29

Syrenn found herself in the healer's ward once again. Not in Gideon's bedroom, like the first time she witnessed a dead body in the castle.

No.

Gideon had intended on her being the victim this time and was probably too ashamed to face Syrenn right now. Not even to keep up the pretenses of their arranged marriage. He wasn't dumb enough to think Syrenn didn't know it was supposed to be her lying dead on that bed.

And Daphne knew.

Daphne. *Daphne.*

Syrenn let her head fall into her palms as the healer rushed for a warm compress. She didn't need to pretend that she was upset. She had lost Maren, who was loyal and innocent. A pawn that had succumbed to this mess—because of her.

And her best friend had let Gideon kill Maren, thinking it was Syrenn.

Something warm was lowered onto the back of Syrenn's neck. She felt the steam of the compress and something else melt into her.

Power.

The healer sent drafts of calming power through Syrenn, easing the ache around her heart only slightly. She choked on a sob, and the healer pressed even harder into Syrenn's skin. She stroked her thumb lovingly back and forth as she murmured condolences into Syrenn's ear. The feeling of the healer's power was becoming so familiar to her own—the two danced together within Syrenn as it did its work.

The door creaked open slowly, shutting almost instantly. She felt soft hands graze her face and knew by their touch that they were her mother's. She didn't even bother looking up or acknowledging her. She sat there and let the two women soothe her in the only ways they knew how.

It wasn't enough.

Her heart was breaking, and nothing would be able to fix what had been done to her.

The cuff around her wrist warmed, it seemed, and then Ender's voice floated through her mind like a soft wind.

You did well, my violent girl.

A tear dripped from Syrenn's lashes as she allowed Ender access to her memories. She showed him Daphne, her surprise to see her, and the agony she now felt in her chest.

Ender said nothing, but she could feel Daphne's betrayal strike him almost as hard as it had her.

"Would you like to talk about it?" the healer asked. Her voice was barely above a whisper, careful not to startle Syrenn.

"No." The words were barely a puff of air escaping her lungs.

The council has heard of the tragedy. I can see them beginning to sway in our favor. Syrenn could see the faces of the men through Ender's mind. *It's getting harder for them to deny what's happening, especially when it was Gideon who found the supposed murderer.*

That didn't turn out well for him.

I don't think he planned on killing anyone else, Ender mused.

No, but then I pissed him off in the garden. Ender startled, then dug through Syrenn's memories until he found the right one.

Ah. His voice was velvet. *You love me.*

You knew that.

You've never said it.

The point is that it angered Gideon enough to murder me. As if he's allowed to be in love with someone else, but I cannot.

What would he have done if he had known how you love Daphne?

Syrenn's gut twisted. The healer must have sensed the shift because she began flowing more of her power into Syrenn.

Probably killed us both, Syrenn said. She felt it was true. The Prince would not have liked Daphne getting close to another lover. He was far too territorial and entitled for that.

I'm sorry, Syrenn. About Maren. About Daphne. About the mess you're currently in. Just hang on a little longer.

Syrenn opened her eyes once Ender left her mind. The first thing she noticed was her mother studying her face. The second was Daphne leaning against the door as if she had just come in.

"Are you alright?" Daphne asked in a small voice. She took a few timid steps closer to where Syrenn sat under the healer's care. She reached a hand toward Syrenn.

Syrenn jerked back, throwing the healer and warm compress backwards. "Don't touch me." Syrenn hissed.

Daphne looked as if she had been slapped.

"Syrenn—"

"Leave, Daphne." Syrenn's fingers dug into her lap to keep from actually hitting the girl. She could feel herself finally beginning to break after all this time caged in the Southern Kingdom. After everything Gideon had done to the girls and to her, it was Daphne's betrayal that was finally doing Syrenn in. "I can't have you here, pretending everything is okay."

"Let me explain."

Syrenn was surprised the girl didn't try to deny it. She didn't even look ashamed that Syrenn had discovered the truth. She looked... determined.

"I can't hear your explanations right now." Syrenn could feel the sting of tears threatening to overflow her lashes.

"I'll come find you later, then." Daphne resolved. She stepped closer to the door before adding, "I love you, Syrenn." She slipped through the crack, leaving Syrenn aching more than ever.

"What happened between you two?" Madge asked, inspecting the doorway that Daphne had just vacated.

"It's nothing," Syrenn said, focusing on her hands that were now folded in her lap. The healer clenched her hand where it rested on Syrenn.

"Perhaps Syrenn could benefit from a rest alone," the healer suggested to Madge. Syrenn was grateful to not be the one to send her mother away. She didn't want her involved—she wanted her to remain in the dark and protected.

"I'll come to check on you later, my girl." Madge kissed Syrenn atop her head before disappearing.

The two women didn't speak for a moment. The healer's powers ebbed within Syrenn before retreating completely. Her pain was less, but it was still ever-present.

"I have a theory," the healer began. "Stop me if you think I'm wrong." She rounded the table Syrenn sat on before coming to a stop before her. They locked eyes before the healer continued, "Daphne is missing blocks of time, and it seems to line up closely with the murders. She has no recollection of harming Aster." She took a breath and gave Syrenn a severe look. "Do you think she is somehow connected?"

Syrenn swallowed past the lump in her throat. The ache in her heart intensified as she said, "She was surprised to see me this morning. As if she already knew about the death that occurred in *my* room. As if she thought I were the one crumpled and lifeless on that bed."

"So perhaps on some level she's aware of what is happening but blocks it out." The healer placed a soothing hand on Syrenn's.

"Maybe subconsciously she thought I was dead, so she was surprised to see me walking toward my room?" Syrenn asked. She wanted to believe it was true—that Daphne hadn't inherently let someone hurt her.

"Precisely. I don't think she approves or condones it, or else she wouldn't be blocking it out. But even she cannot stop whatever it is that's going on." Syrenn wondered why the healer wouldn't all out accuse the Prince, since that was what she was implying.

Syrenn mulled it over. "That's the only explanation. Daphne can't be fully aware of what's going on. She wouldn't let him hurt me." She bit back tears. "She wouldn't."

Syrenn stayed well away from everyone for the entirety of the day. Most of it she spent in the healer's ward alone. The woman was off somewhere working and didn't linger long when she popped in to check on Syrenn.

That night, Syrenn stayed with her parents, her mother not wanting to let Syrenn from her sight. She appeased the woman, though Ender had several shadows lurking about while the three slept—Syrenn tucked tightly between her mother and father.

Just in case.

Asher was still nowhere to be found; Ender had told Syrenn before she fell asleep. He was quite worked up about it, and Syrenn understood why. He was not only a valuable ally, but he was Ender's best friend. She wondered if Prince Gideon hadn't discovered his allegiance to Ender and did away with him.

She shuddered, even thinking about it. She had grown quite attached to the guard and didn't want anyone to suffer for no reason, just as Maren had.

The council was also in an uproar, though Ender didn't share much of the details. Too exhausted to pry, Syrenn left it to him to deal with.

She awoke in the middle of the night with a twisted feeling in her gut. Something was wrong, but she couldn't figure out just what it was.

Ender, she called into the blackness.

They're pinning Maren's murder on Asher.

Syrenn sat upright in a flash, tossing back the covers and startling her parents. "What's wrong?" her father demanded,

She paid him no mind and simply lunged from the bed and into her robe. Before she could even tie the ribbon, blackness swirled around her, and she materialized in Ender's arms.

"How?" The question that escaped Syrenn was guttural.

"I don't know, Syrenn. Some of the guards claim they saw him heading toward the tower. They say he said he was checking on you for the Prince." Ender bowed his head, pressing his forehead into hers. "They're lying."

"But where was he actually that night? He disappeared after we sent him away."

"I don't know. They won't let me see him." Ender's throat bobbed as he swallowed before continuing. "He wouldn't have hurt her—"

"I know it wasn't him, Ender. I know." She clutched him to her, trying as she might to soothe him. "Are they going to try him or just condemn him without hearing his side of things?"

"I don't think it's been decided yet."

"So we have time to set him free." Syrenn didn't know how they were going to manage it, but she knew that if they could condemn Gideon, it would clear Asher's name.

"We need to focus on swaying the council. With the wedding being the day after next, we need them to reach a decision. *Now.*" Ender folded Syrenn into his arms. She wanted to be sick. Everything was turning to hell as her impending marriage crept ever closer.

"Let me meet with them, Ender. I'll show them Gideon's memories. They'll have to believe me."

"That's the thing, my violent girl. They won't believe you. They'll be convinced you're making it up to get away. To overthrow Gideon in the process." Ender pulled back, peering into her eyes with remorse. "They're intolerant and don't like women overstepping their *place.*"

Syrenn's jaw tightened as her anger heightened. "I cannot stand this kingdom."

"We're in need of some change, that is certain." Fingers brushed down Syrenn's hair. "We'll do it together."

Chapter 30

Syrenn was exhausted.

She hadn't slept after Ender dropped the heartbreaking news about Asher. Terrible thoughts plagued her as she went about her day. She had a dinner set with the Queen Regent this evening, and she wasn't looking forward to it.

Avoiding Daphne was no easy task either. Syrenn knew she should talk to the girl, at least to hear her side of things. To see what she knew, what she remembered, if anything. But she couldn't bear the thought of what she might learn. Being betrayed by her best friend, the girl she loved dearly, was something Syrenn didn't even want to consider. No matter how likely it might actually be.

How Gideon was managing the murders while simultaneously manipulating Daphne and everyone else around him was beyond her cognition. How he had gone unseen by all the guards, including those in Ender's pocket, defied all logic. There was no doubt in her mind that those loyal to Gideon would cover for him, but the ones loyal to Ender? They would have confided the truth in the elder Prince if only to help him take his rightful place upon the throne.

Above being confused, hurt, and betrayed, Syrenn felt *angry*. She was angry with her parents for sending her here in the first place. She was angry with Gideon for his entitlement and thinking he could dispose of anyone in any way he wished. She was angry with Daphne for her unyielding loyalty to a wicked man, even when her best friend's life was on the line. She was even angry at Ender for not delivering on his promises. Yes, he was trying, but nothing was coming of it, and Syrenn couldn't help the outrage that coursed through her because of it.

And Syrenn only had today and tomorrow left as a free woman before her fate was sealed forever.

Syrenn was also angry at the Queen Regent, for there was no way she was unwise to her youngest son's *habits.* Madge had been well aware of any and every time Syrenn stepped a toe out of line while she was growing up in Farehail. No amount of absentee parenting could excuse Estia from missing the fact that her son was an emotionless murderer.

No matter how hard Syrenn tried to fill her day doing everything she loved, she still felt horrible and completely helpless for its entirety. The day seemed to slip by quicker than any within the last year as well.

Servants were running about, hurriedly arranging decorations and cleaning bedrooms for the many guests that were to arrive at any moment. Syrenn felt more in the way than anything. But even staying in one place out of the way and reading all day didn't stop the wedding preparations from happening or the clock from ticking incessantly.

She walked to the dining hall that evening, trailed by two guards— neither one her favorite. Asher was locked in a cell deep below the castle, barred from any visitors. Syrenn had tried earlier that morning but wasn't admitted. Shooed away was more accurate.

The doors opened for her, unveiling the Queen Regent, already perched at the head of the table. Syrenn halfheartedly dipped her head in greeting, then continued to her place on the Queen's left.

They were to dine alone, and Syrenn couldn't quell the discomfort that brought her. She didn't know if she would be able to hold her tongue, not after Maren and Asher. It would be hard to avoid telling the Queen the truth without being able to deflect the conversation onto someone else.

Taking her seat, Syrenn composed herself as best she could. Internally, she was a total mess, though the Queen would have never guessed by looking at her.

"You look lovely, my dear," Estia said as she poured Syrenn some wine.

"Yes, well, it's been difficult these last few days."

"We'll find you a new lady's maid. That will make things run smoother," Estia all but dismissed Syrenn's discomfort.

Syrenn gripped her goblet tightly and drained the contents in one swallow. Choosing to drink her retort, she instead said, "I don't believe it was Asher who is at fault. He has always been loyal—"

"The guards saw him. He was the only person with access to that tower."

"They're lying," Syrenn hissed, unable to stop herself.

"I would like to have a nice dinner with my future daughter. We are finished with this conversation, Syrenn. I'll hear no more talk of this. It's done." Estia's face had grown hard, her voice commanding.

Her anger wouldn't diminish, no matter how hard she tried to stifle it. Syrenn did not heed the Queen's warning. "How can you be so blind? How do you not see Gideon is the one murdering these girls? That was supposed to be *me* in the tower. Gideon was trying to kill *me*—"

"*Enough!*" Estia's fists slammed into the table, rattling the dishes and causing the wine to slosh onto the table. Clattering sounded as Estia abruptly stood, knocking her chair backwards and onto the ground. "What you're saying is treason. Do you want to keep your head, girl?"

"How can you let such a wicked, vile human lead your people? When you have the power to stop it. You know as well as I do that Ender is the rightful heir," she nearly screamed with frustration. Syrenn was now standing, not aware of when she had risen to her feet. "He would be just; he is worthy."

Estia rounded the table, her hand shooting out and striking Syrenn across the face. Syrenn didn't so much as flinch. Gripping Syrenn's arm, the Queen's nails punctured the skin on her upper arms from the force with which she held her. "You have no idea what it means to be a mother. When you finally bear your own children, you'll understand. Until that day, Syrenn, you keep your mouth shut." Estia was inches from Syrenn's face now, spewing venom into every word that crossed her lips.

"He murdered your daughter," Syrenn growled, jaw tight. Then she said through her power so that only the Queen could hear, *How can you protect him after he murdered your innocent little girl? You call yourself a mother, yet you favor an evil man over your other two kind, beautiful children.*

The pressure around Syrenn's upper arm disappeared, and the Queen took a step back, acting as if Syrenn had slapped her. "You can't know that." The woman shook her head as if trying to shake the truth from it.

"Did I speak false, my queen? Did you detect a lie slipping from my tongue?" *My mind?* Syrenn quirked her brow, challenging Estia to deny her. "Gideon can't pin that on Asher, now, can he?"

"You are a wretched girl, aren't you?" the Queen hissed as she stomped past Syrenn.

"Just because you do not like the truth does not mean that I'm the bad person here. Your son needs to be stopped, Estia. You know it as well as I do." Clanking reverberated off the walls as the Queen kept walking out of the dining hall. Not stopping her pace to even listen to what Syrenn was saying to her. "Imagine what he will do to our children if, for some reason, they do not please him."

The final echo of footsteps dissipated as the Queen came to an abrupt halt. Silence surrounded them, and Syrenn turned to peer at the Queen. She had come to a stop in the doorway, her hand grazing the stone as if it were grounding her.

Hand dropping, the Queen resumed her steady gate, leaving Syrenn feeling as if she had finally won a battle.

"That wasn't nice," Ender murmured.

"She needed to hear it." Syrenn pushed past him and onto the settee in his room. The fire pulsed and crackled, warming Syrenn's skin immensely. She had been feeling so cold as of late. "We need her on our side."

"You're right."

"I know I am," Syrenn bit out. "Have you heard anything more from the council?"

Ender rounded the couch and took a seat next to Syrenn. "If we move against him, Syrenn, he will kill Asher." He placed a hand atop her thigh.

"Like he's going to set him free if we do nothing? Do you really believe Gideon has an honorable bone in his body?"

"No, Syrenn. But for now, Asher is safe. You're safe. Daphne is safe. We need to make him think he's won—"

"You're not implying I actually go through with this marriage, are you?" Syrenn stood, throwing Ender's hand from her lap in the process.

"I think it's the best course of action. Make him think he's bested us, make him feel safe, then we strike."

"By 'strike?'" Syrenn asked, pacing the floor in front of him. She couldn't believe what Ender was suggesting.

"I mean overthrow him. Half the council is now on our side after the incident with Maren. The other half will be swayed now that you've had it out with my mother. Once he feels safe, he won't expect what's coming for him," Ender explained.

"And what's that? A life in prison, I hope? Under heavy wards and guard?" Syrenn crossed her arms over her chest, trying as she might to keep the heat inside.

"That is what we're leaning towards, yes."

"And then what? Will you be King?"

"The title is rightfully mine."

Syrenn stopped pacing, spearing the heavy weight of her gaze into Ender. "I have no desire to be Queen, Ender. None."

Shadows converged on Ender as he rose and grabbed for Syrenn's arms. "You don't want to be Queen, or you don't want to be *his* Queen? There is a difference, my violent girl."

She looked at him then as if seeing him for the first time, seeing a hunger in his eyes that she could feel within herself as well. It was as if she were seeing a future for herself within the Southern Kingdom that she had never considered.

"Either way, I don't have a choice on the matter. Prince Gideon gets what Prince Gideon wants for now. After our wedding, he will be crowned, and if that's how we're letting this play out, then my fate is sealed." She tried tearing her arm free, but Ender only tightened his grip on her.

"I won't allow him to take you." The words were a whisper, but they rang clear as any bell within Syrenn.

"We have to make it believable, don't we? Or do you have some other plan you're keeping from me?"

Ender only smiled wickedly at her. Finally wrenching her arm free, she watched him carefully, unsettled by the look in his eyes. They had become dark, almost vengeful. She backed away slowly, contemplating what he might have in mind, what he wasn't telling her.

"If what I've seen in Gideon's memories is true, you need to keep your own guards around Asher."

"Why?" Ender waited patiently for Syrenn to form the right words.

"If he did what I suspect to your sister, he may do the same to Asher."

"You've seen it before, haven't you? I thought that was a dream..." Ender contemplated saying more but waited for Syrenn to go on.

"Yes. I believe he took your sister's powers—whatever they were. And he seemed intrigued by Asher's, so please just keep an eye on him."

"So that's what that means? Those lifeless, dried-up bodies? Their powers have been taken." Ender looked horrified.

"Yes." She didn't take her eyes off Ender as she watched shadows begin swirling around him.

Then he was gone.

Chapter 31

One day until the wedding.

Syrenn couldn't help the countdown that kept ticking incessantly in her mind as the hours, the minutes, the seconds passed. She was numb—both in body and mind.

She had her final dress fitting, some poor maid having to lace her into her gown while Syrenn stared blankly at the wall just above the floor-length mirror before her. She refused to feel the scratching of the fabric across her skin. Refused to see the bright white and glittering jewels wrapped around her. Refused to acknowledge that it wasn't Maren behind her.

She couldn't eat. She couldn't sleep. She couldn't do anything but stare off into the abyss, dread coiling deep within her stomach. Her mother flitted around the room, a horrible case of nerves. If only she knew the half of it, Syrenn thought to herself.

After the murder of Maren, Syrenn was given a different bed chamber. The Queen, being kind, even after Syrenn's outburst during their private dinner, told Syrenn she shouldn't ever have to step foot in that tower again. She hadn't bothered to even go and inspect the new room—now in the main part of the castle—since she had been spending her nights with either her parents or Ender.

Today, however, she chose to seclude herself in that very bedroom after her fitting. Lunch had passed, and Syrenn didn't want to see anyone if she could help it. Not even Ender. Not after he blatantly refused to tell her of his plans. There was something more he wasn't telling her, and she was tired of being kept in the dark—only being told things when it was useful to those around her.

Palming the dagger Ender had gifted her, she cracked the door to her room open. If Gideon was waiting for her, she would be ready. She wouldn't put it past him to kill her now so that he wouldn't have to go through with the affair. To rid himself of the problem that was her and be with the girl he truly loved. She was sure to lock her door behind her.

They deserved each other, Syrenn thought. If Daphne truly knew what Gideon was doing and did nothing to stop him, she deserved to be tied to the loathsome man forever. Apparently, his heinous acts did not disturb her. Syrenn's heart constricted with so much broken love for Daphne. Her betrayal was something that Syrenn did not think she would ever be able to heal from.

It was just past midday, though the sun was at the opposite side of the castle. Shadows cast across the courtyard outside Syrenn's window. If she were to open the glass and reach her hand out, she could brush the tree that sat just beyond the stone wall. Wondering if she could keep this bedroom after her marriage to Gideon, Syrenn made herself comfortable on the bed.

Stashing the dagger beneath the pillow, Syrenn lay down and closed her eyes. She needed rest. All this worrying was really wearing on her—her head in a constant ache—and she couldn't even stand for long periods without getting winded and dizzy.

Rest.

The Queen and her lover stood forever—now cast in stone.

Syrenn closed her eyes as she mentally recited her favorite childhood tale. The tale of her once fallen kingdom. The beginning of the end of Farehail. Her lids were so heavy, even with the bits of sunlight still filtering through her window.

Their souls remained within that stone, forever connected and unphased by the changing of times that inevitably happens in all lands.

Her body took on a weight, lead coursing through her as her breathing evened and she drifted off.

Even long after the Kingdom fell into ruin, the Queen and her lover remained, forever protected by the will of the Wildewood.

The bed dipped behind Syrenn, a warm arm looping around her body and nestling close. Syrenn didn't open her eyes. Couldn't even try because of the exhaustion overtaking her. She only felt the love that exuded through the warmth behind her as she drifted off into a deep sleep.

Heart pounding, Syrenn bolted upright.

She was alone, but she knew someone had been with her only moments ago. She slid her hand along the sheets next to where she sat, feeling the warmth that still radiated within them.

That someone had not been the elder, shadowy Prince.

A horrible feeling settled into Syrenn. The fact that anyone could get into her room at any moment made her want to be sick. Made her never want to sleep again. Not that she had been sleeping well anyway. Not that she had been doing anything well as of late.

Syrenn felt as if her life was crumbling into pieces before her eyes, and she could do nothing to stop its cascade into destruction.

She felt as if she couldn't talk to Ender about it either, him being so broken up about Asher's detainment. The truth about what his brother was doing. He would likely just tell her not to worry, that he had it under control.

Syrenn was tired of being belittled about her fears, her wants, her needs. Everyone around her thought she needed to keep quiet, look pretty, and just be thankful that she was chosen by a prince. Whether they said so consciously or unconsciously, the verdict was the same.

No one wanted her stirring up the trouble she had seen. No one but Ender, who was thankful for her help.

Though it got them nowhere.

Syrenn felt more exhausted now than she did before her short nap. She could tell by the pinkish light filtering through the window that evening was closing in. She would take a light supper alone—as was tradition for the bride on the eve of her wedding in the Southern Kingdom.

The Prince was not to see her before the wedding ceremony. The fewer people to see her, the better, apparently, which was fine by her.

She did, however, want to get a book for her evening in—something to pass the long hours of what she knew would be a sleepless night. There would be no more sleeping for her, she thought. Not unless Ender stayed with her, keeping guard and protecting her from anyone who might come wandering in.

Creeping into the hall, she checked for roaming figures within the corridor before leaving her room. The last thing she wanted was a lecture from the Queen Regent. She locked the door behind her, though she now knew it would do little if someone truly wanted to get in.

They would find a way.

She arrived at the library without incident, thankful there weren't many servants in the hall that bowed to her. They were too busy tending to the guests and wedding preparations. She wanted to be sick every time she came into contact with them; the formality too much for her. The reminder of what was inevitable—tomorrow evening's charade—made her want to throw herself from her forsaken tower.

Unfortunately, the library was not as empty as the rest of the castle. This must be where everyone was gathering after traveling so long to attend the Prince's wedding. Faces she had never seen before picked through titles and milled about. There was a spread of tarts and cakes on one of the long hall tables and flutes of sparkling wine bubbling in glasses set upon trays carried by servants.

Syrenn had stumbled upon some welcome party of sorts.

"Don't mind me. I've come to collect some entertainment for my night alone," Syrenn murmured as all eyes turned toward her when she stumbled to a halt before them.

"Oh, you're Gideon's bride. My, aren't you lovely," a large woman with kind blue eyes said to her. "We won't say a word about seeing you, my dear. Collect your book." She smiled sweetly at Syrenn, gesturing towards the expansive shelves.

"Thank you, madam." Syrenn nodded her head and went to the bookcase that held the series of tales she was currently flying through.

"I bet you're excited for your big day, aren't you? The Prince is lucky to have such a stunning bride." A man who had been drinking out of a glass containing an amber liquid turned bright eyes onto Syrenn. His face was polite, and Syrenn was shocked to note that the people of this land seemed much nicer than those who lived within the castle walls. That was not what she had expected.

Syrenn smiled at the man, knowing he didn't actually expect her to reply. Who wouldn't be excited to marry a prince? Plucking a book from the shelf, she flipped through the pages, ensuring this was the correct tome she needed to start next.

The excited murmuring that cascaded through the room upon Syrenn's arrival quieted as another set of feet entered the room. Syrenn ignored the change in atmosphere, sure someone like the Queen Regent or one of the councilmen had made their way to the party and was undoubtedly about to scold Syrenn for being out of her room.

Skimming the first page of the novel, Syrenn turned from the shelf and clamped the book shut. Her eyes bulged when she saw Daphne standing in the middle of the room, eyes unfocused but directed upon Syrenn.

Right. Most of these people knew Daphne. They knew of her and Gideon's past. Knew Daphne was probably mourning the loss of her would-be title, and that was why they silenced at her appearance. Shame. Syrenn could see the now solemn faces of those in attendance. They pitied the girl.

Their pity should be directed toward Syrenn. Daphne got away from a madman unscathed. Syrenn would be stuck with him. Hopefully for only a short time, though nothing was guaranteed, no matter how many times Ender assured her otherwise.

Syrenn was in no mood to talk with Daphne, though she knew that was precisely what Daphne came here to do. Tucking the book beneath her arm, she resolved herself to pass by without a word. Daphne wouldn't pursue her in this crowd, it being socially unacceptable and very unladylike of her. Daphne had always lived by society's rules—them being ingrained in her at such a young age.

Gliding across the floor of the library, the atmosphere was dense with discomfort from the patrons. Did these visitors think their coldness was due to a jealous rivalry? Syrenn didn't care. It wasn't their business, and they weren't her people.

Yet.

Just as Syrenn was passing by, Daphne put out her arm to stop her. Barred from her path, Syrenn had no choice but to clear her throat. Daphne's eyes remained unfocused as if she were searching for the right words to say. No words she found would rectify the situation she had gotten herself into. The betrayal was not one Syrenn could ever forgive, she realized with a pang of remorse.

Daphne didn't budge, and Syrenn huffed an audible sigh. She whispered, "I don't have time for this, Daph—"

Cold.

Syrenn felt a cold so sharp it burned.

The feeling radiated just below the right side of her ribcage— shortening her breath and causing her to emit a sputtering gasp.

Daphne's face held no emotion as it turned to stare at Syrenn head-on. It was as if she were moving in slow motion, Syrenn thought. That, or Syrenn's mind had stilled and wasn't processing actions as fast as they were truly happening.

It took a moment for Syrenn to work out just what that coldness was— sharper now as she sucked in shortened breaths. It wasn't a coldness at all, she assessed. No.

It was pain.

A pain so sharp Syrenn's mind tried, but ultimately failed, to block it out. Her eyes connected with Daphne's—searching for something in them that wasn't there. Searching and coming up completely blank.

Syrenn looked down now—between her and her best friend. Her former lover. They were pressed so close as if in an embrace. White hair cascaded like a waterfall over Syrenn's shoulders—a barrier between their bodies. She peered at Daphne's hand that was pressed firmly into her stomach.

That hand pulled away slowly from Syrenn's flesh, pulling with it something shining and silver—now coated in a bright crimson. As bright as the roses in the courtyard garden.

Beautiful, Syrenn thought before her mind finally caught up with the present.

Shrill screams pierced the air. Glass crashed to the floor, shattering and spraying droplets of liquid onto the polished marble. The book wedged under Syrenn's arm thumped to the ground, but Syrenn didn't move; she only brought her face back up to Daphne's.

Syrenn could see people rushing from the room within her periphery—*yelling, screaming, wailing for someone, anyone to come now. Quick.*

The pain within Syrenn's stomach became secondary to the writhing in her gut. Power ripped from Syrenn, latching onto anything it could. Syrenn blocked out the frantic, incoherent thoughts. Didn't hear any of the chaos that her power absorbed as she reached a hand toward Daphne. Fingers grazed Daphne's cheek, then dropped from the iciness they found there.

"*Why?*" Pain laced the word—the thought—as she directed it at Daphne.

The girl remained near lifeless behind those sage eyes.

That is until something else took hold. Sage turned to gray in barely a moment, Daphne's brow furrowing with anger.

Time sped up as Daphne was raising the knife above her head. Syrenn stumbled back, clutching her wound and putting as much space as she could between her and Daphne. She wasn't fast enough; Daphne brought the knife slicing into the forearm Syrenn had uplifted as a shield. She tumbled backwards and onto the polished floor.

Fire lanced through her skin, and Syrenn let out a growl. Unsatiable rage burst from her as all the pieces of the past month fell into place. Daphne was atop her faster than she could fully process it.

Daphne. The only girl who had been promised the Prince's hand.

Daphne. The one who killed Aster after she had already been detained.

Daphne. Who had been the one murdering the girls for the Prince's heart.

Syrenn's hands shot up, but not of her own volition. Her power had taken over, protecting her from the imminent danger before her. Flesh gave way under her fingertips as she gripped Daphne's wrists with her full strength, knife dangling inches above her face.

Gritting her teeth, Syrenn seethed and pressed her body upwards, trying as she might to knock Daphne from her body. Whatever it was that had come over the girl was no match for Syrenn. It was as if the strength of twenty men had been imbued within her.

As if the year of heartbreak and malice had finally worn her thin.

They were stuck, Syrenn's arms now shaking from the pressure of Daphne bearing down on her. Rage contorted her features further as Syrenn struggled for her life. A guttural yell ripped from Syrenn, a frustration and heartbreak all her own exploding within her chest.

Darkness caressed her wound, sweeping gently over the gaping hole below her ribs. Syrenn felt the sickly hot pulsing from her skin, felt it pooling beneath her as the shadow that had once been secured around her wrist slithered down her body. She felt it wrap its way around her thigh as Daphne leaned farther into her, the blade edging closer towards her mouth.

The dagger at her thigh had never felt so heavy. The shadow tickled her skin as it worked the blade free from its strap. Syrenn knew she couldn't hold on much longer and willed that shadow into hurrying the hell up.

It fell free in the same moment Syrenn rolled, shoving into Daphne as hard as she could. The shadow was around her wrist again in an instant, pressing the blade into her awaiting palm. Pain barked through Syrenn's knees as she kneeled and whirled, thrusting her dagger upward—just as

Wren had shown her all those years ago—meeting Daphne as she lunged.

Syrenn felt the blade as it sank into Daphne's chest, piercing the soft muscle of her heart.

Hot, thick blood seeped onto Syrenn's enclosed hands as the clanking of Daphne's knife echoed off the walls. The room came back into focus, and Syrenn could barely hear the pounding of feet over her own thundering heart as they clambered down the corridor just outside the library.

Syrenn's power leapt out once more, latching onto Daphne's fading life force.

Knock, knock, knock.

The wood reverberated beneath Daphne's knuckles as she rapped on Scarlett's door. It took only a moment before the girl swung her door open, greeting her with a pleasant grin.

Daphne gripped the knife tightly behind her back as she pranced into the room, babbling about the dance class they had earlier in the day. She swung the door shut behind her, waiting for it to latch before she plunged the knife straight into Scarlett.

Horrified, Syrenn fell into another memory.

Vera gasped, eyes wide as Daphne yanked the knife from her neck, tearing the flesh further. Blood spewed from between Vera's teeth, and she stumbled backwards, falling onto the bed in a heap. Daphne leapt upon the body, plunging the blade into her chest again and again and again.

Another memory and it was Iris being butchered before her eyes. Daphne's hands were coated in crimson, causing the blade to slip from her hands and toward the stone floor.

As that blade fell, so did Syrenn.

Aster came to her door, brow furrowed.

"What the hell do you want?" she demanded.

"Can I come in?" Daphne's voice sounded dead to Syrenn's ears.

"No. You can leave. I'm not in the mood for it, Daphne." Aster turned, trying to shut the door and bar Daphne from entrance. Daphne thrust her blade into the crack, swiping at Aster.

She shrieked, bolting back. But Daphne was quicker.

She was upon the girl, but Aster fought like a wildcat. She scratched and thrashed. She screamed and wailed. Throwing Daphne off her, she straddled her to keep her down. A moment passed before Syrenn saw herself careening from the tower stairs and knocking Aster from atop Daphne.

Syrenn begged not to see anymore.

She fell from the memory as silhouettes entered the library and frantic voices began demanding answers.

Syrenn only saw the light spark back into Daphne's eyes a moment before it faded forever.

"I love you, Syrenn," she whispered, a smile ghosting her lips.

Then her face relaxed, her weight became heavy, and Syrenn had to direct her falling body to the side so as not to be crushed by the dead weight of it.

Turning to the opposite side of Daphne's now lifeless form, Syrenn heaved onto the stone floor. Nothing surfaced, for she hadn't eaten in the past day. Waves of nausea rolled through her regardless as she felt warm, thick liquid pooling around her. Some her own, the rest her lover's. Her mind felt light, and just as she was about to collapse into that wetness, rough hands yanked her from the ground.

Ringing pierced her ears, so she heard none of the words that were thrown at her. Numbness had taken over her entire form. She no longer felt that wound that still leaked just below her ribs. She no longer felt the stinging slice along her forearm. Her vision was black around the edges, blurry everywhere else. She was nothing, felt nothing, thought nothing.

Except that Daphne was dead.

And she had killed her.

Her body was being thrashed around, that ringing in her ears ebbing and flowing with the movements. Syrenn became aware that she was being hit. Hard.

Repeatedly.

But still, she felt none of it.

Not until her body dropped to the ground once more, head almost knocking against the floor, were it not for the shadows that gathered beneath her.

That's when everything came crashing down.

"I'm going to kill you!" The words were the first to register with Syrenn. "I'll kill you for this, you fucking *bitch*." Gideon sobbed the words. Actually sobbed them as Syrenn finally came back into herself.

Everyone was there. Everyone. The entirety of the council, Gideon held back by guards and blocked from Syrenn by his mother. Her parents, barred from rushing to Syrenn's side. Ender crouched over her—a protective wall; his shadows still wrapped protectively under her.

She felt a familiar power pulsing through her. When had the healer arrived? She was already working on stitching Syrenn up.

She dared a glance to her right. The world tilted beneath her as she looked upon Daphne's lifeless form—color now fading from the lack of blood.

Shadows held her upright as a dark voice whispered in her mind, *you did what you had to. She was trying to kill you, Syrenn. You had no choice.*

Syrenn didn't bother responding. Nothing she said would soothe her aching heart. She knew that she had no choice, but that choice still irreversibly broke something inside her.

"What happened." The Queen demanded the truth, her youngest son still wailing between the guards.

"Mother, now is not the time—"

"What. Happened." The Queen trudged closer—a beast stalking her prey.

"She was attacked, your Grace. Miss Delphi attacked her," the large lady from earlier shakily attested from the corridor. Syrenn peered out into the hall, noting the crowd that had amassed now that the danger was gone. Why had no one intervened on her behalf?

"Is this true?" Estia's hard eyes pierced into Syrenn, and all she could do was nod as tears pricked from her eyes. She couldn't breathe.

"She speaks the truth, Gideon. Syrenn is not at fault here." The Queen had turned back to her son, who was barely standing as he sobbed—the guards holding him upright.

As if Syrenn's heart didn't hurt enough, she felt another pang as she watched Gideon slowly fall apart before everyone. It was as if someone had reached into her chest and squeezed a hand around her soul.

Gideon was not the monster.

No. Gideon had just lost the love of his life by Syrenn's hand.

She looked at Ender, who stared back into her with horror-stricken eyes. As if he, too, had just put that fact into place. His brother, whom he was so sure had been the murderer, was actually innocent.

But the memories...

"Kaya, please take our future queen and get her cleaned up. Give her something to make her rest. This is a horrible, horrible tragedy, but we need everyone back to normal for the wedding tomorrow." Syrenn couldn't believe what the Queen Regent was saying. She still expected Syrenn and Gideon to wed? After *this?*

The show must go on, Ender solemnly whispered into Syrenn.

The healer stood, grasping Syrenn by the arm and pulling her to her feet. The shadows beneath her helped to steady her legs as she straightened. Leaning heavily on the healer and the shadows, the two women left the library. Insults and threats trailed them, screamed from Gideon's lips as he grappled with the truth that now rested lifelessly on the floor.

Bodies parted, giving them space as the healer steered Syrenn to her new rooms and the awaiting bathing chamber it contained.

Chapter 32

Syrenn had prayed she would never have to mourn the loss of another lover. She had mourned losing Wren, but this loss was nearly unbearable.

There was no coming back from this.

At least Wren was still out there, somewhere. Even if Syrenn had no hope of ever seeing her again. She was alive. She was happy, or so the healer said.

Kaya. The healer was called Kaya.

"You can't blame yourself, Miss," Kaya whispered as she readied a bath for her.

Syrenn swayed in the doorway. "I don't believe it. It wasn't her. It couldn't have been—"

"What did you see when she was dying?" The healer asked the question, but Syrenn could tell that she already knew the answer. She must have guessed. "It would explain her bouts of lost time, Syrenn. It would explain why she couldn't remember. She must have blocked it out, either willingly or by some other force."

Syrenn could only hear the splashing of the water as the healer dumped in soothing salts and oils. She came back to Syrenn, then began unbuttoning her dress. Syrenn let her, only swayed on her unsteady feet and stared into the distance while her mind raced through the facts.

Daphne had been losing bits of time. She had been scared, unsure of what was happening. Perhaps she didn't realize what she was doing.

Had she—

"It was her who killed Maren then. Wasn't it?" Her voice sounded gravelly.

"I would say so. But not everything is always what it appears on the surface, Syrenn. You, of all people, should know that." She was referring to Farehail and the secrets their island held.

"I didn't see that in her memories as she was dying. I didn't see it, but she was so surprised to see me that morning..." Syrenn trailed off, putting it all together.

Daphne had been the one to kill Maren. The one who meant to kill her.

She couldn't breathe.

"Though not exactly the same, I've experienced losses like this, Syrenn. So many of them..." The healer paused. "It's a pain so raw and unrelenting, but it can be managed with time. I promise you that." Her copper eyes held a world of pain, yet there was still a sliver of hope within them.

"Leave us," a dark voice hissed from the shadows, though not unkindly. "Please, Kaya."

The healer dropped her hands from Syrenn's dress, and she could feel the absence of the woman's warmth—her comfort. Ender's soon replaced it.

Before the door closed behind her, Ender asked, "Would you please go check on Asher for me? They won't allow me entrance—"

"Yes," the healer cut him off almost immediately.

And then she was gone.

Syrenn wanted to scream at Ender. Wanted to hit him, scratch him. Stab him. She was so angry that he had been wrong. That they had been looking at the wrong person this entire time. Because of his influence, she hadn't seen what was right in front of her face.

Hadn't seen that Daphne had only gotten so close to her so that she wouldn't suspect who the real murderer was. Daphne had known they were searching for the killer. She had known that night—

"My violent girl," Ender whispered into Syrenn's hair. "My love." His face nestled into her head, and his arms wrapped around her from behind. He gripped her tightly, uncaring of the sticky blood now drying upon her dress—her skin.

"She meant to kill me," Syrenn whimpered as she turned in Ender's arms. Sobs erupted from deep in her chest, and she struck Ender. He stood, unmoving as Syrenn pounded into his chest again and again, screaming and sobbing for her lost love.

Ender did not move, even though each of her strikes was one unto his own heart. He couldn't fix this for her. Couldn't make anything right. So, he took her pain in the only way he knew how.

When Syrenn eventually calmed, or rather, became too exhausted to go on, Ender slipped her dress from her body and guided her to the bath. She allowed him to help her in, not saying a word as the tears still streamed from her eyes and into the water. He washed her carefully, lathering the soaps into her bright hair, washing away the crimson that stained it. He scrubbed until every fleck, every drop marring her skin, was washed away.

Neither of them said another word as he coaxed her from the depths and wrapped a towel around her body. He dried her as best he could before moving her into her bed, where he pulled the thick blankets atop her shivering form and folded her into his arms.

Sleep did not come. Not for hours as Syrenn stared at the wall, unseeing. She played the night over and over again in her mind. Couldn't wipe the memories of Daphne's fading essence from her vision. Couldn't wipe the feeling of her blood from her skin.

Syrenn's head was throbbing when she awoke the next day. She moaned, then turned over and reached out her hand.

The bed was empty. She sighed to herself, squeezing her eyes shut against the blinding rays.

Just like that, her world crumbled once more. It felt as if her chest had been cleaved open as she remembered the previous night. How Daphne had nearly killed her.

Twice. How she had been murdering the other innocent women in the castle.

All because the Prince couldn't marry her.

Not that he didn't want to. Syrenn had discovered that he truly did love Daphne. He did want to marry her. But it was something they weren't allowed to have. So, Daphne had done the only thing left she thought she could.

Eliminated the competition. Disposed of every threat there was to her happiness.

All this pain was secondary to the realization that Daphne had never truly loved her. She had used her as an alibi, then as a way to stay out of her and Ender's suspicion.

It took a moment longer for Syrenn to realize what day she had awoken to.

Dread and pain and loss coiled in her stomach. There was no getting out of this marriage if Gideon was indeed not the killer as both she and Ender had suspected. Since he was innocent, there was no reason the council needed to overthrow him and replace him with Ender.

It didn't matter that Ender was the rightful heir.

Emma Lynn Ellis

It didn't matter that she didn't want to be stuck with Gideon, even if he hadn't killed those girls.

It didn't matter that even though her heart was broken, it belonged to Ender.

Nothing mattered, Syrenn thought as she lay in her bed, unmoving and wishing for death.

The darkness in her recoiled at the thought, and she spent all of one heartbeat feeling guilty before the door of her room opened.

Estia, Madge, and her new maid, whose name she hadn't bothered to learn, walked in carrying an ungodly amount of white fabric.

"You've slept most of the day. It's time to start readying yourself." Estia showed no sorrow for the death of Daphne or the hurt Syrenn now felt. Didn't care that her son's true love had been ripped from him last night.

The show must go on, Ender's voice echoed in her mind. *And a show she shall get.*

Before she could ask what he meant, his darkness retreated from her. She was pulled from the bed by her maid, coming to meet her mother head-on. Madge timidly brushed Syrenn's hair from her face, assessing the damage that had been done behind Syrenn's eyes. She was broken and knew that her mother could tell.

But it didn't matter.

They stripped her, washed her, and pressed oils into her skin. They combed her hair, twisted it into an intricate design. They painted her face.

No one spoke.

For over an hour, no one said a word as they readied the future queen for her wedding. No one said a word as they shoved her into that hideous white dress. No one said a word as they laced up the back. As tightly as they could, it seemed to Syrenn. Though, those laces were the only thing keeping her together at the moment.

No one dared mention Daphne. Or what was to come in just a short time.

Syrenn knew that more guests were arriving. She knew the Prince was dressing somewhere, readying himself as well. She wondered if he hated her.

Of course he hated her.

When they were finished grooming and dressing Syrenn, Estia stood before her, blocking the path of sight to the mirror. Madge stood stoically in the corner of the room as the maid fluffed Syrenn's skirts.

Syrenn met the Queen Regents stare head-on. She watched her, unfeeling, as she assessed the bride before her. Syrenn wanted to gouge her eyes out. She had a hand in this. If she had stepped in, allowed Daphne and Gideon to wed—

"The ceremony is in one hour. You are to wait here until your father collects you." The Queen's gaze was unyielding as she gave her commands. "Do you understand?"

"Where else do I have to go, Your Grace?" Acid was thick on Syrenn's tongue.

"Don't think I'm blind, child." She quirked an eyebrow, telling Syrenn she knew exactly what she had been doing behind all their backs. What she and Ender had been doing.

She chose to clamp down on her retort.

Estia waltzed from the room, maid in tow. Madge stepped gingerly up to her daughter, wrapping her into her embrace.

"I'm so sorry, Syrenn. Had I known what we were getting you into—"

"It's done."

"Syrenn, maybe we can find a way to take you home—"

"It's done, mother. Please, just leave me." Her tone was dry, annoyed with her mother for waiting until it was too late. "I want to be alone before I have to go through with this."

Madge wiped the tears from her own eyes before pulling away from her daughter. She nodded, her face broken as she left the room without another word.

Years, months, days, hours, seconds passed. Time meant nothing anymore as Syrenn stared into her own reflection. As she fell into her dark eyes, that darkness like black holes swallowing her up. She imagined they would consume her from the inside out, leaving nothing for anyone to find. Leaving nothing for Gideon to take his rage out on.

For even if Gideon was not the one who murdered those girls, Syrenn had been on the receiving end of his rage once already. It was not somewhere she wanted to go back to. Not if Ender wouldn't be there to stop it.

Which he wouldn't be. Not after they were wed. He wouldn't be allowed anywhere near Syrenn; she was sure of it.

Gideon knew where her heart belonged, and he would banish Ender just to wound Syrenn as she had wounded him.

A creaking sound pulled her from those black depths, her sight settling back into the mirror before her, attention drawn to the door swinging open behind her.

Bronze hair rustled with the breeze of her open window. Blue eyes found her standing there in that hideous dress, staring at her own reflection.

"I've come to apologize about last night." His voice was barely audible. So broken. She watched Gideon's eyes as they flittered through so many emotions—grief, fear, regret, longing—until they landed on her. The emotion left in his eyes when they connected with hers reflected her own.

Helplessness.

She said nothing, didn't so much as move or breathe as Gideon let himself into her room and shut the door behind him.

"You were defending yourself. She attacked you." He whispered the words as if he didn't believe what he was saying. "I should not have struck you like I did."

She didn't believe what he was saying, either.

So Syrenn voiced the one thing she had been thinking about all morning. The one thing that didn't add up in all of this.

"If she was the one murdering them," Syrenn's body, her mind, her power stilled as she asked the Prince, "Then why did I see memories of their deaths within your mind?"

Gideon froze. His face searched hers, searched for the words Syrenn knew weren't the truth. Still, with only a moment's hesitation, he said, "She confided in me. That's why I sent her to the healer to begin with. She was missing gaps of time. We connected the gaps with the times of the murders. I followed her once, and found Iris..."

"And you didn't think to report it? To tell someone?" Syrenn demanded.

Gideon's eyes became murderous. "And if it were Ender? What would you have done, *my bride*? Would you have him condemned? Put to death?" He seethed. "Or would you do everything within your power to keep him safe? To protect him?"

Neither spoke for a long moment.

"You expect me to believe that Daphne did this on her own?" she whispered.

"Yes. Because she did." His hands were fisted at his sides now as if it were taking all his effort not to strike Syrenn again.

Her power lurched from her, trying as it might to dig into Gideon's mind. It smashed into a hard wall instead.

He smirked. He actually smirked at her as her power reeled back in. Shaking his head, he walked to the door and yanked it open. "I'll see you shortly, my *bride*," he mocked.

"Daphne wasn't just my friend, you know." Syrenn couldn't stop herself from unveiling this truth. Gideon's head turned back, a questioning look directed at her. "We were lovers." Syrenn held his stare and quirked an eyebrow, watching him intently as his face became awash with utter disbelief.

Watched as it turned to rage.

He stomped from the door, slamming it in his wake.

She had wounded him. Had struck deep, just as she intended.

The angrier he was, the less likely he was to touch her on their wedding night. At least, less likely to try and take her to his bed. She had no doubt he would take his anger out in other ways. He would bloody her up for what she said—what she and Daphne had done together.

But perhaps he would be just distracted enough to let her power do its worst. Because Syrenn knew that there was no way Daphne had worked alone. Not the Daphne she knew.

Not the Daphne she loved.

The look in the Prince's eye when Syrenn had told him about the relationship she had with Daphne only further confirmed her suspicions. He was somehow behind this. Somehow forcing Daphne's hand into doing the unthinkable.

Chapter 33

Pacing the room, Syrenn felt as if time had completely stopped. Certainly, it had been an hour. Surely, it was time for someone to come and collect her and bring her to her death.

Figuratively, of course.

On her hundredth pass, the door to her room finally opened. Though, it wasn't her father who stepped inside, but Ender.

Darkness swept in around him as he latched the door behind him, turning the lock. "Don't lose hope, Syrenn. I know it seems like there's no way out—"

"There is no way out, Ender. Not until I'm dead."

"I need you to stop thinking like that. I promised you I would find a way out of this for you, and I will. This is just a setback." He crossed the room, scooping her hands into his own. "Trust me. Please, Syrenn." He was begging her, pleading with her to not do anything brash.

She could make no such promises.

But she also couldn't let Ender think she had given up hope. He would worry, and then he would do something stupid to get himself into trouble. She wouldn't risk him like that, as Gideon had so eagerly pointed out to her just moments ago.

"Dark, broody Prince," she began. She gazed up at him, allowing herself this last moment to fall into those dark eyes. This last moment to hope for a different outcome. "I love you in a way I have never loved anyone else. You are a part of me, and that will never change. Not this marriage, not being parted. Nothing will stop my heart from beating for you." She lifted onto her toes, kissing him sweetly on the lips. Their eyes fluttered closed.

"I love you, my violent girl. I will get you out of this." The promise was empty, and Syrenn knew it.

"I will forgive you if you can't." Her lids remained shut as she breathed him in one final time. She squeezed them tighter, stopping the tears threatening to overflow.

She wouldn't let this be the end of her and Ender. If he truly had failed, then she would take matters into her own hands. She would be the conqueror of her own fate. She would not end with Gideon.

"Just have some faith in me." Lips pressed firmly into Syrenn's scalp, Ender's breath heating the crown of her head.

"You should go. My father should be here any moment."

"He's waiting outside the door, actually." Ender pulled back and studied Syrenn's dress. "I asked him if I could have a moment before he collected you."

"And he obliged?" Syrenn was stunned. Her father hadn't seemed to like Ender in the slightest. Anything that put Syrenn in danger, Cairn would have shut down instantly.

Ender smiled at Syrenn, the light not reaching his eyes as he said, "I think he sees me as the lesser of two evils." Brushing a finger down her cheek, he took a step back and headed for the door.

As the door opened, Syrenn saw her father waiting patiently, pressed up against the wall of the corridor. She watched as Cairn nodded to Ender as he passed by, leaving the door open to allow him access.

Gut plummeting, her father entered the room. "Are you ready?" he asked.

Her body began trembling, dread pooling deep inside her. Her power writhed in solidarity. Lip wobbling, she said, "No. But I have no choice."

"Syrenn, it wasn't the Prince. You said so yourself that you saw the memories of the attacks coming from her as she..." he didn't finish the sentence as Syrenn's eyes finally overflowed with tears. "My girl, I know you didn't want this, but I promise you'll grow to love him."

She couldn't correct him. Couldn't share her fears with her father. He wouldn't understand the dread and fear that had taken root deep inside her. She knew in her heart that Gideon was somehow behind Daphne's acts.

So Syrenn simply wiped her tears, flashed her father a small smile that didn't meet her eyes, and nodded her head in acquiescence. Gripping her hand, Cairn looped his daughter's arm through his own as he guided her from the bed chamber.

The tapping of their shoes against the stone floor was the only sound. Guards lined the hall all the way to the throne room, causing a sense of claustrophobia to shroud Syrenn's mind. There was no getting out of this, was there? Her heart pounded in her chest with every step closer to the throne room.

Every step closer to Gideon.

He would be waiting at the altar for her, ready to accept her hand and condemn her forever.

But there Gideon was, waiting just before the closed doors, watching Syrenn and her father as they crept ever closer.

"Sir, may I have a word with my future wife before we say our vows?" Gideon flashed a sincere smile, one that had Syrenn's power thrashing behind her ribs.

"You best make it quick. The Queen was very clear on how she wanted today to go." Her father handed her arm to Gideon, who then guided her down a hall. And into one of the many vacant offices it contained.

The door shut behind them, and Syrenn fought that force inside her as it tried to claw its way out. She remained close to the door, hopeful that if anything went awry, she would make it to her father in time.

"I know that you lied, Syrenn, to get under my skin." He turned to face her, his expression devious as he continued, "Daphne was loyal to me. She would never have taken another lover. You might be miserable, but there's no need to lash out."

Syrenn stared at him, bemused. He really felt the need to prove himself right over this? At this very moment?

"Oh, but I didn't lie," she said simply and without fear.

"Come now, Syrenn. *Tell the truth about you and Daphne.*" Syrenn knew the command was coming before he even spoke. Knew he had a need to find out the truth. Knew that it had been eating away at him since she opened her mouth in her bedroom.

"Daphne and I were lovers. We shared many intimate moments over the past year, culminating in us spending the night together a few weeks ago." She didn't even try to lie. She didn't even fight the words as Gideon's power coaxed them out.

She smiled, watching him take everything in.

Watched the anger settling into him now that he could no longer doubt Daphne's betrayal. Triumph flared, but it was edged by something else. Syrenn was sure at this point that there was something odd happening around them. She *knew* it had been far longer than an hour since the Queen Regent had readied her and left her to await her father. Why wasn't anyone coming to collect them, to get them moving and on with it?

Gideon's hand was around her throat before she could even process the fact that he had moved. Choking on a gasp, she clawed at his skin.

He only tightened his hold in response as he said, "I'll fucking kill you, Syrenn. I will. But I'll be sure to take my time doing it. Slowly. Over many, many years." A secret smile stretched his lips as if he knew something she didn't.

She only sputtered her response, knowing he was likely to make her hurt, make her bleed for the rest of her surely short existence.

His hand relaxed enough for her to choke down a breath. Since everything was going to hell already, she chose to ask the questions that had been bothering her. Her fate was sealed anyway, so why not taunt the beast? "You made her do it, didn't you?" Her voice was raw but steady as the accusation hit its mark.

"Why would you say that Syrenn?" He smiled sweetly at her.

"Because she blindly followed you since you were children. She'd do anything you wanted her to and you knew that. You took advantage of that. You used her to get us out of the way." She growled at him. Then, quirked an eyebrow just to annoy him as she said, "But it didn't work, did it?"

His hand connected with her cheek, the stinging singed her skin a moment later. Her power writhed beneath her skin. Her power and Ender's lashed at the pain burning her face. It flung itself into Gideon's mind before she could stop it. Before *he* could stop it.

"Why are you taking me to the beach today?" a small girl asked Gideon as she danced along the shore. She couldn't have been older than six, her straight black hair whipping around her face in the early winter breeze. Storm clouds raced overhead, but the two paid no mind to the oncoming rain that was surely about to hit.

"You and Ender always come out here. Maybe I wanted to spend some time with you for once." Gideon feigned annoyance, but Syrenn could feel that giddiness he tried to force deep down into the depths of the soul. Syrenn's stomach soured, knowing what she was about to see.

Annalise shook her little head and kept skipping along the sand, just where the water connected with the millions of grains. She stopped with a bounce, bending to pick a rock from the earth, half-buried within the sand. She chucked it into the crashing waves, watching as the water fountained up with a splash. A soft smile twinkled in her eyes as she reached for another.

Gideon stopped a pace away, staring at the girl in a mix of wonder and greed.

Syrenn's blood chilled.

"Annalise, can you show me your power again?" He intended for the words to sound innocent, but Syrenn could hear their razor-sharp undertone. She knew what he was about to do; she could feel it in her bones. She wanted to scream, wanted to lash at Gideon who was all of eleven. How did he know? How could he do it?

"Why?" Annalise turned fully to face him now, concern scrunching her brow. Syrenn memorized her beautiful brown eyes, so like Ender's. She could see so much of Annalise's eldest brother within her features, and it made Syrenn's eyes prick.

"It amazes me. You have a gift, Annalise. One that is very vital and special." He stepped closer, trying to keep casual.

"Father said I wasn't to use it unless he was there to supervise." Her lips pursed as if debating breaking those careful rules their father put in place for her.

"I won't tell. And I'm your brother. I'll even let you use them on me. But you have to promise to be nice." The grin he flashed scared Syrenn, but Annalise didn't seem to notice—too excited by the prospect of her brother wanting to play with her. Wanting to see what she could do and telling her how important she was. She looked up to him; Syrenn could tell.

"Alright." Her face became serious as she stepped even closer to Gideon. Her brow furrowed, and Syrenn felt Gideon's body still within the memory. His muscles tightened under an unknown influence, and without a second thought, he ran into the depths of the rough sea, submerging himself to his waist.

Annalise howled, and Gideon blinked in surprise.

"I said be nice!" He yelled but then followed it with a laugh. He trudged back to the shore, ushered in by the crashing waves. The sky darkened with every passing heartbeat as if the storm would break any second.

"But it's so funny!" she cackled in response. When Gideon was safely back on the sand, he scooped Annalise into a hug.

Squeezing her tight, he said, "You truly are amazing, Anna."

Syrenn's power writhed. It slashed and clawed at Gideon, tearing at the memory they were inside. Her stomach lurched as she felt what Gideon was doing, what Annalise hadn't realized was happening to her just yet.

A second later the little girl's eyes sparked. Fear and dread skewed her features, and she wiggled in his grasp. When he didn't break his hold, she shoved with her too small arms, kicked with her tiny, booted feet. But still, he did not drop her.

Still, he siphoned that special power of hers from her small body.

Syrenn watched in horror, unable to stop it. Unable to intervene because this was only a memory and nothing more. This was the past, and Syrenn could do nothing to change the outcome.

Annalise's face drained, slowly. So slowly before Syrenn's eyes, the girl took on a bluish, then gray tone. Her skin became sallow, hollow as Gideon still clung to her; concentration heavy on his brow.

Syrenn was going to be sick. But she refused to look away as Gideon finished siphoning every last bit of power from his little sister. She watched as he finally released her from his hold, dropping her now lifeless body onto the sand. Kept watching as Gideon looked upon the mess he made, the husk that was once his sister.

And he turned away, walking from the beach without a flicker of remorse on his face.

Syrenn wanted to leave, wanted to pull back from Gideon's memories, but her power wouldn't budge. Idly, she wondered what was happening to her own body while she was trapped in Gideon's mind; wondered what Gideon was doing to her or if he was watching these memories with her.

Another memory came into focus.

A much older Gideon was walking through the corridors of the castle. It was late at night, nearly black within the stone walls.

He was a teenager, Syrenn guessed, for his face still held a childlike aspect. His features weren't as harsh as they were in the present.

He was heading towards one of the many guest wings held within the castle. Syrenn followed the memory as he turned the corner and walked straight to the third door on the left of the hall. He didn't knock, simply let himself in.

Nestled between the blankets atop the intricately carved bed was Daphne. She was sleeping soundly, and Gideon quieted his steps as he walked through the doorway. Gently, he pressed the door closed and turned the lock. He sidled into the sheets beside her, wrapping her in his arms.

Another memory—this one more recent. Within the last year, but Syrenn could see herself as well as the other girls sitting at the small dining table. Everyone was there, so this must have been before the murders started. The girls were talking about the history class from earlier in the day, and Gideon watched them interacting like a hawk.

He wasn't even listening to what they were saying, Syrenn realized. He was just watching them—their bodies, their lips, the way they looked at each other. Then his eyes came to rest on Daphne. It was as if she could feel every bit of that gaze on her because a heat started to spread up from her clavicle and onto her cheeks. She didn't turn to look at him though, only kept up her conversation with Scarlett.

Everyone was finished. Gideon stood, "That was a lovely meal, ladies. I'll see you all in the morning. Get some rest." He left the room without waiting for them to respond. Heading straight for his wing within the castle, he smiled to himself as he heard the small footsteps following him.

He didn't turn around, so Syrenn didn't see who was following him until he was in his bed chamber. Daphne slipped through the door behind him, grabbing his arm to gain his attention.

"Are you ignoring me now?" Daphne demanded from him.

"Of course not. Why would you think that?" Gideon feigned innocently.

"Don't play games with me, Gideon. I've seen how you've been looking at her." She ripped her hand from him, folding her arms across her chest in defiance.

"Does it upset you? I'm only doing what my father asked."

"Your father is dead."

"But the order remains, unfortunately. I asked the council about it already." He turned from her, heading toward his wardrobe. He began unbuttoning his jacket. Removing it, he started on his under shirt, leaving Daphne to stew.

"He said you could still choose me if none of the others suited you. No one has power. So, you can choose me." Daphne crept up behind him, reaching around and finishing the buttons for him. Her hands scathed across his skin, and Syrenn felt him shudder beneath her touch.

"No one has power? Is that so?" Gideon asked.

"You asked me to check, and I did. No one has power." Daphne's hand had stilled, and Gideon knew instantly that she was lying.

Syrenn held her breath as she watched in horror. He turned, grasping her wrist and pulling her into his chest. "Tell me the truth," he commanded, his body hardening with her closeness and the control he now had over her.

She stilled, and Syrenn could tell she was fighting it. Could tell she didn't want to give up her secret. "It's Syrenn. She can read minds." It was a whisper, but Gideon's face contorted in triumph.

"Was that so hard?" His smile was feral. "Why did you lie to me, Daphne?" he asked, pretending that he was hurt. It always worked on her. She had always been easy to manipulate.

"Because she's my friend, and she's been so nice to me. She doesn't want to be here. I know you and her would make each other miserable."

"So, you did it for yourself? All so you could keep me for your own." He smiled and stroked her cheek. Pressing his lips to hers, he said, "I'll always be yours, my sweet Daphne." He rolled his hips forward, pressing that hardness into her and feeling the surge of pleasure ripple through himself at the contact.

She pressed closer and raised to her toes, deepening their kiss. "I love you. Please let her go. Pretend you don't know."

"I will. But I need you to do something else for me." His tongue dipped into her mouth, danced with her own. Syrenn could taste him through the memory, whether through this one or her own, she didn't know. She shuddered.

"Anything," Daphne breathed, the sound nearly a whimper as she spoke into Gideon's mouth.

His hands gripped her body and pulled her ever closer. His kiss became rough and claiming as his fingers sank into her soft flesh. Panting, he breathed, "I need you to kill Scarlett."

Syrenn felt the weight of the power behind the order as it sank into Daphne. Her eyes glazed over as she nodded, unable to refuse Gideon while he used his sister's power.

Syrenn was thrown from Gideon's mind—horrified. Blinking, she fell back—barely catching herself before she tripped over her gaudy dress. Gideon towered over her, leering down with a smirk on his face.

"Enjoy what you saw?" he asked innocently.

She said nothing. How long had she been in there?

"I hope you're ready for what I have in store for you." He prowled closer, cornering Syrenn between him and the wall. She had nowhere to go. Nothing to defend herself with. Her dagger was still beneath her pillow, where she had left it.

How stupid, she thought.

Hand springing forward, he grabbed Syrenn's wrist and squeezed. Hard. It took every bit of restraint within Syrenn not to cry out as she felt her bones groan beneath his grip. He ripped her closer and brought his face so that it was level with hers. "I can't wait for all the things I'm going to make you do. Perhaps you'll murder your parents before they can make it back home."

Syrenn blanched back, fighting the tears threatening to overflow.

"No. That wouldn't be enough." His smile grew mad. "You'll kill Ender. Two birds, one stone." He laughed at his own joke, his eyes taking on a distant look as if he were remembering something.

"I won't. You'll never be able to make me. I'll kill myself first." Syrenn said defiantly.

"Oh. But you won't. I forbid you to ever harm yourself, Syrenn." She felt the weight of his power—or rather, his sister's power—as it plunged into her. She gasped as it twined into her mind, effectively nullifying any thoughts of self-harm she had ever or would ever have.

Feral. That was the only way to describe the thing that had taken over Gideon.

"You're a madman."

"Mad or insanely clever? I've got everyone right where I want them, and they're completely unwise to it. Why do you think the council wouldn't overthrow me, even though my brother practically got on his knees and begged them?" His grip tightened more, and Syrenn could tell her bones were seconds from snapping. His lips lowered to the side of her head, and Syrenn gagged on his scent. "Why do you think Ender kept promising to get you out but never made an actual move to do so?" he whispered into her ear.

Her heart, her mind, her entire body stilled. The world tilted beneath her. Gideon had used his sister's power on the council members. On Ender. On everyone in the castle, undoubtedly.

The healer. That was why she couldn't leave. Why she stayed in a place she hated, with a prince she knew was evil. Why she—a trained assassin—made no move to take him out.

Gaping at him, she said, "No." It was the only word she could form from the silence of her mind. The only word she could form around the thrashing of her power.

"This has been fun, Syrenn. But I do think it's time for our wedding. I've stalled long enough." A knowing smile flashed, then she felt a tugging deep within her gut.

A tugging from the outside that had her power recoiling, but unable to hide.

A snap, and then a harsh emptiness as she felt a section of her power being ripped from her through the place she and Gideon were connected.

Horror and grief and dread overtook her as that piece of her was yanked from her body and into Gideon. As he smiled down at her after stealing a piece of her power, a piece of her soul.

He dropped her arm, kissed her on the cheek, then left the room.

Chapter 34

Crumpled on the ground, she let her tears flow freely. She would stay here until someone pulled her from the room—scratching and clawing—and forced her to walk down that aisle to Gideon.

The door opened, and she saw her father's head peek inside. It swiveled left and right before he found her sprawled across the floor. The door flew open then, her father rushing forward to gather her in his arms. "What happened?" he demanded.

"Ender," she whispered, unable to stop her voice from wobbling. "Ender." The demand shuddered from her as her body shook, as she reeled from the assault on her power. "Ender Ender Ender *Ender,*" she repeated over and over until her father was rushing from the room.

A second later, the shadows were culminating in front of her. They were around her, inside her, and she yielded to them. Her power dove into them as Ender formed around her, holding her within his arms.

She didn't hesitate as she showed him everything. As she said over and over and over, "He's controlling everyone. You. *Everyone.*" *He's controlling the council. He's used that power on you. Ender...*

Her father was back in an instant, nearly panting as he said, "We don't have time. The Queen is demanding we start *now.*" He was closing the door behind him, giving them the semblance of privacy as he crouched beside Syrenn and Ender. They made no move to break their embrace.

I don't know what to do, Ender raged.

You can't do anything, it seems. He's made it so.

I don't remember him using that power on me.

You wouldn't. Daphne had been out of it during those attacks. She didn't know what she was doing. You must be blocking it out as well.

Syrenn…

"I'm so sorry, my girl. I'm so sorry. I don't know what's happening, but it's my fault." Her father was on his knees, laying his head atop hers now. "I'm so sorry," he whispered to both Ender and Syrenn. "I should have never sent you here."

Syrenn clung tighter to Ender. She flung her power into her father, showed him the love Ender had for her, then said, *I'm glad you did. Even with this mess, I'm glad I found* him.

She felt him still above her as he took in the thought. Could feel the tension and distress in him as the shock from her using her power settled. She had never used it on him, even after he found out those few days ago.

Pulling back, she wiped her face. Ender looked at her with such a broken expression it pained her. "We have no choice," she said as she stood. Both men stood with her, hands still clinging to her in comfort.

She went to the mirror to see what she could do to fix her face. Luckily, whatever the Queen and her maid had painted on her held true. She fanned air to help soothe the redness. Though, the guests would assume she was just another emotional bride, overcome with love and excitement on her big day.

"We'll find another way, Syrenn. If it's the last thing I do." He was so sincere that Syrenn had to swallow the lump that formed in her throat.

"I believe you, Ender. I believe you'd do anything for me."

She whirled back around, setting her face into stone as she took her father's arm. Nodding to her, he steered her from the room. Ender disappeared in the puff of shadow, but the band around her wrists tightened as the darkness within her brushed along her heart.

Syrenn counted the steps to the throne room. Counted them to keep her mind from reeling, to keep herself from vomiting as she walked to her dreary future.

The guards on either side of the doors didn't so much as budge when they stopped before them. Syrenn heard an organ begin to play, echoing against the stone as the notes flowed seamlessly from the instrument.

The traditional wedding march of the Southern Kingdom. The door would open in only a moment to unveil her, signaling for her and her father to begin their parade.

A flicker to her side had Syrenn's head turning. Ender appeared for just a second, pressing his body close to hers. It was just enough time for him to slip something into the pocket of her dress before disappearing again without a word.

She blinked, and in the second her eyes were closed, the guards had opened the doors.

Before her sprawled the throne room she had visited too many times before. Except, it had been utterly transformed for today's event. Purples and whites speckled the aisle that had been constructed between hundreds of chairs. Flowers spilled from every platform, sconce, and chair in sight. Sweet, sickly scents intermingled and tickled Syrenn's nose. She held in her sneeze as her father guided her forth.

Each step lasted a lifetime.

She didn't focus on the time that trickled by too slowly. Didn't focus on the terrifying grin plastered on Gideon's face.

Ender's face—still and stoic beside his brother upon the dais—was the only thing she saw as she marched down the aisle with her father.

Home, she thought. He was her home. Her tether to sanity within this mess. Her unmoving, unchanging star in the night sky. She knew everything would be okay with him by her side through it all.

She kept trudging, her father slowing her pace as she nearly danced down the aisle toward Ender. The darkness inside her—her darkness—danced behind her ribs, danced with her own now fractured powers as she kept her focus solely upon Ender.

Closer and closer he became, and suddenly, she was stepping up and upon the dais. Displayed so that everyone could see, her father guided her hand into Gideon's awaiting palm. Gideon grasped her tightly as if she would run at any moment. But it was not his skin she felt on her own. No. It was Ender who brushed against her, warmed her, as she looked past Gideon and fell into the blackness of Ender's never-ending irises.

She fell and fell and fell into those depths. He held her there—unwavering.

My violent girl...

The officiant began speaking, but Syrenn heard none of what he had to say.

Minutes passed as the man droned on and on about the unity of marriage, the duty to their kingdom, the justice the two of them must uphold within their realm. Syrenn let the words flow through her as she stared into Ender's soul.

A ghost of a smile played at the corners of his soft lips.

"Now it is time for the joining of the two souls we have before us today. From the moment of the sacred vows and forward, the two shall be tethered in body and soul until the day they are called away from this world. Syrenn, speak the sacred words, and so it shall be."

Holding Ender's eyes, she parted her lips and let the words that had been drilled into her these past few days slip from her tongue.

"*I, Syrenn, give myself unto you. From this moment forward, one we shall be.*" She spoke to Ender, let the words land upon him, inside of him, as she continued, "*To seal this union, I freely give you a portion of my power. A tether from my soul to yours, ensuring that we will never be parted from this day until our last.*" Even though Ender already contained a kernel of her power, she sent him another. His eyes remained fixated on her as he accepted that piece of her. She watched as his eyelids shuttered with emotion.

Vaguely, she became aware of Gideon being prompted to make his proclamation to her. But it was drowned out by Ender's voice rumbling through her as he recited those sacred vows into her mind.

I, Ender, give myself unto you. From this moment forward, one we shall be. To seal this union, I freely give you a portion of my power. A tether from my soul to yours, ensuring that we will never be parted from this day until our last. Syrenn felt more of his darkness pouring into her as he continued, *You are my reason for breathing, my home, and the keeper of my soul. I will love you until I'm ripped from this world.*

I will love you until I am nothing but power beneath the dirt.

Gideon did not send a piece of his own power into her when he finished speaking. Not that she wanted any vile part of him inside of her.

The officiant began speaking again, and she felt Gideon closing in on her. It took everything in her not to blanch from his kiss. She closed her eyes, bit back her urge to bite him, and allowed him to press his lips into her.

A show they shall get, she thought.

Cheers erupted from below the dais. Syrenn's stomach dropped, but that now expansive darkness inside her was there to catch it—soothe it. She was still numb as Gideon guided her to the side, and the guests rose to their feet.

Servants swept in and cleared away the chairs. Dropping them to the sides of the room, they brought tables in, seemingly out of nowhere. Before her eyes, the room was transformed for the reception. It took only a heartbeat.

It amazed Syrenn how quickly the people of this realm could move on.

Chapter 35

A party after there was a gruesome death only last night.

Syrenn couldn't believe it. Couldn't believe how these guests went on with their lives as if nothing had happened. As if Daphne wasn't dead.

Her parents weren't in attendance, uninvited by the Queen Regent after the incident.

Not that they would have attended regardless, but it was all about public conception when the Queen Regent was involved. They had to be formally disinvited even after the shame Daphne unwittingly brought upon them.

She hadn't seen most of these guests before tonight. Congratulations were given over and over. So many times, their faces began to blur. One person's features bled into the others, contorting into a blurred mess before her eyes. All the while, Gideon's grip was like a vice on her arm.

Dinner was served, a formal affair that Syrenn stared blankly at while she moved things around on her plate, giving the semblance of eating. If anyone were to pay close attention to her, they would chalk it up to nerves.

She was about to be crowned queen, after all. A title that would be short-lived, if Gideon had any say over it. Which he did. He could end her life at any time he saw fit. He would probably make it look like a suicide, even though he wouldn't allow her to end her own life.

No. He had to be the one in control. Always.

Dishes were cleared along with the tables and chairs. Syrenn let her body be dragged to the dance floor. Let Gideon place his hands upon her as he pulled her into a waltz. Music played, and her body floated along with its melody. She'd learned every step of this dance over the past year. Didn't have to think as her feet found their place over and over again.

Gideon smirked—a viper taunting his prey. She tried to block him out, but with her stolen power within him, she couldn't keep him from her mind for long.

Would a little life behind your eyes be too much to ask for? He growled into her. She recoiled, almost flinching back at the intrusion. *Play by my rules, Syrenn, and I'll let you live.*

What about Ender? Will you let him live? She knew the answer but waited for him to respond regardless.

You know I can't do that. Because of you, he knows too much. She closed her eyes, trying to block out the guilt. It was all her fault. The love of her life would die—most likely by her own hand—because of her. Daunting uncertainty of what Gideon planned for her future made her utterly sick.

As if you couldn't force him to forget everything he knows. I bet you can do a lot of tricks with that stolen power of yours.

You're right, my wife. I can do whatever I wish. Syrenn stamped on his foot as the dance came to a close with as much force as she could. Fingernails dug into her skin as he grunted through the pain.

More cheers erupted. Gideon stepped away, shooting her a hateful look and heading to whisk up his mother for her dance. Syrenn's father joined her, and off they swept into another melody. Safe in her father's arms, she let herself feel for the first time in hours. She let the pain and grief wash over her. She let the uneasiness run its course, leaving in its wake a feeling of resolve and numbness.

Her father allowed her to rest her head on his chest as they swayed. He had never been a dancer, but Syrenn treasured the moment all the same. Likely her last with her father. He and her mother would travel home not long after the wedding, and she would be dead shortly after. Before they had a chance to return. As long as they were safe, she didn't mind so much.

Pressing his lips to the top of her head, he whispered, "You'll be okay. I have to believe that."

Syrenn rolled her eyes, utter annoyance weighing on her. It was just like her father to put his faith in the unknown. Not make a plan to spring his daughter from this cage. No. He would simply hope for the best, just as he had his entire life.

"Luckily, I can take care of myself," she mumbled into him. His arms tightened, and they finished their swaying as the melody came to an end. Her father gave her a sad look, his dark eyes pleading for forgiveness before stepping away and leaving a void in his wake.

Ender was there, ready to sweep her away into another dance. She expected Gideon to step in, to stop them from being close. To drive another wedge between them. He didn't.

Maybe this was his way of allowing them to say goodbye.

She wouldn't say goodbye. Refused, actually.

"About tonight," Ender began.

"We aren't discussing it." She could feel the tension throughout his body. His shoulders were stiff beneath his black jacket, his jaw tight. He ground his teeth with unease. "I doubt he even wants to touch me like that. Not after I killed Daphne yesterday." She choked on the words.

"He wants to hurt you. He'll do it to hurt you." His eyes landed on her. Lined with silver, she had to look away when her throat painfully tightened. "He'll do it to hurt *me*."

"With any luck, we won't have to worry about it." She pressed her body closer to Ender's heat, careful not to nestle too closely, though. Every eye in the room was on them as they twirled and stepped with the rhythm. Syrenn never wanted the song to end.

But end, it did.

For a beat longer than appropriate, Ender held onto Syrenn. His finger stroked along the small of her back, snagging on the many jewels that crusted her bodice. Flickering eyes scanned her face, memorizing her lines and edges. Syrenn returned the sentiment before stepping back and away from that small piece of her soul.

The distance was palpable. Unbearable as Gideon collected her, scooping her off and into the crowd to mingle.

Syrenn was cold as she stood atop the dais, Gideon on her left.

They faced the amassed crowd, but none of their faces registered beyond the different shades as the officiant from their wedding ceremony chanted before them. Facing the crowd, he nearly sang an old verse, spoken in a language Syrenn did not know. The cadence of his voice was like velvet, sliding into Syrenn's ears and soothing the uneasiness in her stomach. It was a song from the ancient Wildewood, she realized.

It was the end.

There was no turning back. There was nothing Syrenn could do as time slowed once more before her. She felt it happen as if time were its own living force. One moment it was a current—wild and untamed—rushing passed her skin. The next, it was mud, slipping between her fingers slowly and dripping onto the floor in a messy heap.

Her tongue was stuck to the roof of her mouth. She tried swallowing to no avail. The voice echoing in front of her slowed but did not falter; each word stretched like a line into the sea. He lifted the jeweled wreath from where it sat upon the cushioned pedestal to his side.

Her crown.

As was the Southern tradition, she would be named Queen before Gideon was pronounced King. This was a show of solidarity; that the two would rule together equally. Would become one within their reign. He, being of the royal bloodline, already held a title that was unwavering. It was not as important to pronounce him King as it was to secure her obedience.

Syrenn could feel Gideon's unease next to her, coiling off him in waves. He was eager to be King; he had been for some time now.

Yet, time had slowed, tethering her to this moment for longer than was natural. She was thankful, though. It gave her time to think. Time to study that jeweled wreath, encrusted in sparkling stones with many facets cut upon their surfaces.

It was beautiful.

So slowly, the man turned, holding the crown high above her head. Syrenn wanted to laugh, his movements nearly comical. But when she went to kneel before him, she felt that thickness in the air around her that was slowing him down. She, too, moved into position in such a slow fashion. Awe and disbelief at what was happening, at how aware she was of it, sat within her.

Her knees hit the ground, and she waited. And waited. Waited for the officiant to place that gold wreath atop her head. The second it was in place, a tether snapped, and time resumed.

Applause reverberated throughout the room. Shouts of contention were bellowed as Syrenn stood and was anointed Queen of Nume.

With her eyes on the ground, Syrenn saw Gideon's fist clench at his side. She smirked, placing her own hands into her pockets.

Hard warmth brushed against her fingers as the memory of Ender slipping something into her pocket surfaced.

Ender.

She smiled, turning to her husband—in name only. His eyes landed on her and instantly became guarded. Gideon watched as a devious smile spread along her lips. As her eyes brightened with intent.

The audience would think it was delight—love, passion, whatever. But it was none of those things that rested upon Syrenn's face. In her eyes.

It was her freedom.

Syrenn tightened her fingers within her pocket and took a step toward the almost King. The officiant began chanting again, readying to anoint Gideon into his stolen position.

From the corner of her eye, lost amongst the crowd, she saw a flicker of darkness weaving toward her.

Yes. She was doing the right thing.

A flash of a second was all it took for her to rip the dagger from her pocket and plunge it deep into Gideon's heart. She didn't balk when the feeling was so close to what it had felt like to pierce Daphne's heart the night before.

For Daphne. She forced the thought into him before his body shut down.

Another second, and his mouth was dropping open in surprise. His face contorted in pain another second later.

Syrenn's smile widened. That thick, wet feeling returned as blood coated her hand, which was pressed firmly to Gideon's chest.

And through that connection—that small, simple brushing of their bodies—Syrenn siphoned her stolen magic back into herself.

Another second passed, and there was a flash of silver. Metal glinted, swiping quick and true.

That was when the first scream sounded, nearly sending Syrenn jumping from her own skin. The shrillness of it had her refocusing on the scene before her and not the feeling of her power melding back together within her body.

Gideon's head slipped from his body, unveiling Ender, who stood just behind him. Sword still raised and coated in blood, and he, too, had a hand upon Gideon's flesh. Vaguely, she heard the thumping of Gideon's head as it rolled from the dais and onto the floor at the feet of the crowd.

Syrenn could feel the siphoning through her own connection with the now-dead Prince. His heart still beat even with the metal that pierced it. Its force waned quickly, though. They had mere seconds before that power died with the Prince, and apparently, Ender knew it too. He wouldn't let that last piece of his sister die with this wicked man. It was the only thing remaining of the lost girl, the girl that had meant so much to her true husband.

She felt Ender pull his sister's power from what was left of Gideon's body. Felt as he didn't stop there. No. With a surge of panic, she felt as Ender pulled Gideon's own power from his flesh. As that power became lesser and lesser within what remained of Gideon's form, Syrenn felt something more slithering inside of Gideon's depths. It wasn't her power, nor his own. Nor was it Annalise's power. No. It was something entirely foreign, and it pierced its way through the connection she still held with Gideon. She felt it reach out and into her body, then coil submissively beside her own.

Both she and Ender let their hands drop simultaneously as Gideon's body fell in a heap on the ground. More screams ensued as everyone realized what they had done. Together.

Always.

With blood now coating Syrenn's dress, the new Queen turned to face her people. She placed her blade—that beautiful gift from Ender—back into her pocket. She felt rather than saw as Ender sheathed his sword next to her.

The screams stopped instantly.

Syrenn stepped forth, plucking the remaining crown from where it sat. The metal was cold in her hands, blood marring its sparkling surface. Her heart beat wildly as Ender knelt before her, and she lowered her hands to his bowing form. When the crown rested elegantly upon his beautiful, dark head, Syrenn brushed her fingers across his shoulder.

He stood and faced their people.

"Bow to your Queen," the Southern King commanded.

And so, they did.

Chapter 36

Amidst the chaos, the calamity, and the utter mayhem that ensued after the Prince's head had finished its descent down the dais steps, a lone silhouette skulked its way through the Southern castle.

Completely unseen by those around, it darted around corners—agile as a cat. Keeping to the darkest portions of the corridors, it began its own descent down, down, down into the dungeons deep beneath the castle proper. There were no guards here—not with the havoc that the elder Prince... King and his new Queen had wreaked upon them. If one could make out the face of that silhouette, they'd be able to see the smile that the new monarch's actions had brought to its face.

At last, it was free.

But first, a debt was owed.

The silhouette sauntered through the long corridor lined with many different cells on either side. Most were full of the younger Prince's... experiments. There wasn't much left of those poor people. Barely more than husks remained. It was lucky the prisoner it searched for hadn't been here long. The silhouette knew good and well that the younger Prince had his eyes on this one's power.

It was rare, though not too rare. But useful. Very much so.

The keys it had hidden in its pocket chimed when they were pulled free—the only sound the silhouette had made thus far on its journey.

The form beyond the bars rose to its feet, peering between them to see who was coming.

"You got lucky, Ash," it said to the man.

"What's happening up there? The guards all took off. No one would say anything." He gripped the bars as the silhouette worked, selecting the exact right key on the first try. It twisted easily in the lock, the metal groaning as the barred door swung free. Asher scooped the silhouette into a hug, nestling his face into its neck as he breathed in its scent.

"Our girl took down the Prince."

"Syrenn?" he gaped.

"Stabbed him right in the heart with a smile on her face," It chuffed in amusement.

"Perhaps she would have made a good assassin after all," Asher mused.

"I think one of our own loved her enough to teach her a thing or two." The silhouette dropped the keys into Asher's awaiting palm.

"Prince Ender is okay as well?" The worry in his voice was palpable.

"Your King is fine. As is your Queen. By Southern law, this realm belongs to them without question." The silhouette shook its head. It was dirty—what they had done—but so very necessary.

"With Gideon dead, you're free." He said it as if the thought had just crossed his mind. "Will you leave, then?"

The silhouette's steps faltered. It hadn't given it much thought over the past six years as to what it would do once the Prince's influences were no longer holding it there. But that force of its own slithered beneath its surface.

Go, it seemed to say.

Demanded, actually.

"I think it's what I'm supposed to do. I think it's time." It kept walking, taking the stairs two at a time—feet light and quick.

Asher followed close behind, his own steps silent. They had been trained together, after all.

"Are you sure you're ready for that? You could always stay here with me, you know." He reached a hand to the silhouette's shoulder, stopping it and pulling it so that it was facing him.

"You know I don't belong here. I never truly have."

Asher's fingers traced the dip in the silhouette's shoulders, caressing the curves he knew so well. They skimmed up along its neck, landing on its cheek. His head dipped forward, allowing his lips to press lightly onto the ones before him. "Promise me you'll be safe."

A catlike grin cracked the silhouette's ever-stagnant features. "You know I can take care of myself."

Asher smiled in return, remembering all those years as children—teenagers. It was right.

The silhouette backed away slowly, that smile still playing on its lips. Asher waited until it was out of sight before heading towards the throne room. Towards the chaos he could hear all the way from across the castle.

Towards his new Queen and King.

The silhouette scurried from the castle. It was the dead of night by now, but the land was lit by millions of twinkling stars above. Leaping between buildings, unseen by all those who passed, it made its way to the docks.

To the ship it knew was about to set sail to Farehail.

To home.

Epilogue

The Queen of the Southern Realm—so light and fair—ruled with a grace that had been unknown to their people for a long, long time. She was generous, just, and true. She had a way of knowing exactly what her people needed and never hesitated to deliver.

The shadow at her back did what he did best. He watched from the darkness, ready to defend his Queen from any awaiting threats there might be. Though, none were foolish enough to threaten her reign.

Not since the day she was anointed. Not since the day he stepped back from duty—knowing it was she who must rule the land.

The two were a pair, together in their every breath until their last. She was the light to his dark, and he the dark to her light. Forever two sides of the same coin.

They broke every tradition known to the South—so outdated and dusty. A mockery of everything that was meant to be.

The South rejoiced in their presence.

They grew.

They loved.

They upheld.

Fin.

Acknowledgments

Without you, the reader, none of this could be possible. You give my dreams life every time you pick up on of my stories. I am forever grateful for all the support that has been shown to me thus far by each and every one of you. Never stop dreaming.

I am indebted to my sisters for always being there to be the first eyes upon my work. You're never afraid to tell me when I've gotten too excited and need to slow down and retrace my steps. I need your kind of honesty in creating the perfect story and couldn't do it without each one of you. You each bring something different to light due to your personal perspective and they are insanely valuable.

Don't get me started on the cover of this book. How gorgeous is it? It's beyond words. Without the help of two of my best friends, it would be so very ugly. I'm no artist, nut they are. I can't thank you both enough for your talent. You take my vision and turn it into reality without fail.

Last but not least, this book would be a mess without my husband. He's the reason these words are in book format, and not completely sloppy within these pages. After spending hours formatting the first book, this one was a breeze! As well as his insanely adept skills at formatting and his ravishingly good looks, his commitment to me and my passion has kept me going. He believes in me, supports me, and encourages me in every avenue of my writing journey. I love you. Always.

Made in the USA
Columbia, SC
24 February 2025

54314248R00188